O'Malley

Paul John Hausleben

Cover design by Jacqueline Sweet Designs
Cover Concept by Paul John Hausleben, Mr. Amine Abidi,
and Ms. Lydia A. LaGalla
All photographs by Paul John Hausleben

Published by God Bless the Keg Publishing LLC
Henrico, Virginia, U.S.A.

ISBN: 978-0-9986300-6-9

Dedication

To old-time hockey, to the players who played the game rough and tough but fair, to anyone that ever donned a pair of ice skates and glided across a frozen pond in the dead of winter, and to that magical noise that a hockey puck makes when it strikes the wooden blade of a hockey stick.

O'Malley

Paul John Hausleben

Contents

Acknowledgements

Thank you as always to Mr. Harry M. Rogers Junior for his support and his profound friendship. Thank you to my family and friends for the support during my endless writing adventures. A special thank you to Ms. Lydia A. LaGalla for her beta-reads of snippets of this novel and her invaluable advice and critique of my work as well as the assistance with the cover of this novel. Thank you to Mr. Amine Abidi for bouncing cover concepts together and landing on the locker room scene. Finally, a tip of the goalie mask to Ms. Jackie Sweet for listening to our concepts and for bringing James T. O'Malley to life before our eyes with your amazing talents on the cover design.

"To the many guys that I tangled with on the ice, well, sorry, but my name is James Thomas O'Malley and well, I never, ever give up. I play the game to win, I fight for respect, and I fight to be a winner. I always will until the end of all time."

Paul John Hausleben

15 June 2019

Preface from the Author

Over my many volumes of various drivel, the character of James Thomas O'Malley has been a wonderful character for his creator to have in his back pocket. O'Malley contains a certain amount of magic. He drops into a story and instantly, his fierce reputation turns a story in a most peculiar direction. It could be a scene of characters happily skipping hand-in-hand through a garden of precious roses. Roses cultivated in care, and roses that are broadcasting glorious scents into the air from their heavenly pedals, and if O'Malley appears in the scene, the reader's expectation is that O'Malley would trample the roses, tear the heavenly shrubs out of the dirt by their roots and then angrily eat the remnants of them. Thorns and all.

Could it be that poor O'Malley is a tad misunderstood, and that he has anger issues?

Ever since James T. O'Malley arrived on the scene in my novel, *The Night Always Comes* and he becomes the ice hockey nemesis and rival of the character of a certain goaltender wearing the number twenty-seven, and also known as Paul John Henson, readers have had an infatuation with the character of O'Malley. O'Malley's toughness, his meanness and his ultra-competitive nature and wild on-the-ice behavior combined with his gentlemanly behavior when off the ice, make him a character for the ages. Without a doubt, there is something special about the character of O'Malley.

I must confess to utilizing O'Malley here and there for a certain influence upon the story. Yet, in the aforementioned novel, I purposely tickled the reader with a hint or two that there might be more to the character's wild behavior than the stereotype of a traditional hockey goon that the storyline indicates. In the scene from *The Night Always Comes,* when Jim visits Harry, Paul, Binky, and Rose at dinner in the exclusive, Black Bear Club, O'Malley is a perfect gentleman. So much so that the women initially do not even recognize Jim!

Jim's very eccentric creator made careful note of such influences. I tucked it away in my writing notes for use later on down the line.

The character of James T. O'Malley continues to make various cameos here (the opening to *Harry's Resort* in the *Time Bomb in the Cupboard and Other Adventures of Harry and Paul* contains an often-overlooked appearance by James T. O'Malley) and there in other novels, and in short stories. Rather predictably, Jim enjoyed a starring role in my hockey novel, *Geyer Street Gardens.* In that novel, the reader gains the deepest insight yet into O'Malley that I so far chose to reveal.

Yet, my idea for the character still had more evolution to occur and by the time the final adventure of Harry and Paul rolls around in the epic novel, *Heaven's Gain,* the reader finds O'Malley a close friend of Harry and Paul and their families and O'Malley, emits a powerful and dynamic role in that novel's storyline. In reality, as I did with most of the characters from the various *Adventures of Harry and Paul,* I intended to tuck O'Malley away on my dusty shelf of characters and allow Jim to remain there for posterity.

Often, my writing adventures take me down other roads and I have to reach for characters on that dusty, old shelf of sleeping characters. . ..

During the summer and autumn seasons of 2017, while composing the emotional short story *Mirror* for the collection titled *The Chronicles of Henson*, I found the perfect spot to reach for the formerly resting O'Malley and drop Jim into the storyline. A spot which required his reputation as a tough guy, and from thereon, my mind whirled with questions.

'Just why was O'Malley so mean? Why did he play the game of hockey so brutally? Why was he so angry on the ice? Yet, deep down, he had this incredible warmth and genuine love in his heart. So much so, that, as his former rival and nemesis did, James T. O'Malley quit professional hockey, became the pastor of a large nondenominational church and committed his work and life to the work of The Lord.'

Interesting thoughts, indeed. . ..

My eccentric mind dissected my own character, and I was so intrigued with those questions that I set to work. In a fever-pitch display of writing behavior, I wrote and completed the draft for this novel in just less than four weeks. Suddenly, James Thomas O'Malley had an entire life, a background, and those questions that nagged his creator finally had answers.

I loosely based the fictional character of James T. O'Malley upon an actual hockey player that I encountered in my old hockey circles a long ago. The actual O'Malley was a brutally fearsome and tough player, and a feared hockey fighter of legendary status, but unlike the fictional O'Malley, the nonfiction version had little to offer in the way of hockey skills. He was a poor skater, I suspected that he was actually a converted boxer, and he was more of a brawler than he was a hockey player.

What a wild brawler he was too!

So much so that it was a well-used catch phrase in our circles to label a person flipping their lid or losing their temper, as "Having gone, O'Malley!"

Whether it might be true or not, or just a humorous rumor about the magical transformation of the wild personality of the nonfictional O'Malley, the word was that years later, the former brawler repented of his evil ways and he did enter the ministry. I confess to finding that fact, regardless of truth or fiction, rather hilarious and I stole it for the fictional James T. O'Malley.

Writing the novel, *O'Malley* was a rewarding experience and although writing novels steals large portions of my soul while I write them, and I find my best writing strength in shorter works, I do find my mind toying with the idea of reaching for more characters on that dusty, old, shelf of characters. There are quite a few of them sitting there, resting and waiting for the perfect moment to jump into their own adventure.

Time will tell.

Until then, I hope that you enjoy reading this novel as much as I have enjoyed the experience of writing it.

Thank you for reading *O'Malley.*

Paul John Hausleben

15 June 2019

Prologue

The restaurant was within walking distance of the hotel that we were staying in for the night. When I asked the hotel desk clerk about it, he did not really answer me. Unless a shrug and grunt counted for an answer. I thought, what the hell, you have wandered into worse places, Henson.

Off I went into the cold January evening. No snow in the air, but no stars in the sky either. Lots of crusty ice along the way. The restaurant sat there, dimly lit and very sad. Sort of like a lost dog on a city street corner. Piles of plowed, dirty corn snow from the last snowstorm sat here and there in the parking lot. I opened the door, wandered in, made my way past the booths, and gravitated toward the bar. This was a normal behavior for me because after hockey games, especially games where O'Malley was on the other side of the ice and he was whizzing pucks around my head, it seems as if I always made my way to the bar.

I walked past two old chaps asleep in their whiskey sours. Their noses were up to the cherries in the glass, and then, next in line, I passed a young couple playing touchy-feely with each other while giggling at their love. Their drinks sat untouched on the high-top table. Their mouths and hands were too busy to drink.

No one even noticed me. This was my kind of joint, even if it smelled similar to old socks dipped in sweat and mended with threads of shame.

Picking a bar stool was easy.

They all were empty.

After a quick scan of the well-worn selection of bar stools, I picked one that I thought would not give me a splinter in my ass, and I carefully sat down. My intention was not to wiggle around too much.

There was one bartender working this particular drink slinging shift. A woman bartender who currently stood on the far end of the bar while she was washing glassware in the sink underneath the bar.

I sat there for quite a long time while she washed the spent bar glassware. A long time indeed. After all, glassware washing is very important. To keep my mind from wandering and my eyes from burning from the view, I occasionally stared at a neon, blinking light, hanging on the wall in a dusty corner of the barroom, while it slowly winked "COLD BEER" at me in glowing red neon.

The bartender was tall for a woman, very tall, and her dyed blonde hair was huge. The kind of hair that went on forever, teased up in great waves of frill and frizz. It reminded me of a whipped parfait. Huge hair, worn in the style that was very similar to what all the movie stars wore in the 1970s.

This gal was not a movie star.

Finally, she noticed me, and turned off the water. With a great heave and a sigh and a mouth that pointed Deep South at the edges, she slowly walked over to me. With a swoop, she grabbed a bar napkin with her hand and made her way over the rest of the way. Her huge breasts were the size of the Green Mountains of Vermont, but not as pleasantly shaped. Her girdle pulled her excessive parts and pieces in so tightly that I prayed for no fast moves.

The explosion would be hell to deal with, and it had been a long day. I dodged enough missiles for one day.

The eyeliner and lipstick and all types of other makeup on her face held on in desperation of not peeling off, sort of like a crow holding onto a high wire in a windstorm.

"Whadda, ya want?" Ms. Happiness growled as she slid the napkin over to me.

"What type of beers do you have on tap?"

"Ya got eyes?" She pointed to the tap handles.

"Okay, you pick it, then. Tall glass. Bad day, huh?" I asked the second stupidest question that I have ever asked in my life. The first was when I was seventeen years old and I asked my old man if I could borrow twenty bucks in order to take a gal on a date.

"Life's a bitch and then ya die," she said as she wobbled to the taps with a tall glass in hand.

I leaned back and despite her misery, I smiled, because I thought of one of the old man's most famous sayings, "A bartender should never be grouchier than I am."

When she dropped the glass in front of me and without another word, went back to washing glassware, I lifted the glass, made a toast to the old man and took a long sip.

I took another sip and made another toast. This one was to James T. O'Malley. I flexed my sore shoulder and thought, damn, how that O'Malley could shoot one deadly, hard-ass shot. Glad it was my shoulder and not my head. O'Malley was an amazing player. Dealing with him was like dealing with the unleashed Furies of Hell. My body and soul ached from the game today and O'Malley was the cause of the majority of the pain.

Geez, this beer was cold, and it tasted good. When I mustered enough courage, and I put on my goalie's equipment and mask, then I would ask this congenial bartender what brand it is.

Later. Not now.

As I said, it had been a long day.

A very long day.

Chapter One

James Thomas O'Malley

There we sat. Three washed up, old hockey players, all sitting in a row. Two of us old geezers nursed mixed cocktails, while one sipped slowly from a frosty mug of Big Boulder Beer. There we sat, sipping our drinks of choice and rehashing old memories of glory days. Left side to the right side, or better yet, from the far-left bar stool to the far-right bar stool, straight out from the corner of the bar where the jukebox sat, was number thirty-five, number twenty-seven and then number eleven.

Three ducks floating on a murky pond of memories.

Three magpies sitting on a high wire of bullshit.

Three pigeons sitting on a ledge of a city skyscraper while braving the winds of huff and puff that blew hard from a bunch of blowhards.

Dear reader, you get the idea.

Now, for the real names. Left to right, was Harry M. Redmond Junior, Paul John Henson, and James T. O'Malley.

I am your chronicler of sorts, the narrator, the writer, and the remote observer of all of these events and the recorder of a most amazing person's remarkable life. For lack of any other descriptions above and beyond that one, then I am number twenty-seven, Paul John Henson. Harry M. Redmond Junior is my brother from a different mother and James T. O'Malley is well, let's just say Jim is our mutual best friend.

It was not always that way between Jim and Harry and

especially Paul! Oh no, it was quite the opposite. At one time, we were mortal enemies, ice hockey players on opposite teams vying for the same coveted championship. The animosity was more so with Jim and number twenty-seven. Harry did not have as long a history of on the ice battling with the legendary James T. O'Malley as what I did in my hockey career. Harry left the hockey world earlier than I did, due to a serious injury, while I played on. However, Harry was there, on my side, rooting me onward in my quest to defeat the notorious number eleven and win a hockey championship. Now, in an amazing twist of fate, we were the best of friends and I could not see my life for being quite the same without the presence of James T. O'Malley. I am quite sure that Harry felt the same way as I did, and we were both sure that Jim had a certain affinity for the two of us, too.

If you looked up the definition of intense in the dictionary, there should simply be a picture of James T. O'Malley. Ditto for the two words of commitment and honesty. And many other words too.

In another twist of irony, after Jim and I left the hockey world, we both entered the ministry. Jim became a nondenominational minister, leading a large congregation for over twenty years and I became a Lutheran clergyman, first serving as a senior pastor for a Lutheran church in semi-rural northern New Jersey and then as the Bishop of the Northeast District of our Lutheran Synod.

Life is full of twists and turns.

Pastor Jim was now retired and he and his lovely wife, Kate, both were sitting back and enjoying life together. In retirement from the ministry, Jim kept busy coaching a local high school hockey club and his talents were instrumental in shaping many young hockey players' lives both on and off the ice. No surprise here, Jim's hockey club won championships, and they always led the league in penalty minutes.

As far as the legend known, as Mr. Harry M. Redmond Junior is concerned, well right now, I will use his own words as a description of his life and his many careers.

"Harry M. Redmond Jr. is the name. Inventor, businessman, entrepreneur, hit songwriter, welder, womanizer, and general, all around windbag and a loudmouth, but overall, I am not a bad guy!"

The endless adventures of Harry and Paul would fill many pages of books, and dear reader, I promise that I will do my best to do so. Right now, suffice it to say that Harry was very successful. He earned more money than he could ever spend and for two humble and poor kids from a rough and tumble Paterson, New Jersey neighborhood, we did fairly well for ourselves. Harry was now semi-retired and he and his lovely wife, Rose, kept very busy running many charitable organizations and functions. Harry always wanted to return good fortune to people of the inner city of Paterson and to contribute parts and pieces of his success to the heritage that we knew so well.

As far as Pastor Paul John Henson goes, (I still used the title of pastor because the bishop title was far too stuffy for me) I was still working. In fact, I was now slowly trying hard to recover from the tragic loss of my wife a few years earlier and with the help of my friends, my family and a brief return to the hockey world for the three of us, I was gaining strength to go on in my life. I knew that I would never forget or fully recover, because that was nearly impossible, but every day, I recovered portions of my soul. That recovery is another story for another set of pages, but dear reader, without the love, courage, friendship, and support of these two men sitting on each side of me, I am sure that I would not even be walking this earth right now.

Now, here we sit, three old friends and while we jumped from game-to-game in the discussion, indeed, from play-to-play to fistfight-to-fistfight, we shared a lifetime of memories and friendship. I knew that this invitation to share drinks, to share glimpses into our past and jump once more on the ice surfaces of hockey rinks now long since turned into apartment complexes or shopping centers, was part of my two friend's efforts to assist me with my healing process. For that, I truly loved these two men as if they were my brothers.

You see, dear reader, in this life, it is not always what you have accomplished as an individual, rather, it is what you accomplished and shared with others that makes this life so special.

This gin joint was in O'Malley's adopted New Jersey hometown, a small nook in the corner of this quaint town's main street. The inside was dark, a little dusty, and it smelled like a combination of stale beer, ground out cigarettes, whiskey, and a touch of armpit sweat and work boot odor. It was quiet, and the patrons mostly kept to themselves. A few regulars, a few visitors, a young man or two chasing a pretty gal or two, but for the most part, it was a typical New Jersey gin joint.

In New Jersey, there were quite a few of them. As in, on almost every street corner.

A mirror reflected colors and the faces of bar dwellers as it smiled at us from behind the endless display of bottles. The décor of this gin joint was a mix-match of vintage and modern doo-dah and local memorabilia. Tastes of Americana, with American flags, military flags and patches from military uniforms, law enforcement, emergency responders, firefighters, assorted heroes and other items donated from the local crowd of patrons. Touches of New Jersey with a picture of the Great Falls of Paterson and snapshots and postcards from the beaches along the Jersey Shore. One particularly, cool piece of décor, which hung proudly over the top of the mirror to the right side of the liquor display, was a framed vintage number eleven, hockey sweater from the New York Colonials hockey club with the name "O'MALLEY" emblazoned upon the back of the sweater.

O'Malley was a legend, and he was a regular.

If you asked me to tell you the year that this meeting and celebration occurred, then I would find it impossible to do so. Honestly, I would not even want to venture a guess. After my wife left this world to become Heaven's gain, I lost track of the years. What I could tell you from the hallways of my memories was that it was mid-September, and it was a Saturday. A late afternoon on a Saturday and the owner of this establishment had left his daughter to tend bar and run the gin joint along with a handful of servers working the dining room floor behind us.

Rachel was the owner's daughter, and she was cute and petite, with a nice figure and a bubbly personality. A guess at her age was that she was between twenty-five and thirty years of age and she was gifted with blonde hair and stunning blue eyes. Jim knew her quite well, and she knew Jim too. Rachel was an excellent bartender. She knew her profession quite well and her spirit kept time spent at the bar, a perfect mix between quiet and lively.

Rachel's happy demeanor reminded me once again of one of my old man's more famous sayings, "A bartender should never be grouchier than I am."

The bar was almost full; there were only a few empty seats between a long row of patrons and us. Some couples, a few older men, a young couple who laughed and kissed more and more while the drinks flowed harder into them. A television mindlessly broadcasted a baseball game while it hung in a dusty corner of the bar, its screen filled with remnants of nicotine and a touch of grease. The game was a lopsided contest between two Midwest teams. Since the local teams, as usual, were long out of playoff contention, the local stations switched to the network broadcasting some more "interesting" games. The haze on the television screen made the game seem as if they were playing the game in the middle of London in a thick fog.

When the three young men slipped into the previously empty seats next to Jim, I only lifted my eyes briefly to gaze at them. Harry was right in the middle of demonstrating a technique that he used to body check an opponent when he needed to move a puck slowly along the boards to kill some time for me to recover from a hard and difficult slap shot. Harry's demonstrative motions and passionate testimony had me longing for a comeback in the net-minding duties. Well, it was not quite that passionate, but it *was* entertaining. I saw Jim turn around and look at them, then back to Harry, and Jim, sensing the growing crowd at the bar, even stood up and scooted his bar stool over a little to allow the three men a little more elbow room along what was now a full bar.

When the one young man, now seated next to James T. O'Malley, pounded his fist on the bar and hollered out boldly and rudely to Rachel, "C'mon, shake ya beautiful ass, baby, and get us J.D. and cokes. Lots of ice and dip ya cute, little, titties in the ice first so ya all hard and ready to go for me. I like ya ass in those tight pants, wish ya had bigger titties, but love the blonde hair and swingin' hips. Betcha' ya blonde down where it counts too. Ya skinny, but ya will do for a quickie later on before I go and get me a'nudder hottie. Cuz, baby, I am da man!"

His two sidekick pineapples mimicked his actions and beat on the bar counter to play a little game of, "Let's all be jackasses and play follow the stupid and foolish leader."

Now, Harry stopped speaking, and demonstrating his body checks and holds, and he walked over to his drink, thumbed a thumb to me and then to Jim, rolled his eyes in disgust and took a long sip of his Wallcrawler cocktail. Everyone else in the entire gin joint looked over to where the young man was now making a lewd spectacle of himself, and while no one said a word, they all wore equally disgusted faces. The middle-aged couple on the far side of these three young idiots scooted their bar stools over and away from them. In unison, the entire bar did the same so that the distance between the other patrons and these nitwits was as far as it possibly could be.

Everyone moved away, except for one person.

A certain James T. O'Malley stood up just a little and scooted his bar stool back over to where it formerly sat. Jim looked over at the young man, and I watched as his eyes studied the young man's smug face, his cut-off tee shirt, displaying his exposed and sculptured chest muscles, and his tattooed arms and the inked designs over parts of his neck. The loudmouthed punk's eyes briefly glanced over at Jim, and then at Harry and me, and he adjusted his ball cap with the sales tag still stuck on the lid of the cap on his head to make sure that it tilted at just the correct sideways angle.

There goes the end of a quiet and enjoyable afternoon sharing drinks and memories with my buds.

Bye-bye enjoyable and hello, "Happy Hour?"

I knew that look in O'Malley's eyes, since I spent a good part of my hockey career studying those same eyes for clues as to where Jim was going to shoot, what he was thinking, and as to when the cork was ready to blow out of the volatile bottle of the notorious number eleven.

While James T. O'Malley was a supremely gifted hockey player with incredible skating skills, a wicked hard and accurate shot and a desire to win that I never encountered with any other hockey player that I ever met, played with, or against, he also was the most feared hockey fighter, and player of all time. I sincerely believe and mean that statement. In the semi-professional circles, O'Malley was just as feared a legend as he was at the big-league professional level. Everyone, and I do mean everyone, in the hockey world at all levels, knew of and heard of the legend known as O'Malley. When I first arrived for a stint with a team in Kansas City after playing on Long Island, New York, the first questions my teammates had were about what it had been like playing against O'Malley.

How he never made it to the big-time is a question that I feel I have the answer for safely contained within my heart. It was not part of God's plan for O'Malley. Ultimately, he had a much more important mission as Pastor James T. O'Malley rather than number eleven. Regardless, Jim's reputation for having the willingness for beating the hell out of his own grandmother to gain possession of a hockey puck was well earned and deserved. He was a fearless man and Jim backed down from no one or anything. I know it well. One afternoon, in a hockey game of so long ago, in a rare fit of my own rage and frustration; I, too, battled O'Malley. Since I was a goalie and therefore, I seldom fought, and despite the fact that I outweighed and towered over O'Malley, I had all I could do to hold my own with this wild barbarian known as the notorious number eleven. I was a very strong man and at that time; I was a mass of solid, fine-tuned muscle and a veteran of many Paterson, New Jersey street battles, with my own reputation of being a very capable fighter. It felt as if I was fighting the Tasmanian Devil. Maybe four devils. The consensus was that I won the battle; I am not too sure about that. The fight was neutralized by game officials after a few blows, and in my opinion, it hardly even qualified as a fight due to the brevity, but in the end, O'Malley did not care because, he actually never lost any fights, he just circled back for a kill shot later on down the road.

O'Malley often said, "I will meet you here on the ice, or in the alley behind the rink, or in the parking lot, but I will meet you."

He meant it too. He fought small players, medium-sized players, the biggest players, the toughest players. O'Malley did not care because if it meant winning the game, then that was all O'Malley needed and wanted.

Yet, off the ice and in "normal" mode, James T. O'Malley was the most articulate, eloquent and soft-spoken gentleman that you will ever encounter. In mere seconds, under the right conditions, a Jekyll and Hyde transformation could occur. All it took were a few "trigger" words, or a hockey game, or a hockey puck, or a stick to the face and boom! O'Malley transformed into a wild barbarian, hell-bent on turning you inside and outside and grinding you up into a little ball of mush. The Gospel, according to Pastor O'Malley, took Peter, cutting the ear off the Roman Soldier part to heart.

Harry and I both sensed the storm clouds of transformation building upon the horizon. . ..

Rachel stood with her hands on her hips, shook her head, and proudly reported, "We do not accept or tolerate behavior and language like yours here in this establishment. So, kindly move along. I will not serve you or your friends."

"Oh, a feisty one, huh, guys? I bet she screams in bed. C'mon, baby ya gotta recognize me as Ray Campagna, mixed martial arts professional champion and rapper artist. I am dropping a new record this week and I have me a new video too. This is my hometown and the way that I see it this is my hometown bar. All I want is to have a few drinks and a little lovin' too. This is my brother and his buddy. They are in training too. We are big, bad, but handsome. Like I said, I am da man."

Rachel pointed at the door, and walked away while saying, "I never heard of you, and don't care who or what you are. I am a part owner of this establishment, and you need to leave now. Goodbye and good riddance."

I watched the eyes of this supposed big, bad, and stupid jerk grow wide and anger filled his face. When Rachel walked by him, he stood up, leaned over the bar, and tried to reach and grab her arm as she passed by him.

Rachel avoided him, glared, and the jerk yelled out, "No one says no to, Ray! Now, get ya tight ass over here and serve us some damn drinks."

When Ray decided to lean back, he did so into the outstretched arm of James T. O'Malley. The punk turned around and looked at Jim who now was arm barring him from sitting back onto the bar stool.

Jim stared at him with those deep, black eyes and his lip with the scar from a long-ago high stick, lifted in anger while he sneered and said, "I believe that you heard Rachel's request. It is time for you and your associates to leave this establishment."

I went to jump off my stool, but Harry reached out, grabbed my arm, and held me in place.

"No, twenty-seven. Please, let it go. Sometimes, punks like this need to learn hard lessons. Otherwise, they think they can always get away with bullshit and terrorize women. Today, it is drunken smartass jokes and, in the future, it is ugly and disgusting stuff. Let it go, Paul. God will sort it out. Sorry, my brother, but it is not the right time for any of your usual old lady bullshit right now."

I nodded my head and knew that Harry was correct. Ray glared at Jim and he stood up next to number eleven, who simply stood his ground and remained expressionless. The two cronies jumped off the stool and surrounded Jim and while it was killing me to do so, I held my position. The rest of the bar's patrons grabbed their drinks, cleared their stools, and stood to watch the scene unfold.

As I had mentioned, O'Malley was a legend, and he was a regular.

Ray spun around, and then he sauntered up and bumped into O'Malley's chest, flapped his arms in a display of his perceived toughness and curled his hands into fists. Ray was not a small guy and O'Malley was not a huge or imposing man, which was one of the reasons so many men had made grave errors when confronting O'Malley. It was not his physical size that made him the notorious number eleven. Instead, it was the size of his heart and the power of his soul. I could see O'Malley's pulse throbbing in the temples of his head as the flow came over the legend.

"Establishment. What are you, a newscaster or sumthin'? Ya speak like ya got sumthin' stuck up ya ass. Yo, old man, I am a bad guy. A hood kid! A badass gangsta! I just told the hottie who I am. I am da man! Rapper, undefeated champion and I have street cred to back it all up too. Go back to ya buddies and stay outta of this. I hate to have to beat an old man's ass silly and raw. Ya buddies look like they are smart or they are pussies, cuz, they are not standing up to help ya old ass. Big guys too. One looks like he eats too many cheeseburgers and the other is a washed-up old hippie, but they are big guys. Must'b pussies. Ya a pussy and ya buds are pussies, too. Now, sit down, finish ya drinks, rock in ya rocking chair and shut the hell up while I have my way around here and with the cute hot chick."

Jim shook his head and pointed at the front door.

Then Jim said, "It is with heart-felt assurance that I can inform you that my friends are not cowards. Quite the opposite. They are both ultimate warriors. Men who are very respectful and men who play the game to win. Just as I do. We never, ever give up. We play the game to win, we fight for respect, and we fight to be winners. We always will until the end of all time. You have no idea who they are and what they are capable of doing. They are not intervening because they know I do not need them to do so. Because, they know me."

Jim was so well spoken.

Harry leaned in and said, "He has not fully transformed into wild barbarian mode yet, twenty-seven."

I nodded in agreement and whispered, "Any second now."

After hearing O'Malley's words, Ray laughed and turned to his minions and right on a queue, they laughed too. Monkeys see and monkeys do. In this case, jackasses see and jackasses do.

"Play the game to win, huh? Whatever game ya old ass plays. Sounds like ya are a loser to me. Are you stupid or just thick in the head, or too old to hear? I am Ray Campagna, mixed martial arts undefeated champion. I will knock ya old ass into the next county." Ray then turned and pointed at us and said with his finger pointed at us and his tattooed arms exposed, "I know youse guys are pussies and shaking in ya shoes, but ya better come and git ya old friend and protect him from the ass-beating he is about to git."

Harry shook his head, smiled, while saying, "He does not need any protection. I can assure you that we are not pussies. It is just as Jim said. We know him. But honestly, we promise, we will jump in when it is required to save and protect ya ass and ya buddies' asses from . . . Jim." Harry then smiled and added, "Just let us know what hospital youse guys want us to tell the ambulance dudes to take ya to."

Now, Ray looked around. His eyes darted from Jim, to the crowd that was now watching and smiling, then to his buddies and finally to Rachel. It seemed as if for a mere few seconds a few hints of doubts crept into . . . "Da Man."

Rachel caught his eyes, pointed at the front door, and said, "Last chance to leave on your own or leave on an ambulance cart."

"Bullshit! Up ya ass, ya old asshole. I gave ya a chance!"

And, with a loud yell and a scream, Ray assumed a martial art's stance, and then he jumped in the air, performed a martial art high kick, and nailed O'Malley right across the jaw with a ferocious blow that snapped Jim's head back with a terrific force. Everyone gasped in horror and Ray's face turned from smug to shock when he watched Jim stand his ground, touch his lip and shake his head, side-to-side just a little. Jim reached up to his mouth and his finger caught a little blood trickle that formed in the corner of his lip. Jim looked at his finger, licked the blood off his finger, his face broke into his patented smile, and he shook his head once more.

I settled in now. This was a scene that I had watched a few times before and it was about to get really good. The transformation was now complete.

Hold on tightly.

"Undefeated, huh? Professional, huh? As in a registered and licensed fighter? Bad guy, a rapper, with street credentials and you are a gangster? Is that all you have, punk? That is what Da Man is all about, huh? Well, now, since I am a reasonable man, and I am very fair, I am gonna give you one, more, free shot and then, it is my turn. A subtle warning, I dabble a little in dentistry, but I only do extractions."

Ray shuddered, screamed, and nailed Jim with a solid left hook punch across the jaw. Jim took a step back and smiled that same smile, but this time, Jim held his hands up and spit his false teeth into his hands, and then he smiled a toothless and wide smile.

Jim's original teeth are in the dirt under some of those shopping centers and apartment complexes.

While Jim put his teeth into his pocket, all we could hear was Ray say, "Oh shit."

"Yup, smart-ass, now, it is my turn."

All that it took were about six or seven deadly accurate and crushing punches to his face and body and Ray, also known as "Da Man" was on the floor of the barroom and begging for mercy. Despite Ray's best attempts at defense, the force of Jim's blows blew right through his defensive maneuvers.

It was as if sledgehammers had hit him.

It was needless to say that Ray was no longer undefeated, and he was certainly not a badass. He lost his street credentials too.

His two buddies unwisely jumped into the fray and

when O'Malley had Ray on the floor and was stomping his body with his foot while simultaneously, holding the two minions by their necks and beating their heads on the bar counter, Harry, elbowed me and said, "Okay, twenty-seven. Let's go save them from, O'Malley, before he really turns it up on these fools."

I nodded and jumped out of my bar stool and followed Harry to the scene of the "Return of Number Eleven."

We scurried over and rescued the previously undefeated champion and his fallen comrades from the wrath of O'Malley.

Harry bear-hugged Jim, and the big guy tugged him away, while saying, "Okay, number eleven, break it up. Put ya false choppers back in ya mouth. Ya are going to have to sit in the penalty box now. It is over. They now have learned that they need to respect their elders and young women too."

Harry was still a big, strong and powerful man and his bear hug could break you in half. Jim stopped teaching his lesson and allowed Harry to pull him away from the melee. One of the male bar patrons and onlookers took the incensed and possessed O'Malley and led Jim over to his bar stool to re-transform and cool down.

Harry grabbed the two minions and held them by the waistbands of their pants, and the big guy examined their injuries. They were bloodied, swollen and shaken, but we had rescued them in time before they required resuscitation and hospitalization.

"Ah, ya punks are okay. A little aspirin, a few stitches or butterflies and an ice pack or two and you will be as good as new. Old twenty-seven here would not even get any medical attention with these little winky-dinky-doo injuries. O'Malley must 'a felt sorry for youse guys, cuz, he went easy on ya."

The two shocked punks only shook their heads and checked their teeth, and they held their heads in their hands.

I reached down, picked the man formerly known as "Da Man" off the barroom floor, and held him on his feet until he was steady.

Ray was a mess.

Blood flowed from his mouth and from a few cuts over his eyes. He spit one of his teeth out and held it in his hand, looked at it, and then stuffed it into the pocket of his pants. A souvenir and a reminder of the ultimate lesson learned. Ray's eyes were already swelling shut. Some facial bruises appeared in glorious colors of red, black, and what I must say, was a rather pleasant shade of blue.

"On your feet, there, chief. Not as big and as bad as you thought you were, eh? It looks as if you are no longer undefeated, but I hope that you are wiser. Eating fists for brunch has a strange way of teaching some serious little lessons. Hopefully, you will think the next time that you are disrespectful to a woman and your elders."

Ray only looked at me, and I knew he felt my strength as I picked him off the floor in one swoop and held him.

He examined me carefully and then finally spoke, "Shit, man, are all youse guys giants?" He then put his fingers in his mouth and checked the status of the rest of his teeth. Rachel handed him bar napkins to hold over the blood flowing out of his mouth and above his eyes. "I hit him with all that I had and it did not even faze him. I rode those kicks and punches to a clean knockout record."

"Well, sorry, Ray, but you are the one who got knocked on your ass today."

Ray held his head in his hands and dismally asked, "Who in the Hell is that guy?"

I pointed at the framed jersey hanging above the bar and said, "James Thomas O'Malley. That is his famous, notorious, number eleven, hockey sweater. A dentist who only does extractions. Welcome to the world of old-time ice hockey. I have to say that . . . you have a broken picker for choosing people to harass and try to convince how big and bad you are. Of all the people in this entire world, you just messed with the absolute wrong guy that you could have possibly messed with. Harry warned you, but you were too busy convincing all of us that you were such a big, bad, gangsta, in order for you to heed his words. Well, now, you know that you are not really, Da Man. I should also mention that Jim is also known as Pastor James O'Malley, but he is retired now."

"Hockey! An old-time ice hockey player! And, a pastor! As in a church type of pastor?" Ray gasped at the thought that a minister and old-time hockey player had just kicked his ass.

"Yes, in-deedy. Can you imagine what he was like thirty years ago? The body count after hockey games was incredible. Maybe you should consider a change of attitude and some church attendance too. Don't mess with hockey players, pastors, prophets, saints, angels, the Holy Spirit and God. They can all kick some major ass. After all, Peter cut the ear off the Roman Soldier and Jesus turned the moneychangers inside and out too."

Ray had no response, and it seemed as if he might have held some remorse for his behavior even if he did not say it or overtly display it. Ray simply stood there and felt his swollen face. I smiled and manhandled Ray, as I led him toward the rear door of the bar. He was too weak and bloodied to fight back, and even if he was not, I was ready to kick his ass now too. I nodded to Harry, who grabbed the two minions, and while holding each of them by the scruff of their necks in his powerful hands, Harry followed my lead.

As we led them to the back door of the bar, Rachel held it wide open for us.

I explained, "Since you are supposedly a licensed and professional mixed martial art fighter, who was previously undefeated, I am quite sure that the last thing you need is the world to know that you threatened a supposedly old man and then proceeded to get your ass kicked by the same supposedly old man known as, O'Malley. Since you would not leave when the owner asked you to leave and you threw the first blow, we are going to cut you guys a major break. My buddy and I, who are also ex-hockey players, are not going to call the police and instead, we are unceremoniously going to throw your sorry asses out the back door and into the alley behind this, as Jim says, establishment."

With a heave and a toss, Ray went head over a teakettle into the alley and he rolled for a few feet until he stopped.

Harry then launched the two sidekicks in the air and they joined their buddy with a thud and a roll.

Rachel leaned out the door and tossed Ray's hat out the door and in his direction. It spun and flipped in the wind and then landed close to the former champion.

"Don't forget your fancy hat, jerk!" Rachel yelled, along with her golden toss.

With a loud shout, Harry said, "Bye-bye, Ray. Who is the pussy now? Ya little dumb-ass punk. When your ass heals up, go get a tattoo of a cupcake on ya ass. Because, Ray, ya no longer Da Man but ya are Da Cupcake. We would like to stick around and watch you lick ya wounds, but it is time for me to order a'nudder cheeseburger. By the way, the drug store is two blocks down on the right side. Bandages are on sale today. Tell 'em that O'Malley sent ya sorry asses!"

Rachel mouthed, "Thank you" to us and we returned to the bar where the bar crowds were on their feet, giving the famous number eleven a standing ovation.

It was not his first standing ovation.

Harry bellowed out, "Rachel, c'mon, drinks for everyone on my tab! Here is to the legendary, James Thomas O'Malley!"

The bar jammed with patrons, and after Rachel and the

servers poured all the rounds of shots and drinks, we toasted the real man!

"Here is to O'Malley! Long live, Jim, and all that he stands for and all that he honors!" Harry yelled out with his arm hanging around the famous number eleven.

The crowd yelled, "Here! Here!"

Since Jim had returned to his "normal" mode, he smiled, and he spoke in his gentle voice, "Thank you. It is my sincere hope and prayer that my little lesson allows those three young men to reexamine their previous evil behavior and wretched ways. Perhaps, they will even attend church and come to know, The Lord."

He tugged at his pants, humbly sat down on his bar stool, turned to Harry and said, "Now, Harry. Please, before that unfortunate interruption by those ill-fated and rude young men, where were you in explaining that move along the boards? Perhaps, you could show, twenty-seven and me in a little more depth. I am most curious as to how you kept the puck between your skate blades. Fascinating. I wondered why I could never dig it out when you did that."

Jim then turned and smiled at the beautiful bartender, who beamed with pride at her protector.

"Rachel, please, my dear, would you obtain my best friends here another round on my tab? We are going to take taxicabs home. This is a most interesting discussion, and a fun filled afternoon. I am sure that we will continue well into the evening. There are so many stories, hockey games, adventures, and potentially, some more little lessons to cover."

Jim abruptly stopped speaking. It seemed as if he was gathering his thoughts. Jim leaned in, and Harry, Rachel, and I could tell that the intensity of his words was capturing his heart and soul. His black eyes flickered with raw emotion and combined with the dim lights of the bar.

Jim pointed his finger into his own chest as he spoke in a deep, but low whisper, "You always need to play the game to win. Just as I do. I never, ever give up. I play the game to win, and I fight for respect. I always will until the end of all time. You can play the game rough but fair, but have respect for the rules and for your opponents. If you never stand up for respect and if you never play the game to be a winner, then you are everyone's best friend. James T. O'Malley is not interested in being everyone's best friend, but I am interested in winning and for standing for The Lord and for respect. If I do lose, then I make sure that I gave it all of what I had to give and I give the winners the respect they deserve. And mark my words, I might have lost, but I will return with all the power in my soul and wearing God's armor. Peter cut the ear off the Roman Soldier. Peter played the game to win, and he stood for his friend and for what he believed in and so does Pastor James T. O'Malley and number eleven."

Jim leaned back; he folded his arms across his mighty chest and smiled. A slight transformation, into the notorious number eleven, but now Jim returned.

"Rachel, please, I apologize for the interlude. Please, those drinks, my dear. You are such a glorious young woman. A gift to this world from God. Some young man will be so lucky to hold you on his arm and within his heart and call you his wife and lover."

Rachel leaned over the bar counter and gently kissed the cheek of the notorious number eleven. The mighty heart of the warrior melted, and Jim's face turned twenty different shades of red.

Rachel whispered, "No, Jim, you are a gift to this world from God. Thank you for those little lessons."

Dear reader, please meet Pastor James Thomas O'Malley, also known as the notorious number eleven.

Did I happen to mention that O'Malley was a legend?

Amongst many things, he was a legend. However, most of all he was our friend and a great man.

I am sure that this world was a much better place

because of James Thomas O'Malley.

There is no doubt in my mind that I am sure of it, because along the way, Jim just had an uncanny knack for teaching those famous "little lessons."

Chapter Two

The Last Shift

When the telephone call came from Mrs. James Thomas O'Malley that we might want to head to the hospital right now, if we wanted to see her husband one last time on this side of Heaven and while he might still be vaguely aware of our presence, a million or more thoughts ran quickly through my mind. In many ways, I found it difficult to sort the thoughts out from those related to hockey, to those related to our other common profession, which was serving as clergymen, to our remarkable friendship. It even influenced my choice of attire to wear to visit with Jim, or as Harry and number twenty-seven, as well as countless other teammates, players, coaches, and a multitude of others, who knew James Thomas O'Malley from his famous playing hockey career, lovingly called him, "O'Malley."

Even though I was now retired for about two years, (although I was now on the "retired but able to preach list") I kept my usual black suit and white pastor's collar handy for times such as these times, but something told me to dress differently for this visit. From professional ice hockey, is where O'Malley and I came to be where we now were in our lives together, and in retrospect, I guess, somehow, that is to where we ultimately will end. With those thoughts in mind, instead of my clergyman's attire, I chose my old throwback Long Island Rooster's number twenty-seven hockey sweater, black dungarees, and my black canvas sneakers. I did slip my rugged old wooden cross on a cloth lanyard over my neck and ran a comb through my still shoulder-length hair and a brush through my beard.

"Okay, Paul, I have to be honest that I did not expect to see you dressed in a hockey sweater," my wife, Rose Henson reacted, when she saw my choice of attire.

At first, I did not answer; instead, I pulled at the front of my sweater, stared at the logo on it, and then smiled. Rose sensed my mood and reasoning and she warmly smiled at me, then walked over, wrapped her arms around me, and gracefully set her head upon my chest.

I heard her whisper, "I understand. It is what you two shared and what you represented. To return to your roots is what you feel that you owe to, Jim. I understand."

We are always in tune. My wife's mind is remarkable and perhaps that is not the correct word because it does not encompass enough of what she is. Extraordinary in every way.

That works.

"I am ready if you are," Rose said as she puckered her lips up to me and I leaned over and kissed her gently.

"Thank you for you. I am ready. Let's roll."

We wrapped our arms around each other and made our way to the garage. The hospital was about an hour or so away from our townhouse. It would be an emotional ride, because I knew that we would rehash some of what James T. O'Malley and I shared in our lives as well, as some memories that Rose had shared with the man known as "O'Malley" too.

We jumped in Rose's sports car and I drove.

Once out on the main road, Rose leaned in and gently placed her hand over mine as I rested it on the stick shift for car and she gently asked, "You, okay? Do you want to talk about Jim and your lives together, you know, let it out and chase away, as you say, the ghosts?"

I smiled and nodded, and as soon as Rose said those words, I felt the memory of a special afternoon and evening rush into my mind. A time when O'Malley and I shared memories of his life and some of the stories that made up the life of a very special person. A man who God shaped, molded and generously allowed to be a part of so many lives. This world was such a better place because of the life of Pastor James Thomas O'Malley, also known as the notorious number eleven. A man, who when we played together on the ice in an era that now seems as if it were ten lifetimes ago, was the mortal enemy of a certain goaltender who wore number twenty-seven.

As I said, maybe ten lifetimes ago, or even more.

"I need to write it all down, you know, someday, in one of my books. O'Malley told me his story a few years ago. One afternoon in the summer when he stopped by the bishop's office and honestly, we goofed off all afternoon and part of the night too. We ended up at The Elusive Lion Pub, and well, it was quite the memorable experience. I can say that it was one of the most extraordinary experiences of my life. Jim told me things that I never knew before about his life and how it formed him into the pastor, the hockey player, and the great man that he is."

Rose jumped into the conversation and with her glorious laugh lacing the words, Rose added, "That is going to be a fascinating story, Paul. You must write it down. Twenty-seven and number eleven rehashing a lifetime of battles and memories and I am sure some emotions. I bet both of you took taxicabs home."

"Hell yeah, we did, and the next morning and a good part of the next afternoon were brutal, while I recovered from far too many beers. After that long day and discussion, I asked Jim to write notes of his life, and he did. Jim gave them to me under one condition. He said I could only write the story and publish it after he left this world to reside in Heaven. For some reason, Jim was convinced that he would go before me. It looks as if he was correct. I understood, and I agreed to his terms. The notes are simply amazing and I have them in a file on my desk. Jim hand wrote them and my plan is to combine them with my own writings and our adventures and turn them into a book. It will be a tribute to a great man and it will tell his story."

I turned and smiled at Rose and my wife smiled back and gripped my hand tightly.

Rose gently spoke while holding my hand, "It will be. You know that he is so much more than the tough guy and wild man reputation that followed Jim around. He is a great man and your idea for a tribute is wonderful."

I nodded and said, "He is a legend. I am proud to know him and call Jim, our friend and our brother. I know that Harry loved him, too. I am quite sure that Jim's feelings are mutual."

I turned onto the main drag, shifted gears, and the big engine responded as the memories began to flood my mind and the story of the remarkable life of O'Malley flickered to life.

"You know something, Rose? Did I ever tell you about the first time I ever met, O'Malley?"

"Not sure, Paul. Maybe, but what does it matter? I could listen to your stories endlessly. Just to hear your amazing voice and that illustrious Paterson, New Jersey accent melts my heart and is music to my soul. I am all ears."

"Well, it was a hockey tournament and Harry and twenty-seven were. . .."

Mrs. Kate O'Malley met Rose and me at the hospital room door and her face broke into a huge smile as her eyes caught my attire. Kate nodded her head, wiped tears from both of her eyes and waved for us to come closer and when we did so, she leaned in while the three of us warmly embraced. Rose and I took turns kissing Kate's cheeks, and I studied her eyes. Jim's wife was a part of Jim, and I am quite sure as many stories that I had told my wife, friends, and family over the years about Jim, number eleven had told a few about me too. Kate knew that I studied eyes for many reasons and one of them was to discover clues about a person's soul.

She smiled and knew my intentions and before I could say anything, Kate spoke, "I am okay, Paul. I assure you that I am. Staying strong. My mind knew this was coming for a few weeks now. It is time to convince my heart to let go of him now."

"God is great, and God and all the Angels in Heaven, are with you and holding you and Jim right now, dear Kate."

No words, just a nod and she warmly held me once again, while Rose held her hands on Kate's back and my wife and I joined together in an effort to absorb some of her pain.

Kate was a gorgeous woman; she was tall and shapely with striking facial features and long, flowing brown hair with touches of auburn that sported licks of gray along the edges and tumbled gracefully in charming waves of glory over her shoulders. Over fifty years ago, this gorgeous woman stole the heart of the formerly elusive O'Malley and never returned it. They made an awesome couple and remained glorious partners in sharing the twists and turns of life. For a reason that neither Kate nor Jim ever chose to share with us, they never had any children, but they shared a glorious life.

Kate took Rose and me by our hands and she quietly said, "Come along, my dearest friends. Come and visit my James. I hope he opens his eyes and can share just a moment or two with you this afternoon. The last few hours have not been very good. The doctors and nurses seem to think we might be down to the last few days of this horrible struggle."

The three of us approached the bed, and we stood next to James T. O'Malley as he laid there in the bed, not moving his eyes or stirring in any way. Tubes and wires of all types crisscrossed his body, leading to many electronic monitors and instruments standing as if they were silent sentries next to Jim, telling the final tales of his life while they stood guard over him. It had been about a week or thereabouts since we had last visited Jim, and the regression in his condition took me by surprise, as I am sure it did my beloved Rose too. Gaunt did not begin to describe Jim's appearance because it was beyond gaunt. It was shocking.

Dear reader, I will leave it at that.

I tried hard to remember what Jim really looked like before cancer ravaged his body and his appearance, and I closed my eyes as I felt Rose squeeze my hands tightly. I knew that my wife was struggling with the memory, too. This was the last battle for the great number eleven. Even O'Malley could not win this one, but he was going to be in a glorious place very soon. Jim knew it and I took great comfort in that fact and I know deep down, Jim did too.

In my profession, both as a pastor and as a Lutheran bishop, I had faced loved ones, parishioners, and many persons, while they closed in on death and neared the end of their lives as they lay upon countless deathbeds. It was never easy, nor was it something that you somehow became "used" to facing. Quite the opposite because I had come face-to-face with this situation more times than I wanted to admit or recall. This one was particularly difficult.

I let go of both the women's hands, dropped to my knees, and knelt to pray next to the bed.

Lowering my head and clasping my hands, I first prayed silently that God would have mercy on Jim and take him to Heaven quickly, and then aloud, as I prayed, "Dear God in

Heaven. All praise to you for the life of our beloved, Pastor James T. O'Malley. He remains your faithful servant. Thank you for James T. O'Malley and what he means to Kate, Rose, and to me. Mostly, thank you for what he means to this world. I pray for Jim's comfort, in this time of need. In Jesus' name, we pray. Amen."

"Thank you for the prayers, Pastor Paul, and thank you for wearing your hockey sweater."

I heard the words and felt a gentle tug at the collar of my hockey sweater. I opened my eyes to see Jim gently holding the sweater by the neckline and wearing a wide smile. I smiled back and stood up. Jim reached out his hand and I took it. His eyes motioned for Rose and for Kate to join our clasp. They did so and the four of us laid our hands on top of each other's hands.

Jim spoke in a weak voice, but somehow even though my words cannot capture the emotion of the moment, his voice was as powerful as it always was, "Some of my fondest memories of this world are of you wearing that number twenty-seven jersey. All we shared, all we battled for and all we meant to each other. Be sure to carry on with the mission, twenty-seven. Take care of my beloved Kate, hold Rose close every day of your life and always play the game to win. Some people will think that O'Malley lost this game, but we know better because it really will be the ultimate win. Carry on, Paul. Please continue to play the game to win. I cannot think of any man who is better for the mission than the world famous, number twenty-seven."

"I can never fill your skates, Jim."

He shook his head, smiled, and then coughed a little. After struggling and then catching his breath, he mumbled, "This dying stuff is not for pansies . . . no, Paul, you can fill them. Now, it is time for my last shift and soon, I will hang my skates up for good. Make sure they resurface the ice for the next game. No ripples, not too much water and no hard edges. Falling on your ass, only means you have to get back up again."

I held his hand tighter, and Jim smiled widely. "You got it, Jim. I am here and will skate the next shift for all of us."

He nodded and mumbled, "Harry and I will meet you on the other side. Buckle your mask straps, cuz, number eleven does not cut any breaks. Even in Heaven. No breaks. I always play to win the game."

Jim then allowed his eyes to wander around the room. They landed upon his wife, and then on Rose and once more he smiled. I knew that he was recalling some words from a long time ago. A special time that we shared together.

"Twenty-seven, I will tell you, I will meet you there, my long-haired friend. I will meet you there."

I smiled, hugged him and said, "Jim, I am counting on it! I would not want it to be any other way. Would . . . you?"

O'Malley smiled while saying, "Hell no, twenty-seven, hell no."

"Me too. I would not want it any other way. I am counting on you, Jim. Counting on it."

Rose's warm embrace around my neck felt so comforting and loving. While I was focused intently on my laptop, my wife had crept into my office and snuck up behind me. She now wrapped her arms around me while placing her head on my right shoulder.

"You have been so quiet since we returned from the hospital and visited with Jim and Kate. You hardly said a word the entire ride home. I know that you are suffering and I knew that this is where I would find you. I see that you are going to begin to release some more ghosts."

"I am, my love. Yes. It is time. The doctors seem to think that Jim might be into the last few days here, and I need to shift some emotions from this world to my other world.

This world of words and adventures that I have created."

I could feel Rose nod her head and then her arms released from her grip around my neck. She slowly walked over to the side of my desk and stood for just a moment or two, and then she smiled at me. I looked away from the laptop screen and smiled in return. Rose gently moved some papers, and then she sat on the edge of my desk and continued to stare at me.

"What, is it, Rose?" I was somewhat puzzled by her intense stare.

"Nothing, just that I am so proud of you. That is all. My pride and my love for you are equal within my heart and my soul." Rose gently reached out and motioned for my hand and I took it and we held each other's hands for a few moments without saying anything.

"Thank you for that. Pride in a spouse is very important and you know that my pride for you is endless and overflowing, Rose."

"I do know that. Above all, the honor that you will bestow upon Jim is more than just a release of emotions for you, dear Paul. It is a mission and, in your heart, it is an obligation that you need to fulfill. I know you so well. You will not rest until you tell Jim's story to the world. Away you will travel, to hockey rinks of the past, to pulpits, to fistfights, to all that Jim has shared and all that you now know. This is going to be one of your famous writing marathons. I can feel it. No rest, until you feel as if you have paid O'Malley back for all he has given to you and to this world."

If I was not riding so high on emotions right now, from our hospital visit, then I think that I would have been able to force the tears back from my eyes upon hearing my wife's words. Right now, it was hopeless, and I felt my eyes rim up with the tears and Rose's eyes did the same. I stood up, Rose did too, and we kissed, and then warmly embraced.

After wiping away our tears and sharing some deep kisses, I said, "I am not sure how one person could be so deeply connected to my soul, as how it is that you are, Rose. You are amazing and you are correct. I have to write this. Jim is a special man and I owe him so much for what he taught me about so many things. Not quite sure where I would be right now if it were not for James T. O'Malley in my life."

"I understand. Therefore, write you will, number twenty-seven. Write as if you are a glorious man with a grandeur mission and a man, possessed by amazing words. Because . . . you are."

Rose let go of me and I saw her eyes catch something on my desk. She picked up some papers and thumbed through them rather quickly, and then Rose looked at me.

"Are these the notes that you told me that Jim compiled?"

"They are. I will use Jim's own words and testimony to piece together the book. At least that is my plan. I will weave my own memories and the hockey adventures within. His life story is amazing."

My wife's dark eyes darted back and forth from the pages to me, and then she replaced the papers on the desk and said, "I cannot even imagine how much James T. O'Malley has crammed into one remarkable life."

With her words and the tone in which she delivered them, Rose seemed to latch onto and feed off of my own passion to write this story. Her beauty surrounded her as if it was an aura from Heaven.

With an intensity that I had not seen until a few minutes ago, Rose continued, "I am here to love and support you. It seems to me that you are busier in your retirement than you were when you worked, but at least, I have you here right next to me and I can love you and come in and disturb you for passionate sexual interludes whenever I want to."

"Okay, needless to say, I gotcha covered on that one. Is that the plan? This book could take a long time if we start off like that."

"Of course, that is the plan. You bet it is! Time means very little right now. Often, it is how you end, not how you begin. In between, will be our time. With a few glorious words, woven into that amazing memory of yours, you will begin. How about a glass of Scotch to start off the flow of inspiration?" Rose asked, while she waved to the wet-bar along the wall of my office. She looked as if she were one of those beautiful women displaying the latest lineup of new cars in an automobile showroom.

"Works for me. Thank you for all that you do and all that you are in my life, Rose. I love you to the moon and beyond."

My wife smiled at me, winked, and melted my heart. I watched Rose select a top-shelf Scotch whiskey from our selection, she poured a neat Scotch into a glass etched with the number "27" and with a seductive smile on her gorgeous face, Rose, gently swayed her gorgeous hips and glorious backside, while she sashayed over to my desk.

When she gently handed me the glass, leaned over and gave me a kiss, and whispered, "Write on and good luck. I will be back for one of those interludes when you need a break."

I knew that I had to be the luckiest man in the world. To have lost a glorious love and then God provided number twenty-seven in his various incarnations, with another chance at immense love was more than I, as the rather weak wordsmith that I am, could find words to describe how it made me feel. Without saying anything else, Rose waved and walked out of the office.

Her rear view was quite amazing, too.

Now, with love in my heart and the story on the edge of my memories and the tips of my fingers, it was time to write on and get rolling. I shuffled Jim's notes, and I knew right where I needed to begin. And, with a sip of Scotch, I began to release some ghosts and slowly they rose from the keyboard and floated above my head and then drifted gracefully into every corner of the room. There, the ghosts waited and watched as they considered my next move. Alone in my office as the trickle of Scotch warmed my veins, I smiled, because in my heart, I knew that I had this game covered. Words are the magic keys that unlocked the doors to my soul.

Initially, I did not require Jim's notes; this book will begin with one glorious memory effortlessly pulled from deep within my own memory bank.

"Now that our business is complete, what do you say if we goof off the rest of this Friday, Pastor Jim, and head for the Elusive Lion Public House?"

Pastor James T. O'Malley put his finger to his chin and pondered my offer.

After a few exceedingly short moments of contemplation, he replied, "I must say, Pastor Paul, that you do come up with grand ideas. Even though I am now retired and I should not even consider our meeting today to fall under the classification of work, I do so. What is that idiom or name that you call every Friday? It has religious overtones and if I try very hard, I can make it all fit into my mind. Sort of, a justification type of angle for supporting Jesus when he decided it was a grand idea to turn the water into wine."

Even after knowing James T. O'Malley for over twenty-five years and our relationship spanning our mutual careers with first professional hockey and now in the ministry, his flair for off-the-ice eloquence never ceased to amaze me! Jim had stopped by to work on some plans for an upcoming project that together we had a mutual interest in. Jim and I were both serving on a recently formed board of directors for a not-for-profit project in my home city of Paterson, New Jersey. A project of community outreach and even though Jim was correct, and he was technically retired, he was very willing to assist and serve on this project. It was a worthwhile cause, and Jim was a devoted and honorable man. Whenever he could support his motto of fighting for respect and playing the game to win, Jim did so.

"Well, Pastor Jim, I declared my own holiday and renamed every Friday to be God Bless the Keg Day."

"Ah yes, the perfect name and laced with your profound wisdom and covert humor. No doubt that you inherited it from your mother's side of your family. English humor. What would the world be like without it? Cold and stark. Conveniently, as the presiding and closest Lutheran bishop to the Elusive Lion Pub, I suppose you're the honorable clergyman to convey the blessing upon the said keg?"

"I am."

Jim smiled, and I saw that corner of his lip go straight up as it did whenever he smiled or sneered. The lip that had a slight fold over in it due to about twenty or so stitches he received as the result of a stick duel with a known hockey "high sticking expert."

There were quite a few of them in our leagues back then.

The famous incident occurred before I arrived in the league where Jim and I battled each other on opposing teams and I never asked Jim too much about that particular battle, but rumor has it that the high sticking player did not fare so well in the ensuing onslaught of blood and fists. Further rumors detailed how the local police had to come out on the ice and slap Jim in cuffs to haul him off the ill-fated hockey stick user.

They were just rumors.

Perhaps.

With the smile still locked on his face, Jim managed to

speak between his smile, "I have to admire Lutherans, all that rabble rousing over there by your leader and going and causing a Protestant Reformation and such. It has turned out rather well for all of us, even over here on the nondenominational side of the camp. With that in mind, I say we quit work early and enjoy a few frosty mugs of a special brew. Perhaps, we can rehash some old times."

"Jim, a perfect idea that works for me and since Martha is off on her summer vacation to the Jersey shore, there will be no witnesses to our waywardness. Please, just give me a minute or two to shut down for the day."

I stood up, pushed the "off" button on my computer, and grabbed some papers from the desk. While I stuffed the papers and my laptop computer into my backpack, Jim stood up and he wandered over to the wall of my office. I could see those famous dark eyes studying the various photographs, certificates, degrees and artwork on the wall and he paused over a black-and-white photo of me standing with Harry on the ice at Ice Land, which was our home rink in Great Falls, New Jersey.

The photo was my late wife's favorite photo of the two of us together.

Binky always said, "It looked as if you were brothers and not just friends in this photo. Anyone that is viewing this photo can feel the special bond between Harry and Paul. The aura around you two is awe-inspiring."

Harry and I were standing next to the hockey goal, wide smiles on our faces, with our arms flung over each other's shoulders. Harry stood proudly in his defensive hockey gear, and I was fully dressed in my goaltending gear. My goalie mask flipped back on my head, my long hair tied behind my head in a ponytail and we each held our respective hockey sticks. I could not even tell you what the year was, or the situation was, but since we were both wearing practice jerseys, then I had to say it was from a senior league team that we both played on. The photo must have been from shortly before Harry's terrible on-the-ice injury and his last shift of hockey. Harry had taken on a slap shot and lost that battle. Most hockey players do. The hockey puck hit him straight on in his mouth and face. The surgeons put the big guy back together. However, the injury was so devastating that Harry hung up his skates after that and only dabbled in skating and some practices here and there. The great number thirty-five remained my biggest fan, and from the sidelines, he pushed me onward and upward. Harry also returned to the ice and assisted me on an important coaching stint. But that dear reader is a different story.

Jim pensively studied the photo for a long time and he mumbled, "Martha, yes, on her summer vacation. She is wonderful, dedicated and full of honor. Martha has been your assistant forever and even a little longer if I recall correctly."

I could tell by the waver in Jim's voice when he made his statement that his mind was wandering, and he looked emotional as he studied the photo. I saw him reach up, touch the glass covering the photo, and run his fingers reverently along the surface of it.

"Yes, we have been together forever. Since I began in the ministry. I love dear Martha and I would be lost forever without her assistance." I walked over and put my arm around Jim, and we studied the picture together.

"This is a remarkable photo, twenty-seven," Jim said with considerable emotions now rising in his voice, "you can feel the incredible bond between the two of you. Amazing. Just the smiles on your faces. Two warriors ready for combat. In those days, hockey was a war on ice." Jim turned and looked at me and studied me for a reply.

"It was Binky's favorite photo of Harry and me. She said the same thing that you did about the bond."

Jim nodded and turned back to the photo. "Must have been before his injury, eh?"

"It was. Right before."

"I miss him every day. Harry was quite the man. Full of courage and honor. Full of life and love. I imagine that there are no words for you to describe how much it must hurt for you, twenty-seven. No words, eh?"

"None."

Jim bowed his head, and I placed my hand on his back as I could tell that he was silently praying. I heard him mumble something about the last shift on the ice, and then he smiled and warmly patted me on the back.

Jim pointed to the door. We began to walk out of the office and I saw Jim look at the case in my hand as the notorious number eleven said, "Well, looks as if you are ready, Pastor Paul. Let's go drown some memories. Did I ever tell you about my last shift on the ice in professional hockey?"

I shook my head and replied, "No, I do not recall that story, Jim. Let's go, and please, tell me that one and a few more. Does it involve a fight?"

"Now, twenty-seven, what in the hell would make you think that!"

"Lucky guess."

Jim was already standing out in the main hallway of the building and even from that distance, I heard Jim roaring with laughter.

I turned and shut the lights out in the office and locked the door.

Chapter Three

Where it all Began

"I see that your friend, the bartender, is not working this shift today. Perhaps, I am mistaken, but does she not generally work the lunch and afternoon shifts here? Gorgeous woman. Stunning. Jennifer, I think her name is," Jim spoke while we settled into two chairs at the bar of "The Elusive Lion Pub."

"Jim, yes, you are correct on all your statements. Especially the stunning part. Jennifer is her name, and she is off to visit her mom and dad in upstate New York for a spell."

Upon hearing my words, Jim nodded and rubbed his chin thoughtfully.

"Upstate New York, eh?" Jim asked, and I nodded. While adjusting the chair closer to the bar counter, Jim said, "This place does not have the usual crowd today, no doubt, because the gorgeous woman is not here. Bet she hauls in the business. Men cannot take their eyes off of her. You two are quite close. If I recall, she is single. Never married. Any romantic aspirations, twenty-seven?"

"Yes, she never married. We are very good friends. Honestly, maybe a bit more. We have dated, gone to dinner, movies, you know, hung out here and there. Honestly, Jim, I can share this with you, well, we are on and off lovers. One night, it turned quite heated, and we were certainly, ah, how shall I say, very romantic, but I never imply that I want to become serious and steady with only her. One night turned into another and well, you know. As you said, Jennifer is stunning, and oh my, she is in many ways. Perhaps that one night that began our relationship was a mistake, but we are passionate lovers without any commitments or schedule. Jennifer understands. She says that I am worth the wait to see how it all shakes out."

"I see. No mistakes, you are just not ready for any serious commitment yet. God will bring you there. My dear, longhaired friend of so many adventures together, I am not telling you what to do. Just some advice. I bottled my emotions for too long in my life and for that, I paid the price. Kate unlocked my soul in so many ways. Only you know your own heart and your beloved wife has been gone for many years now. Until you feel your heart and know your path, then, please do not bottle up that gift of love that you have within you, Paul. God wants you to share it with this world. No one cares or loves harder than you do and I assure you that it is a gift from God to you."

The notorious number eleven was actually a very insightful, brilliant, and deep-thinking man. I often wonder if those hockey players of so long ago, who Jim leveled and pummeled in hockey games of old, could see James T. O'Malley now . . . what they would think?

"Thanks for the advice, Pastor Jim. I will be sure to follow it."

"Of course. Say, what is this bartender's name?"

"Perry. He is usually the closer during the weekends."

Jim smiled while waving hello to Perry.

He then commented, "My goodness. This is a home away from home, eh, Paul? You even know the bartender's schedules. The stunning bartender and romantic evenings have little to do with this being a hangout, eh?"

"She has considerable influence and the fact that my cooking sucks, has a lot to do with it too. Honestly, unless Heather Sarah or Rose come over and cook for me, then I eat here or grab a pizza."

"Understood. I had your spaghetti when we bunked together for that week or so when Harry was so terribly ill. It did suck. Never knew anyone could ruin spaghetti and prepare it so terribly."

"Geez, Jim, ya ate it."

"I did. Not without immense amounts of prayers for blessings for my stomach and digestive systems. I am a man of God and I figured God would get me through it. Harry even warned me that you could not even reheat frozen pizza." Jim patted me on the back for comfort at the reality of how awful my cooking skills are and with a smile, Jim turned to Perry and said, "Say, Perry, please open a tab for Pastor Paul and for Pastor Jim. We will alternate the rounds. Big Boulders, tall mugs. Please. Thank you, sir."

Jim then turned to me and said, "Rose." He carefully studied my eyes as I reacted to Jim mentioning her name. Jim took a deep breath and then spoke again, "Now, there is an immaculate woman. She deeply loves you, Paul. I can see it in her eyes. She is a great woman of faith and you two have climbed many mountains and walked many valleys of your lives together. More so than I imagine anyone can ever realize. Look into her glorious soul and absorb her love deeply into your soul, my longhaired friend. Rose is very special. You owe it to number thirty-five to guard her heart."

Jim's words were profound and honest and I agreed, "I love, Rose too, and yes, we have been through so much together."

Jim reached over and grabbed my arm, and he shook me. Even at sixty years of age, his power and strength could rattle your bones and your soul.

"Not only love her as a friend, twenty-seven. What I am saying, Paul . . . is to love her entire heart and soul. You need to love her very being, and not only just love *her*.

Sharing your love and body with the stunning bartender is one thing, but awakening to the love that Rose projects and feels is a love of a higher plane. God's gift to us, to you, and as you search to find your heart and way while you return from your grief, please be aware of the magnificence of Rose and her profound love for you and the glory that it holds for both of you. A love so beautiful, no matter what the circumstances of it are—should never be overlooked or dismissed."

Jim let go of my arm. His eyes were wide, and his soul exposed.

With a glint of a smile on his face, Jim said, "Please, consider it."

The words washed over me in great waves and I felt an awakening at the power of them. Jim had the unique ability to strike me with more than just his famous wrist shots and slap shots. His words had even more power than his shots did. To escape the grip of the words and their influence on me, I welcomed the fact that Perry came over, greeted us; he shook our hands and hustled off for the beers. When Perry dropped the mugs, and he hustled off to take care of another patron, Jim lifted his mug and I did the same.

"Here is to the great number thirty-five," Jim proclaimed.

"To the great number thirty-five." I answered.

"Upstate New York, huh?" Jim asked, while dropping his mug on the bar. His question caught me off-guard. I was still lost in the toast to Harry, and the words about Rose still stirred my emotions when I realized that Jim was referring to Jennifer visiting her parents.

"Yes, in and around Saratoga. I forget the name of the town. I think it is Clifton Park."

Jim nodded and after another long sip he said, "I know of Clifton Park. Nice town. I am from Mohawk City. Nice area, horrific winters."

I was puzzled because I thought Jim was from New

York City and spent some time playing hockey in upstate New York. Not lived there. Jim sensed my next question, and he spoke before I could even ask it.

"I was born in New York City but grew up in Mohawk City. That is where I first played hockey. On the frozen ponds of upstate New York. My father was a police officer in New York City. He was the typical, tough Irish guy, who became a cop in the city after returning home from serving in the Vietnam War. My father left the force there and took a job with the police force in Mohawk City."

Jim paused, and his eyes lowered before more of an explanation arrived.

"Because of circumstance, we, ah, ah, needed to move. I was only born in New York City. No memories. When I was born, my father moved us. He had to, or I should clarify that it was the correct thing to do so, but I often wonder how things would have been if we stayed in New York City."

I sensed a mood change in my friend. As if the thoughts of his father and the move hung with heavy emotions over Jim's heart and mind.

"What is your father's name? Your parents are both gone now, correct?"

"They are. Sergeant James Reilly O'Malley and for the record, my mother's name is Lillian Patricia O'Malley Odell. My father has . . . been gone . . . for a very long time and my mother about ten years or so."

We both sipped our beers, and some silence lingered as I sensed both Jim and I were thinking of loved ones long since passed from our lives. Perry dropped another round of beers, and Jim ordered shots of Irish whiskey for us. He mumbled that he could not mention or think of his father without toasting his honor and memory.

He only briefly knew my father, but in Jim's words, "Mr. Henson was a great man of honor and strength and we need to toast both of our fathers. I might be a retired nondenominational pastor of a Bible church, but I am Irish. Through and through."

Perry delivered the shots and after a toast to, "Both of our fathers," we tossed them back.

This was going to be a memorable God Bless the Keg Day.

The liquid worked some magic on our inners and as Jim fiddled with the empty shot glass, he leaned over and looked at me. His dark eyes grew even darker, and I watched as raw emotion washed over Jim's face. The emotion began in his eyes, and then it slowly overcame his entire spirit.

I leaned back and waited to listen to his words because I knew they were going to be profound and from Jim's heart.

"Paul, I cannot even think of what my life would have been like if not for the various things my father taught to me. He was a man of immense courage and he taught me as a little boy to fight for respect and always to play the game hard, but fair. The game of hockey and the game of life. Never back down, never lie or twist things. James, he would tell me . . . when you play the game, play it to win. Always play it hard and play it to win. No one ever says that we want to play to lose, so be honest with your own soul. Kick ass and win the game. If you play hard and lose, then come back another day in order to win. Be fair and be hard, James. He loved hockey. Loved it. I think my father only loved my mom and me more than he loved hockey. He played on an ice hockey team with the policemen. Each year they faced off against a team from the firemen. A kick ass, brutal, ice hockey game. War on ice. The bravest versus the finest. He taught me to skate; he taught me to shoot and stickhandle and he taught me how to fight. He taught me how to punch a man's lights out, where to aim my punches and he taught me to win."

I seldom, if ever, heard James T. O'Malley speak so openly about his family or his personal life. I have heard him preach many times and, in the pulpit, dear reader, as you can easily imagine, he was a fiery and animated preacher. However, until now, I have never seen him act or heard him speak so introspectively.

"He was a great man, full of courage and full of honor. In my father's own way, full of faith, too. A man who refused to wear his faith on his collar as if it was a badge of honor to broadcast to the world. Instead, my father kept his faith quiet and used the manner in which he lived his own life to demonstrate it."

I nodded and commented, "That is the best way. Beware of those who broadcast how righteous they are."

"Correct. All of us fall short, Pastor Paul. All."

Jim lifted his mug and downed the last drop of brew, and he glanced at my mug. When he saw that I could also wipe out the remaining brew with one long swig, Jim smiled and waved for the bartender. Perry was on it.

When Perry dropped the fresh beers in front of us, Jim fiddled with the handle of the mug and after some time, he finally lifted the brew to his lips and took a small sip. I could see that he was very deep in thought and I am sure the brews and whiskey were working at his mind, and his body, and as I was about to find out, Jim's soul.

"When I was eighteen years of age, a horrible, wretched thug, and a conspiracy full of evil and malice and possessed by more demons than you and I could even imagine, stole my father from this world, from my mother, and from me. In reality, and technically, he was not even my biological father, but in my heart and in my soul, he was the greatest father that a young man could ever wish for, dream about, and imagine. Stolen from us. Unfairly, stolen from the world. When he left this world, I lost so many important parts of my life and of my soul along the way. Yet, I am not angry with God. God sent me love. Because of the glorious love of my amazing Kate, I was finally able to forgive. Just as you did, when your precious wife left this world so unfairly, I eventually grew stronger in my faith. Tomorrow, after our hangovers from this evening subside, I would like to take a road trip."

Jim stopped looking down at the counter of the bar and his beer mug, and he turned and looked me squarely in the eyes.

"Paul, I would like to show you parts and pieces of my life, and I want you someday to write my story. I think it will help others and I will create some written notes to assist you."

This offer took me by surprise because Jim was an intensely private man. Before now, he never shared with Harry or with me many details of his life.

"Twenty-seven, you are a brilliant and emotional writer and I know what I cannot detail, you will do a magnificent and fair job at filling in the missing pieces. Please, I need to request from you . . . will you someday write my story for this world to read? Perhaps, when the time is correct? When God and your heart tell you that it is time. When I am gone from the Earth and you remain."

"I might go first, Jim."

Jim shook his head and said, "No, you won't. I can feel certain things. God is always with us. Please promise me that you will write the story."

"Of course, I will, Jim. It will be my honor to do so," I said, while I gently patted him on his back.

Jim nodded, smiled, and said, "Thank you. You are, in many ways, my pastor. You reinforced honor and epitomized respect when we played against each other. You helped me understand that winning is not always about the score of the game, but it is about your honor and respect and it is about regaining what is important to you. For that, I thank you. I think that I have reached a point in my life where I need to cleanse my soul. As you were able to do."

I nodded and mumbled, "And you are *my* pastor, Jim."

"Thank you, Paul. It is my honor," Jim said and then his eyes wandered and he spoke again, "yes, taken from me."

I stirred uneasily as I saw that famous and very much feared sneer appear on Jim's lips, and his dark eyes grew supremely intense. I watched in silence as his fists clenched tightly and uniformly in rage at the thoughts of what had occurred. Jim was transforming, but still under control. I almost wanted to change the subject to hearing about his last shift in professional hockey, but I knew that Jim needed to talk about this to purge his soul of some hidden pain.

"Yes, evil took my father from this world in horrible and vile ways. Nevertheless, a few years later, with the help of God and his armor on my body and in my soul, I circled back and evened the score. As you know, twenty-seven," Jim stopped speaking. He reached out and grabbed my arm and intensely looked at me with those dark eyes flickering and shining in the light above the bar. "I might lose the battles, but you can always count upon James T. O'Malley to put on the armor of God and come back to try to win the war. I can tell you my long-haired, God-fearing and righteous friend . . . I won the war."

At a loss for words and allowing my imagination to wander at all that Jim had shared with me, I simply nodded my head, patted his shoulder, and grabbed my mug of beer. I lifted my mug into the air and nodded my head toward the mug suspended in the air as an indication for Jim to do the same. Once we both held our mugs in the air, we touched them as we toasted to his words, memories, and actions.

Yes, indeed, this was going to be a very long, God Bless the Keg Day and tomorrow morning's headache and stomach ills were going to be hell.

Yet, somehow, I knew that it would be worth it.

Jim's notes spread out haphazardly upon my desk as I sorted them out and tried hard to put them into some type of order. A quick glance at my watch told me that it was still hanging onto the late afternoon hours. I might have a chance to work through this before Rose came looking for me to check if I wanted to eat some dinner or not. My whiskey glass was empty, but my mind was full. The papers shuffled before me, like a spilled deck of cards, and after some searching and maneuvering, I spotted the one that I needed. Now, if I could just pick up where I left off.

Here we go now. This is where I wanted to continue with the story. It will be just a matter of reworking James T. O'Malley's own words, into some type of chronological order. Some assumptions of dialogue, some filling in, but I can do this.

I owe Jim and I owe the world.

It was just another farm pond located on a road on the rims and on the outskirts of Mohawk City in upstate New York. Named after an old farming family that originally settled the area, Summer's Pond was roughly an acre or two, and in the warmer weather, it was the local fishing hole, in the dead of winter it became a haven for ice skaters and it transformed into the local hockey rink. On this bitter, cold, winter's day, the pond did not live up to its namesake. Summer's Pond was nothing like summer today. Out on the frozen surface of the pond, the wind blew hard. It chased the little wisps of snow across the ice and they gathered in the corners of the pond, in and around the edges of the frozen dirt. The sun dipped low; the temperature dipped even lower, and the black ice grew thicker and deeper. Yet, the howling of the wind met its match with the sound of ice skates cutting the black ice hard, and the sharp blades created wisps of ice and lines that crisscrossed on the ice surface haphazardly in all directions. The echo of the wooden blades of hockey sticks striking the hard ice sounded in and around the wind and the distinct sound of a hockey puck hitting the same blades echoed across the pond in all directions.

Tonight, on Summer's Pond, there were only two figures left on the ice. The cold, the wind, and the dipping of the sun, chased all the other hockey players and figure skaters and other leisure skaters to their homes for warm fires, hot soup and warm houses to try to thaw their frozen toes and other body parts.

To these two hockey players, the cold meant very little. They remained impervious to the bitter wind and the dipping temperatures. After all, there were hockey lessons to learn and sometimes, those lessons come along the hard way.

Nothing worthwhile in life is ever easy.

"That's it, James. Good. Good. Pull the puck back a little, then move your blade in front of the puck, grab the puck and allow it to nestle into the curve of the blade. Now, flick your wrists, and whip the stick forward as if you were slapping a person, standing right in front of you, on their ass."

James Thomas O'Malley was about eight years of age, he was short, but stocky in his build, and the boy was red-faced from the bitter cold and whipping winds. He had skated on the pond for hours and hours today. Since early in the afternoon. Endlessly, practicing his hard cuts, stops, and starts, his twirls, his crossovers, skating backwards and flipping forward in quick spurts. His legs, knees, and elbows told the story of how many times that he fell, but the young O'Malley always jumped right back up and persevered.

Always.

The young O'Malley fell, but he never stayed down too long.

His father's words echoed inside of the young boy's head whenever he fell and the pain of hitting the ice resounded through his body.

His father had told him, "Take advantage of the frozen ice while it is there. God's gift to hockey players does not last. Skate, until it becomes second nature. Just as if you are walking."

The student of hockey nodded at the teacher's instructions. A furious nod, a nod of understanding that hockey was not as easy as it looked, while standing on a frozen pond about a mile from his home in upstate New York, with temperatures around zero and an unforgiving wind. Young hockey players are impervious to the cold. In fact, all hockey players are impervious to the cold. Especially James T. O'Malley. The boy easily ignored the envelope of cold and the bitter taste of winter.

It was late in the afternoon on a Saturday in late January and Sergeant James Reilly, O'Malley, taught his son the ins and outs of how to shoot a hard wrist shot. Sergeant O'Malley had promised his son that he would take him out on the pond after he finished work, and despite how long the shift was, and how bitterly cold it was out on the surface of the frozen pond, he was a man of his word. The sun was fading, and the night loomed with even more intense cold and bitter winds. The father stood there, wearing a pair of ancient hockey ice skates, with old leather boots that were tanner from wear than they were black, and nicked blades, hand sharpened by a stone kept in a basement toolbox. His hockey stick was from a bygone era, a stick with a long-gone clear finish of protection, made of hard maple and veneered oaks, scarred, and nicked, but still powerful. A stick that had delivered, absorbed, and survived many slashes, scored a few goals here and there, and a stick that had been lifted high above his head in celebration a few times too. The stick felt comfortable in Sergeant O'Malley's hands; it was as if it was part of his body. An extension of his arms. He spun it around and around while watching his son attempt the wrist shot.

This shot, just the same as the many others before this one, was a dud. The wind up and intention was solid, but once again, the puck rolled off the edge of the blade and it spun off weakly before the young O'Malley could flick his wrists. They were firing pucks toward a small wall of cement blocks that surrounded and guarded an inlet pipe that fed water into the small pond. With some sidewalk chalk, the local hockey "club" had marked out a rectangle that was close to the dimensions of an actual hockey net, but they were inaccurate dimensions upon the wall. For shooting practice, the markings on the wall sufficed as a target.

"No quit in you, son! Head up! Never quit, James." The instructor tapped the heel of his hockey stick on the ice in a display of inspiration at the boy's efforts. "Try harder and fight harder. Try it once again, James. You need to feel the weight of the puck on the blade as if you tied the puck to the blade with a loose string and you are trying to break it and snap it off."

The boy nodded once again, and he skated off to retrieve the errant puck that had skipped and sputtered across the ice. Once more, the young O'Malley gritted his teeth, bit into his chapped lips and tugged furiously at the wool watch cap on his head to pull it down in a vain defense against the cold. He was going to whip off a wrist shot and make that puck sing if he had to stand here until he froze solidly in place. Young O'Malley hated the very thought of defeat and of losing. Defeat was not a part of his soul. He picked the puck up, bent at his waist too much and skated quickly, while stickhandling the puck back to the spot where his father stood watching.

"Stand up, James, only bend at the waist a little. Stick out straight in front of you! Work the puck smoothly back and forth on the blade, eyes up and looking at me! Practice weaving through defensemen trying to steal the puck off your blade. Guard the puck with your strength and your speed. It has to become a second nature, son. As if the puck is glued to the blade."

The teacher made a correct observation on the stickhandling technique, and his instructions resonated across the pond. His words hung in the air as if they were frozen icicles and the warm breath from Sergeant O'Malley's mouth created white puffs while drifting silently into the air.

"Nice skating! Great strides and balance! You are dramatically improving in your skating ability. That is an impressive display of skating!" A glorious statement of pride hung in the frozen air, too. A father's pride. Love is love, but pride is love laced with respect and with honor and with joy. Pride is a glorious emotion.

For a hard-boiled Irish policeman from the mean streets of New York City, Sergeant O'Malley was very well spoken and surprisingly eloquent. His son noted the trait very carefully.

The young player performed a hard spray stop, the ice flying in a haze of an icy mist, mixed with small chunks of ice. He bit his lip once more and this time, after a few quick movements of the blade, and a piercing stare at the target with his dark eyes, he whipped off a perfectly executed wrist shot. The puck whipped off the blade, rode hard and flat with just the slightest tilt to the edge of the puck as it sailed towards the wall.

"Nice!" The teacher shouted as he watched the shot ride in a blaze of glory and intensity towards the wall. Putting aside his obvious pride at the fact that this was his son, Sergeant O'Malley admired the speed and power of the shot. In his mind he thought, 'Damn, this kid is gonna be some kind of great hockey player.'

The young player marveled at how good it felt to whip the shot off the blade, the feel of the shot, and his exhilaration of the execution of the movement of the stick and the resulting shot. It sent shivers throughout his body and was more satisfying than anything that he ever did before in his young life. Right then and there, he knew that he was going to be a hockey player. It was his fate.

Young James took his eyes off the flight of the puck for just a half-second, in order to look at the flash of his father's pride and the young player was about to learn another lesson on top of how to shoot a wicked wrist shot. He was going to learn that you never take your eye off flying hockey pucks. The puck hit on its edge and it hit a hard and sharp edge of a course of cement block that stuck out more than the others did. When the puck hit the hard edge, it bounced back with a hard ricochet. Young James was already skating toward the wall in order to retrieve his successful shot, and the puck rode back hard and high and it struck the young hockey player just below his right eye.

BANG!

The impact of the hockey puck would have brought most boys of eight-years of age to their knees and exploded their emotions into tears.

Not this particular boy. He simply shook his head and watched as the offending puck rolled away and then stopped on the ice in front of him.

The first of those little life lessons came the way of James T. O'Malley on this frozen pond in upstate New York. The boy was just beginning his journey. There would be many more.

Suddenly, there was a strange feeling of warmth on his face, as the trickle of blood running down his face and cheek cut through the cold air and warmed his numbed skin. In a second or so, as the young player dropped his stick and peeled off a glove to touch the cut and confirm the presence of blood, the teacher was at his side, carefully inspecting his son's face to determine the extent of the damage inflicted by the puck.

"The puck clipped you rather hard, James. A little lesson for you today, never take your eyes off the puck. Never trust a hockey puck. In many ways, it is as a woman is . . . at times . . . difficult to determine their direction and hard to trust."

The boy nodded, but he might have been too young to understand the statement. Someday, he would understand, and James would look back on his father's words within a different perspective. The teacher's eyes peered in at the cut, while gently moving his son's hand away from the cut to examine it.

"You might need a stitch or two here, James. Let's put some ice on it and keep the swelling down."

Sergeant O'Malley knelt down on the ice and scraped at the surface with the blade of his skate. He scooped up some snow and ice chips, stood up, and gently placed it on the cut. The boy did not even flinch, and the father thought, 'Hell, yeah, this young man is gonna be a special hockey player.'

"It does not hurt, Dad. Please, can I try one more shot?"

"No, not now, James. It is growing dark and your mother will be looking for us soon. We might need to take a side trip here to the emergency room if old Doc Hornsby is not in his office. A side trip that is—if I cannot stop this from bleeding."

The teacher leaned over and pulled the ice away from the student's face. He smiled widely, and the young boy studied his father's face.

The father said with immense pride, "I will say, James. That was one helluva wrist shot. It was a thing of beauty and a work of art. The rebound was hell, but the shot was golden."

The boy nodded at the teacher's words, and he felt his chest swell with pride.Love is love, and pride is pride.

Sunday afternoon was even colder than Saturday had been. After church services and a fine Sunday dinner, the sound of hockey pucks hitting the cement wall once again echoed across that same frozen pond. Young O'Malley whirled and twirled on his skates, while shooting wrist shot after shot toward the wall, while this time, never taking his eyes off the puck.

Lessons learned. Under his right eye, there was a small bandage, and underneath it was a few black stitches that twitched in his skin while the young boy moved and darted. Old Doc Hornsby was still in his office late yesterday afternoon. After all, it *was* hockey season. While the hockey pucks flew through the frozen air and the skates cut ridges across the ice like some type of obscure jigsaw puzzle pattern, words of pride shouted in the air from the voice of a father. The words mixed with the sound of skates cutting the ice and the clap of the heel of an old hockey stick tapping on the ice surface. An old hockey stick from a bygone era, a stick with a long-gone clear finish of protection, made of hard maple and veneered oaks, scarred and nicked, but still powerful.

"Nice skating. Now watch as I lead you in a pass, James. Concentrate! Skate hard and fast and try to capture the puck cleanly while on the fly!"

The teacher snapped a hard pass off as the young boy burst across the ice. The puck skipped and skidded across the uneven ice and the boy cleanly and deftly caught the puck on his blade in one effortless motion and at full speed. Sergeant James Reilly O'Malley smiled widely and marveled at the skills of his son. He took a deep breath and watched as young O'Malley stopped on a dime and sent a spray of snow high into the air. The boy then snapped a pass to his father and the blade of his old stick bounced as the teacher captured it.

Once more in his mind, Sergeant James Reilly O'Malley thought, 'Yes, indeed, this young man is gonna be some kind of special hockey player.'

Chapter Four

The Birth of Number Eleven

"I need a new radio!"

James Thomas O'Malley looked up when he heard the words and his dark eyes caught Fredrick Spieth as he tore the transistor radio from the hands of Dexter Zimmer. O'Malley was a few feet behind them as they all walked home from high school on a crisp, but early October day.

Autumn in upstate New York defines and encompasses the word spectacular.

Fredrick "Fred" Spieth was the classic school bully and the high school's athletic superstar. All high schools have them. Fred was in his sophomore year of high school, one grade ahead of Jim. Fred was older in age for the grade, he was around sixteen years of age, because he was as dumb as a wall of bricks and had to redo a grade or two along the way. Spieth was tall, in fact, he was huge, and very muscular; a star athlete in all the sports, and the rumor was that his parents had tons of money. Jim knew that his father drove a nice car because he had seen his father pick Fred up one day from the local hockey rink. A rink that Jim was hanging around while watching a local senior league practice. Fred played organized ice hockey and while Jim never saw what team that it was that Fred played for or what league he was in; Jim was itching to play against him someday. The young O'Malley dreamed of the day that he could hit the ice and join an organized team. His father and mother were saving the money for the fees and for the official hockey equipment. It was very expensive to play hockey and police officers do not earn a bundle of dough.

In his mind, Jim thought that Fred played defense, but he determined that only by guesswork, his physical size and the puck marks that Jim spotted on the blade of his stick. Jim shook that thought off. Because guys like Fred, always need to be the star. In this day and age of old-time hockey, most defensemen usually hid on the back-line and stayed far out of the spotlight. Staying out of the spotlight would not work for Fred's massive ego. Fred was a star pitcher on the varsity baseball squad, even though he was technically an underclassman. In fact, he played at the varsity level in all sports. He was the star quarterback on the football squad and the center on the basketball team. Even the seniors accepted Fred because he was so huge and overwhelming.

All the cute girls made eyes, swayed their asses and hips at him, and rumor had it that he was kissing the gorgeous Kate O'Leary in the school parking lot last week. All the guys, younger and older, all the way down to freshman, wanted to kiss Kate O'Leary. She was in her sophomore year too and was the envy of all the guy's eyes. Oh well, on and on it went and all of it inflated Fred's already immense ego.

Jim thought about how all of these jerks always get the pretty girls.

Dexter reached and tried hard to recapture the radio that Fred just tore from his hands.

It did not go so well when Dexter reached for it and told Fred rather forcefully, "No! I got that radio for a birthday present! It is mine. Give it back!"

Fred laughed and planted his fist on the chest of poor Dexter and gave him a hard shove. Dexter fell backwards; his lunch pail and books went flying in different directions, and his papers and schoolwork flew into the air. Dexter tumbled into a hedgerow in front of old lady Hansworth's house, and Jim could see Dexter grimace at the pain of the shove and of the hard landing into a group of sticks and twigs that were now poking and stabbing at his body. Dexter Zimmer was also in his sophomore year of high school, but he was what everyone called back in this day, "slow." It was obvious that he had a mental disability of some sort, not severe enough to be in any special education type of program, but enough to be noticeable and to be the subject of laughter, be the subject of cruel jokes and comments and most of all to be the target of bullies such as Fred Spieth was.

"Get lost, ya dopey half-a-head goofball. Ya brains got left in ya daddy's sack," Fred cruelly spouted.

The air filled with cruelty and Dexter's eyes filled with tears as he watched his beloved radio, now in the hands of Fred. Fred laughed along with the three sidekicks that always tagged along as if they were a bunch of drooling groupies. The perception was it was cool to be part of Fred's gang.

Everyone wanted to be a part of Fred's world.

Well, not exactly everyone.

James Thomas O'Malley's fists tightened, his dark eyes grew even darker, and in his chest, his heart thumped with rage. The young O'Malley walked up to Dexter and set his lunch pail and books upon the sidewalk. Jim helped him out of the hedgerow and the stickers, and then he helped to gather his books, papers and handed him his lunch pail.

"Come on, please, get up, Dexter. I will help you with this stuff. Then, I will get your radio back," Jim said as he assisted poor Dexter.

Dexter seemed shocked that someone, anyone, would actually help him and at first, he looked puzzled and then, he smiled and almost in a whisper he said, "Thanks, ah, O'Malley. Ain't that ya name?"

"James Thomas O'Malley is my name."

Fred and his gang had now turned around, and they

were walking back to the scene of the crime.

"Did I just hear that you are going to get this radio back? *My* radio?" Fred said with spit flying out of his mouth.

James Thomas O'Malley nodded his head and stood on the sidewalk.

He handed the lunch pail to Dexter and then said, "That is correct. It is not your radio. You stole it from, Dexter, and please, you need to return it."

Fred turned to his minions and pointed, while saying with an element of shock in his voice, "Is this punk kid for real? Ya'a midget and are, what, a freshman? Get lost, O'Malley, and go play with rubber ducks in your bathtub. Ya still must suck on ya momma's titties!"

Laughter erupted and when Fred turned his back and the gang followed, Jim walked up, tapped Fred on the shoulder, and said, "The radio. Please, give it back."

Fred whirled around and handed the radio to a minion standing next to him.

"Here. Hold *my* radio while I kick this punk's ass."

After handing off the radio, Fred stomped right up into the young O'Malley's face, leaned over into him, and gave him a solid push in the chest. Fred towered over the young O'Malley and, despite the size difference—Jim held his ground.

It is the love within your heart and the power of your soul that counts the most in this life.

Fred seemed very surprised that even with intimidation, laced with his immense ego, that someone actually was not afraid of him. It gave Fred a touch of pause, and then he resumed his bullying.

"Why should I give it back? Ya gonna get ya father the cop to come and arrest me?"

Jim shook his head and said, "No. I do not need my father's assistance. I will procure the radio back on my own. I will get it back and give it to Dexter because it is the respectful and correct thing to do and you are wrong to have stolen it from Dexter."

"Big words from a little kid. Who told you that bullshit?"

"My father. He told me that I should always stand for respect. You are not respectful to Dexter. The radio is not your property."

"Even if it means eating ya teeth?"

"Yes, you do not scare me, Fred. Peter cut the ear off the Roman Soldier to defend what he felt was correct. Now, please, give the radio back."

Before Jim could even finish his statement, Fred hauled off and with a crushing right-handed punch; he landed his fist cleanly on the face of James Thomas O'Malley. Fred's fist caught Jim just below the right eye, in a place where he already had a little red scar from a duel with a hockey puck from years earlier. O'Malley had not seen the punch coming and had little chance of defending the blow. He had taken his eyes off the game.

Another little lesson.

The punch staggered the young O'Malley, and he fell backwards toward the sidewalk. He caught his fall with an outstretched right arm and he fell to one knee as Fred stood over him with both of his fists clenched.

"Well, I guess ya little ass ain't Peter, now are ya, punk?"

As Jim knelt on the sidewalk and looked up at the monster looming above him, he thought how that was not so bad. The hockey puck and stitches hurt a helluva lot more than that punch did. Jim touched his face, and he felt the swelling under his eye and felt the telltale warmth of blood on his face.

Old wounds open easily, and sometimes, they never heal.

Jim reached up to the cut and his finger caught a little blood trickle that was rolling down his face. Jim looked at his finger, licked the blood off his finger. His face broke into a wide smile and he shook his head.

"Stay down!" Fred screamed, and Jim continued to shake his head and slowly rose to his feet. This time, he kept his eyes clearly focused upon Fred's fists.

Lessons learned.

"No. James Thomas O'Malley always gets back up. I never stay down for long. Now, give the radio back."

Fred's face told of the shock that this guy had just absorbed his best punch and rose to his feet as if it was nothing. For a few seconds, he did not know what to do. This never happened before this time. Most of the time, Fred did not even have to punch anyone. They all ran away before he needed to lay them out on their asses. His eyes darted to his gang members, to Jim's face, to the distraught face and emotions of Dexter Zimmer.

"Stop this nonsense and brutal behavior! You, Fred Spieth! I know who you are! I know your mother from church! Stop picking on kids half your size or I will tell her of your abhorrent behavior. Now, give the radio back or I will call the police!"

It was old lady Hansworth, and she was irate and yelling from her front porch. The old lady had seen everything, and Fred was now trapped.

"Okay, okay, I am leaving," Fred said as he waved his hand in the direction of the old lady. "Give 'em the radio," the bully said to his crony, who nodded and tossed it to Jim O'Malley. Jim caught it deftly in the air and he smiled at the minion. Fred waved to his gang, and they followed him as he began to walk away. When he heard the front door of old lady Hansworth's house slam, Fred turned around and stuck his middle finger in the air at O'Malley.

"You will pay for this, punk. You will pay," Fred spewed, with more spit flying out of his mouth.

Jim handed the radio back to Dexter, who smiled widely and patted Jim on the back while repeatedly thanking him.

Dexter had tears in his eyes.

The radio was a cherished birthday present.

James Thomas O'Malley shouted, "Just, say the word, Fred. I will meet you there! Anytime, anywhere. In fact, I am counting on it."

Fred said not a word, but still hung his middle finger in the air behind his back while he and his gang of followers walked away.

Dexter thanked Jim once more, and he said, "I gotta turn here at this corner. I live up on Southside Avenue."

"I know. No thanks needed, Dexter. It was the correct and honest thing to do. Fred has no respect for anyone and he is a big bully."

"I don't know big words, but I know we were right and that you are honest. He stole it from me. He is mean, and he is evil. Is your eye going to be okay? It is bleeding a lot," Dexter said as he leaned in and examined the cut.

"It is fine. See you around, Dexter."

The two boys went their separate ways, and Jim gathered up his lunch pail and his own books and made his way toward his home. He put his finger to the cut and wiped the blood away from his face. He flicked the blood off his finger. He did not want to wipe it on his pants. Clothes were expensive. How he wished he had a tissue or a handkerchief with him.

Jim was still on full alert and he quickly turned around when he heard footsteps behind him. Running footsteps. Jim prepared for an ambush by Fred Spieth; instead he received a huge surprise as to the source of the footsteps. Jim turned around and his face reflected the surprise when his eyes caught the amazing green eyes of the lovely Kate O'Leary. She stopped running and stood behind Jim. She reached in her purse, took out a handkerchief, and handed it to Jim.

"Here. It is clean. I thought that you might need it." Jim's heart melted at the sight of her. Her brown hair had auburn highlights that flickered in the sunlight. Her hair was all around her and it was gently tumbling down over her shoulders while enhancing her perfect facial features. She was gorgeous and her face glowed while she battled the wind, gently blowing wisps of her hair in front of her face. Even at such a young age, when his first hormones had begun to bounce, Jim was not sure there could be any lovelier girl than Kate O'Leary was.

Besides, as his old man would say, she was Irish. . ..

Jim reached out, took the handkerchief, dabbed at the cut, and then looked down at the handkerchief, which was no longer clean. Blood soaked was an accurate description.

"Thank you. That is very kind of you. Sorry, but it is a mess now. I am a mess too."

Kate laughed and waved as she pointed at the blood-soaked handkerchief.

"You can keep it. You are not a mess, James. You are very brave and wonderful to stand up to that horrible and disgusting, Fred Spieth. He never had anyone stand up to him before. I saw what you did for Dexter. It was amazing. I was . . . walking behind you and Dexter."

Jim's face displayed some surprise at her knowing his name and of her description of Fred. He had heard the rumors.

"What?" Kate asked, while reading the surprise on the combatant's face.

"I did not know that you knew me or my name."

Kate did not answer, at least not with words. However, she did answer with the wide smile upon her face and the gentle flicker of budding love in her green eyes.

Jim continued, "I did not know that you felt that way about, Fred. I mean, I heard it said, the other day, that you and Fred, well . . . it was just something that guys whisper about here and there." Jim was fumbling awkwardly with his words. That in itself was unusual. It was her green eyes.

Kate nodded and smiled, and said, "Oh, I know what you heard. That Fred kissed me. Well, he tried, until I kicked him in the nuts. His little, puny, nuts. I bet that he needs a magnifying glass to see them."

Jim laughed and thought, 'Yes, indeed, Kate was Irish.'

"Say, Kate, I think you live over on Lee Avenue. I have to go that way. Do you mind if I walked you home?"

Kate studied his dark eyes, his small but sturdy build, his handsome face, his overt confidence, and his jet-black hair. All she wanted to do was to hold his hand and then run her hands through that jet-black hair and feel it between her fingers. He made her heart flutter and her spirit dance.

Her father would say, "Of course, he is brave and handsome. Even at fourteen or so years of age. He is Irish."

Her young heart melted.

"Don't you think you should go home and take care of that cut? I think you might need stitches in it."

Jim shook his head and said, "It is fine. It can wait. Just a little blood. I have bled before and I will bleed again. Besides, it will be worth it."

She smiled, nodded, and they turned in the direction of Lee Avenue.

When his father started the car, and put it in gear and they pulled away from the front of Old Doc Hornsby's office, Jim's father said, "Well, you might have a real scar now, James. It might take some time to heal. Six stitches this time. How many was it when the hockey puck hit there?"

"Four. I think."

His father nodded.

"Okay, well, when we arrive home and after we eat some dinner, I will begin to give you boxing lessons. Something is telling me that you will need them. First, I will teach you defense. I will teach you how to land punches that will make a man beg for mercy. No matter how big or strong they are."

The young O'Malley nodded and said, "Thank you. I

would like that. I think that you are correct. I am going to need boxing lessons. It seems that there are lots of little lessons that people need to learn."

The truth was that right now, the boxing lessons were all well and good, but in reality, all he could think about was her smile and those lovely green eyes.

A year or so later, after the incident with Fred and Dexter, found James T. O'Malley deep into his relationship with his two great loves. Ice Hockey and Kate O'Leary. It was late September and that meant one thing: it was hockey season. Right before the beginning of the local hockey league's final roster tryouts, Jim had heard through the local hockey circuits that there were some roster openings on the local senior league hockey club. Some players backed out due to injury and other commitments. James T. O'Malley never backed down from a challenge. He felt this was his big chance. Just a few weeks earlier, Jim's parents had finally saved and scraped some money together, and Jim combined the money they gave him with some savings from his part-time job at the local grocery market. Together, they purchased the long-awaited and coveted hockey equipment. Sensing an opportunity, Jim approached the senior league coaches and convinced them to allow him to skip the junior league tryouts and try out for the higher level.

At first, most people did not think he would make the roster cuts because he never played junior league hockey. He was small for his age, and most of the boys on the team were a few years older than Jim was. One coach was a believer, Jim's parents were believers and a young woman with captivating green eyes was on the list of believers too. One coach was convinced, and the others were not. There was little doubt that Jim was on the smallish size for this league and for his age, however, they all admitted that the young man brimmed with confidence.

His first practice and one or two shifts on the ice were all that it took, and now everyone was a firm believer.

The coaches were in awe while they watched as James Thomas O'Malley ducked and spun his way through waves of an overwhelmed defense and then he ripped a wrist shot into the top shelf of the net past a bewildered and overpowered goaltender.

One coach leaned over to his fellow coaches and the coach whispered, "Damn, this young man is gonna be some kinda great hockey player."

After scoring the goal, the coaches waved James Thomas O'Malley over to the player's bench and the one coach leaned over and put his arm around Jim's shoulders.

"That was some display of center ice hockey skills, James. We heard that you were good on the ponds and in street hockey, but damn, that was amazing. Congratulations, James. You just made this hockey club. Be back here on Tuesday afternoon at five."

Jim smiled, nodded, and said, "Thank you."

In the stands behind the benches, a man wearing a police officer's uniform and a woman holding her hand on the back of the police officer cheered, clapped and whistled. A certain lovely young woman with captivating green eyes cheered and clapped wildly too.

Jim had a small fan club.

"Hey, heard you made the team. Congrats. What number do you want, James? These are typical center icemen numbers." The team manager of the senior league team asked while he held out a display of hockey sweaters with various numbers. James Thomas O'Malley studied them carefully and when he spotted the number eleven, he smiled and pointed at it. His father's police badge number was the number eleven. This was now his first organized hockey team, and this was his first official hockey sweater.

Jim did not count the old hockey sweaters that his mother and father bought in the used thrift store in downtown Mohawk City.

"Gotcha. Number eleven. I will get the letters on the back for you. I have them peel and stick letters right here. This is a practice jersey. You are yellow. Fourth shift and a substitute. The game jersey will have your name embroidered on it."

Jim nodded and said, "Thank you."

Tuesday meant scrimmage day and for James Thomas O'Malley it meant it was his first organized hockey game. Scrimmage or not—a hockey game is a hockey game and Jim felt the thrill of it from his head to his toes. The coaches divided the squad into individual groups of blue sweaters and red sweaters, and yellow sweaters. The blue players were the first line, and the red were all the second line players. The yellow sweaters were substitutes and third-and-fourth-line players. While they were all dressing in the locker room, Jim noticed a player that he had not seen before today in the locker room. He was huge, tall and powerful, and Jim recognized his smug smile and cocky attitude right away. He knew most of the players on the team and he knew Fredrick Spieth too. While he watched Fred dress, Jim recalled a teammate telling him that Fred had received a suspension for a few practices and scrimmage games from the league and from the coaches. Something about high sticking and spearing in a practice game. . ..

The regular season had not even begun and already Fred was in trouble. That explained his absence from the tryout practice.

Fred ignored Jim and Jim was very happy to do the same. They never had the promised showdown from the incident of a few years ago, and now Fred was finally a senior on the cusp of leaving high school. It had taken him a few tries to make it to his senior year because while he did grow older . . . Fred sure did not grow any smarter. The word was out that he was working hard for a scholarship to a college to play either hockey or football. The last that Jim heard was that Fred had not yet made a decision. Jim covertly watched as he stripped down to his bare chest, and his ample chest and arm muscles rippled as he chatted to a teammate. He pulled a white tee over his chest and then slapped on his shoulder pads. Then came the jersey and Jim watched carefully as he pulled a blue colored number ten practice jersey out of his equipment bag and pulled it up and over his head. Number ten, blue color, first line and a number, which was a typical center iceman's number. Jim felt his heart thump and his fists tighten. Of course, he had to play center. Defense would never work for the star of every show.

Jim knew that he would be competing against Fred for the starting center iceman position, and he could not hide his joy at the challenge.

A smile broke across his face as he mumbled, "James Thomas O'Malley always gets back up."

The warm-ups for the scrimmage game went by quickly and while Jim passed by Fred a number of times as they whirled around the hockey rink and loosened their legs in a hard skate, he did not say a word. Fred was a very powerful skater. Long strides, long legs and powerful edges into the ice. Fred was a marvelously gifted athlete. Everything came so easily to him.

Their eyes never met and the two players did not exchange any words between them. Jim preferred it that way. His plan was to do his talking with his stick.

Blue hockey sweaters were starters, red was the second shift and the yellow sweaters were all third and fourth shift and substitutes. The red and yellows warmed up their goalie on one end of the ice and the blues warmed up their starting goalie on the opposite side. The blue goalie was the same goalie that Jim had burned with a hard and high wrist shot during his tryout. Jim stood at the red centerline and studied the opposition. Even though they were teammates, James T. O'Malley sized them up to win. If they were going to be a superior hockey club, it all started and ended here. At practice. The team had to work hard to be winners and James T. O'Malley was a hard worker at everything he did. His boss at the grocery market told Jim that he wished that he had ten O'Malleys on his workforce. Jim always tried his best.

His father taught him, "James, always play to win. Always. No one plays a game with the intention to lose and if they do, they are very poor liars."

In the regular season, no team was going to cut them breaks so why should practice be soft. As far as O'Malley was concerned, the word soft was not in his vocabulary. Jim studied the blue goalie and while he seemed very good with pucks down and around his skates, he struggled with shots up high. Particularly like the shot that Jim took the other day in his tryout, which was a shot high on his stick side. Jim made a note of that fact and when his turn came to shoot on his goalie, Jim ripped a wrist shot high on the stick side and it blew by the goalie who only managed to weakly wave at the puck in a feeble attempt to stop it. Jim needed to practice shooting at that location. He had already made a note that the blue goalie could not handle high shots on his stick side, and that was where Jim planned to attack. The head coach had been cruising by on his skates when Jim took the shot and the coach looked at Jim and he shook his head at the power and accuracy of his shot. Some of his teammates commented on the shot too. The goalie only shook his head in awe of the shot and swept the puck out of his net.

James T. O'Malley's little fan club cheered in the stands. They would not have missed this game for anything in the world. Even if it was just a scrimmage.

Jim whirled on his skates, and when the whistle blew to

begin the game, Jim headed for the bench to take his seat and wait for the third shift to have a chance.

The coach grabbed Jim by the sweater, turned to another young player wearing number thirteen, and tapped them both on the shoulders to get their attention.

The coach then said, "O'Malley and Stephens! Listen up! Quick shifts, boys. Stephens, ya red, ya take the opening face-off and if blue wins then forecheck hard and force them to dump it into your zone. After they dump it and chase, then you bail right to the bench. I want to see what this number eleven can do with Fred."

Stephens nodded, smiled and said, "You got it, Coach Hess. Good luck with that. Fred is rested and all full of bullshit, piss and vinegar."

Jim heard the coach whisper, "Yup. Even more so than he usually is. Exactly, why I want O'Malley on the matchup after the face-off."

Stephens skated out and took the draw from an assistant coach, acting as a linesman and a referee. Fred won the draw and Stephens raced after Fred on a hard and furious forecheck. When Fred sensed the intense pressure, he quickly stickhandled the puck a few times and then he dumped the puck into the red zone, while Stephens skated directly to the bench. Classic dump and chase strategy, and Fred had dumped the puck to the right face-off circle and did so in such a skilled way as to not cause an icing. It was a nicely organized and neatly performed play. O'Malley had already been sitting up on the boards to make the quick shift change and his dark eyes carefully followed the bounce of the puck. Jim did not yet know the ins and outs of playing on an actual hockey rink, and Jim did not know how fickle the boards could be, but he knew when an opponent was going to make a mistake and cough up the puck. A blue-team right-winger fumbled with the puck when it took an odd bounce off the boards and O'Malley hit the ice hard. In a few seconds, the shifty and speedy skater had closed the distance between the boards and the right-winger and when the puck danced off the blade of the right-winger, O'Malley adroitly snatched the puck away from him and turned on his skates and broke up the ice.

Fred had pinched in, as did the left-winger and the right defenseman, and as O'Malley turned up ice and gained speed, he could hear Fred loudly swear, "Shit! Catch that little, punk, bastard!"

Fred had certainly noticed O'Malley now. . ..

Jim had his head up. He stood straight up and the puck remained glued to his blade. It was just as a certain police sergeant who knew a thing or two about ice hockey had proudly taught his son.

Love is love and pride is pride.

The left-winger was skating with Jim and even if they had not played together before, hockey instincts took over as it boiled down to a classic two on one matchup. The two players crossed the blue line and when the blue defenseman edged over to Jim's side, Jim whipped a pass over to his left-winger, who cleanly captured the puck as Jim broke even faster to the net. The left-winger faked a slap shot and instead, perfectly passed the puck and with a fantastic, one time effort, James T. O'Malley whipped his classic wrist shot high on the stick side into the net. The twine of the net rippled with the force of the shot, and the hockey puck bounced out almost as quickly as it blew by the goalie. The goaltender never moved, the assistant coach blew the whistle to signal a goal, the little fan club cheered and Coach Hess smiled and whispered, "Damn, this young man is gonna be some kinda great hockey player."

The assistant coach acting as the linesman and referee blew his whistle, pointed at Fred, and called him out on the missed assignment, "That's your man, there number ten! You pinched too deep and paid the price. Looks as if you need to pull your head out of your ass and get your skating legs back. O'Malley just blew you all up! Face-off at center ice!" He blew the whistle and pointed at the face-off circle as Fred slowly skated in and fumed at the blow to his tremendous ego.

Jim's teammates celebrated the goal with some exuberant back slaps and some high-fives with Jim, who congratulated the left-winger on his amazing pass. O'Malley was going to skate to the bench and switch with Stephens when Coach Hess waved Jim back to the face-off circle.

"Take the draw, O'Malley. Quick shift, 'bout one minute or so."

Jim nodded and scooted back to the center face-off circle and he met the glare and stare of the irate Fred Spieth.

"So, we meet again, asshole. How old are you now, punk?" Fred asked with a hard stare as he bent at the waist and leaned on the bridge that his stick made across his legs.

"Old enough to burn your ass and clean your clock," O'Malley answered, and the assistant coach laughed as he dropped the puck.

Jim won the draw and when the puck skittered back to a red defenseman, Fred took the opportunity to cheap shot James T. O'Malley with the end of his blade. When Jim turned his back, Fred deftly lifted his blade, aimed for the edge of Jim's mouth, and caught O'Malley across the lip with the blade of his hockey stick. Instantly, blood spewed out of the cut, and O'Malley skidded to a stop when the pain shot through his face.

A red teammate shouted, "Hey! That is a cheap shot, bullshit high-stick, there, Fred!"

Coaches blew whistles and players screamed in protest.

The assistant coach screamed at Fred, "WHAT THE HELL? YA TEAMMATES, SPIETH! CHEAP SHOT! LOCKER ROOM FOR YOUR ASS!" The coach pointed at the locker room as he turned to check on James T. O'Malley who had dropped his stick, thrown his gloves off and was checking the blood pouring out of a cut that folded over the entire corner of his mouth.

The little fan club was silent as worry enveloped their faces.

Fred glared at Jim and even under the coaches' reprimands, Fred managed to say, "That evens the score. Plus, someday, somewhere, I will have my way with your little bitch girlfriend and she will moan at how good it will be compared to your pencil dick."

When he heard the disgusting words, O'Malley's fists tightened and his face turned to rage.

He licked the blood off his hands and fingers and smiled as he said, "The cheap shot and the cut is one thing, but you just crossed the line when you disrespected, my Kate. Besides, you never called me out until now and as I told you years ago, jackass, I was counting on it. I gave you a fair chance, now, I am going to even *my score.* It is time for you to learn a little lesson. You should never disrespect women and never cheap shot a teammate. Yup, smart-ass, now, it is my turn."

Teammates and coaches went to break up the fight when Coach Hess jumped over the boards by the player's bench, skated out on the ice and held his arms out to stop them.

The cagey old coach said, "No! Let, O'Malley go. He deserves a chance to even the score after that disgusting comment about his girlfriend and the cheap shot to his mouth. A cheap shot from a teammate. Nothing's worse. Let it go. I have a feeling that this is going to end very badly for Fred. Very badly. Fred has this coming. For a very long time now and I have a feeling that he just met his match."

The old coach was very wise, and he had seen a few hockey players along the way. Deep within his heart, he knew that he had never seen the likes of a certain player named James T. O'Malley, and his heart told him that this young man was something very special.

The old coach was not going to be disappointed.

"Bring it on, punk," Fred said as the two young men faced off and squared up for a fistfight on ice skates. O'Malley spit gobs of blood out of his mouth; he then carefully skated around in circles, his fists held high and in the perfect boxing position, with his dark eyes glowing. Jim sized up the much larger young man and you could see Jim studying the posture of Fred in order to determine his style and defense before attacking.

It was just as a certain police sergeant taught him.

And, when he did attack, it was as if Fred met the ferocity of Hell. Within seconds, Jim landed punches that had Fred spouting blood from his nose and mouth and had him begging for mercy.

It was as if sledgehammers had hit Fred.

For a small, young man, Jim threw a heavy punch, and he knew exactly where to land the blows to inflict the maximum pain.

Young O'Malley paid close attention to the boxing lessons.

Blood poured out of Jim's lip, but it only took five or six blows and Fred was down on the ice, Jim on top of him, pouring blood on Fred and pummeling the living daylights out of the much larger young man.

Coach Hess smiled and then shouted, "Okay! THAT'S E'NUFF! BREAK IT UP!"

Teammates and assistant coaches rushed to break the fight up, and in reality, to save Fred from the wrath of fury known as James T. O'Malley. Teammates piled on top of O'Malley and it was difficult to determine who was bleeding more. With great and combined efforts, they finally pulled the raging O'Malley off the top of Fred, who remained on the ice in a silent pool of blood and layers of a destroyed ego. O'Malley stood over him with his fists clenched and his face filled with rage. Jim stood there ominously and while he stood there, with blood pouring out of his lip, Jim glared at him with all the fury that a young man who just stood for respect and his woman's honor could muster.

Just a teenager, but wise beyond his years.

O'Malley wiped the flow of blood away from his lip and said, "If I were you, jackass, I would take that scholarship in football. You are too much of a pussy to make it in ice hockey."

In the stands, two women, one very young and one older, stood with horrified looks on their faces and their hands over their mouths. With all their hearts, they both loved the young man known as James T. O'Malley. Next to them, a very proud and honorable man stood. He draped each of his arms over the two women and held them closely to comfort them. To somehow indicate to them that it was all right. To protect them as well as honor them. Despite the apparent horror of the situation, the smile on his face was a mile wide; because he knew that his son had just stood for the defense of a level of respect.

And all that comes along with it.

Love is love and pride is pride.

On the ice, an old, cagey hockey coach watched as teammates slowly picked the embattled Fred Spieth off the ice and held him as he shakily skated to the locker room. Out of the corner of his eyes, he also watched as James T. O'Malley skated off for an appointment with old Doc Hornsby.

The old doctor was making a very good living off ice hockey in Mohawk City, New York.

The old coach blew his whistle and waved his hands over his head.

"Okay! It's over! Back to the game. Let's go! Stephens, take the draw! Mickey, git ya ass in the face-off circle. Ya moving up to the red squad. O'Malley will be the starting center once old Doc Hornsby stitches him up. Even if I took Fred back, it would not matter. I have a strong feeling that after being on the wrong end of that ass kicking, Fred is not returning and is choosing football over ice hockey."

Coach Hess smiled as he watched James T. O'Malley reach the door in the boards, jump off the ice and make his way to the locker room, while holding a towel over his mouth and the cut lip.

The old coach smiled and whispered as he slowly skated back to the bench, "Hell, yeah, that young man *is* one helluva hockey player and one helluva young man. Hell yeah, he is very special."

That evening, after a visit to the good doctor for a few more stitches and a recommendation that James Thomas O'Malley visits a plastic surgeon to eliminate the fold-over in the corner of his lip, the O'Malley family sat around the table in the dining room of their home. Everyone had joined in, clearing the table of dishes and leftovers. Kate and Mrs. O'Malley had stayed in the kitchen to do the dishes. Kate was always over at the O'Malley's house or Jim was over at the O'Leary's house, and they were inseparable now.

Young love, but powerful love. It always withstands the test of time and all the pitfalls of life.

While reaching into the refrigerator to grab a beer, Sergeant O'Malley waved and said to his son, "Come and sit with me at the dining room table, James. I want to talk to you."

James Thomas flashed a look at Kate and his gal flashed her glorious smile back at her James, as did Mrs. O'Malley. After today's events at the scrimmage game, they all expected this time to arrive.

"Sure, Dad," was all James Thomas said as they made their way to the dining room table.

Father sat opposite his son and in silence; he twisted the cap off the beer bottle and took a long sip, all the while keeping his eyes focused upon James Thomas.

"Okay. The truth. Why did you beat the living hell out

of Spieth?"

"Because it was a long time coming, Dad. You might recall the incident a long time ago when he tried to steal Dexter Zimmer's radio. I called him out then and we never settled it. I owed him for this scar."

Jim fingered the scar under his right eye and his father took another sip of his beer.

"A hockey puck originally gave you that scar, James. Spieth only glamorized it, and now, you have a lip scar from his hockey stick. A terrible cheap shot, and yes, it sucks to receive it from a teammate, but I am not surprised because Spieth is a bully and a loser. That will not change. Despite the aura, he will never amount to very much. Regardless, cheap shots are all part of the game of hockey. It is territorial and intimidating in nature and there are times when you have to do what you have to do to win the game. There is more to this than old incidents, unsettled scores and a high stick. What did he say to you to invoke such an explosion and cause Coach Hess to allow you to beat his ass silly?"

Obviously, the policeman knew how to conduct an investigation. Another sip of beer and he grew impatient with his son.

"James? Don't bullshit your old man now."

James nodded and waved his father in close over the table while casting an eye toward the kitchen. Jim wanted to make sure the women were out of an earshot. His father understood and set the beer bottle aside and leaned in to listen.

In a low whisper, James said, "Spieth said, someday, somewhere, I will have my way with your little bitch girlfriend and she will moan at how good it will be compared to your pencil dick."

Sergeant O'Malley nodded and leaned back and took his beer bottle, and this time, he took a long sip. James Thomas could see the temples of his father pound a little and his free hand tighten into a fist while pondering the evil words of Fred Spieth.

After finishing the long sip, the father said, "I know you are still so young, but do you love Kate with all of your heart, James?"

"I do, yes. I want to marry her someday. I *will* marry her someday. You knew and loved, Mom, when you were our age. Correct?"

"Yes, I did. James, I believe you that you will marry Kate someday. Be smart in your young love. Children are great responsibilities. Always treat Kate as you just treated her today. The woman you love, the woman you defended. With honor. With great respect. There will be obstacles in your love, James, but always return to her with honor and with respect. Hopefully, your love is built on trust."

The father's eyes blinked, and they wandered, and then he spoke again.

This time, the policeman's voice was lower, "Your mother and I, we are, much as Kate and you are, James. We are high school sweethearts, but it has been painful for us. Very painful. Partially, my fault, and a great deal of hers, but much of it was circumstance. After I returned home from the war, I chose to stand for a purpose and that caused us much pain. Someday, soon, I will explain. Not now, but soon. We owe it to you. Besides, your mother and I agreed to tell you of the past and of the pain when you became a man. After watching you today and hearing of all the reasons that you beat Mr. Spieth's sorry ass, I know that you are now a man."

Jim nodded and studied his father's eyes. It was one of the few times in his young life that he could see deep pain within the layers of strength that made up his father.

"I am not sure why standing for a purpose would cause pain, Dad. I thought that is how we are supposed to live our lives."

"When you commit to a purpose and for what you

believe to be righteous and correct, it is, but it is not the easiest thing to do. There are many evil persons out there that want to control this world and the righteous are comparatively few in numbers. Not too many are willing to stand for what is righteous, and it comes with a tremendous burden. I think you are up for it, James. Just remember that you play the game hard and fair and always play to win, but just do not beat player's asses for the hell of beating them. Spieth deserved it. I am proud of you. You stood for your woman and you stood for honor and respect." Sergeant O'Malley rather mindlessly fiddled with the beer bottle, and he turned it around and around in his hands while he pondered his thoughts in silence. He stopped turning the bottle, looked up at his son, and repeated his pride once again in a voice just above a whisper, "Yes. I am very proud of you, James. More than words can ever convey."

"Thank you, Dad. I understand. I am very proud of you, too. Your boxing lessons worked."

Sergeant O'Malley took one last sip of the beer and set the now empty bottle aside. His face broke into a little smile at the words of his son.

"Yes, they did. Sure did. You will need to go to confession this week. Do not miss it. Father Callahan is a hockey fan too. He will hear of the battle and he will be at your first regular season game. Father Callahan loves hockey. Everyone goes on Friday nights. Not much else to spend three dollars on and be so entertained around here. This is hockey country."

"I will take care of confession. It is the right thing to do. I love and respect God."

Jim's father made sure his son went to church, but he seldom spoke of religion. Jim's mother was the driving force behind her son's Catholic faith and she made sure that Jim attended mass regularly.

"Good. What are your plans? You are an amazing player

and have a great future. You graduate in June, and I know that you are not so naïve as to think that the son of a lowly policeman will have some college scholarship for ice hockey thrown at your feet. We are not rich as the Spieths are and I cannot manipulate colleges that I am an alumnus of, although, I am betting that after today, Fred takes the football offer."

Jim laughed a little at the comment, and his father's smile broke some tension.

"Not many American hockey players make it to the pros through college, James. Perhaps, someday, but not now."

Jim nodded. He was mature beyond his years.

"Mr. Rutledge at the store says he wants to promote me to a grocery supervisor when I graduate and he knows the manager of the market in Albany. He thinks he can get me a job there and I would eventually like to attend junior college part-time here and there. There are many semi-pro teams in Albany. Or, I hope to get an invitation to the Iron League or a league downstate. Maybe in Orange or Rockland counties. I am going to work and play hockey. Work hard. Play hard. I will always play to win, Dad. I will always love Kate, too. Hockey and Kate. And I love you and Mom and God too."

"We love you too, James. Church is important. Not much, you will ever do without God on your side. The Iron League and downstate, huh? Kick ass leagues. Might run into big city players and some New Jersey players. Hold on to your ass with them. Tough as Hell. Never underestimate those Jersey guys. Eventually, you will need to skate with the speed of the Canadians. You can do it."

Jim's father waved his beer bottle in the air and asked, "What about, Kate?"

The young and confident James T. O'Malley leaned in again. His eyes darted to the kitchen and he smiled.

"I will marry her someday, Dad. When I settle into my career, I will marry Kate. Be it in ice hockey, or whatever it is that finally calls me to do in this life. After all, she is gorgeous, full of love and spirit and she is Irish."

The old sergeant smiled and whispered, "Yes, she is." His smile grew wider. He pushed his chair away from the table and in a much louder voice, James Reilly O'Malley said, "I think . . . I need another beer."

Chapter Five

Badge Number Eleven

"Are you taking a break for dinner?" My lovely Rose asked me as she snuck up behind me and then lovingly hung her arms around my neck, leaned forward, and kissed my cheek. She smelled as if she was a bed of fragrant sweet pea flowers dancing in the late spring wind.

"Wow! You smell so amazing today," I commented as I leaned into her kiss.

"Does that mean that I usually don't smell very good?" Rose asked with a chuckle while she let go of me and in a quick motion, she sat her gorgeous backside on the corner of my desk. I realized that for a wordsmith that might not have been my best sentence. Perhaps, I should have added one word, "always" to the sentence and omitted the word, "today."

It is quite amazing how one word can control a person's fate.

I paused and looked at Rose, who was smiling at her, catching me in my own words. My wife had already moved on from the coy remark, because I saw her eyes darting from the papers on my desk to the screen of my writing laptop.

"I deserved that one. Let me rephrase that . . . you smell even more wonderful than you usually do because you *always* smell amazing. New perfume?"

"No. It is a new shampoo and body soap. I missed you in the shower. You could have scrubbed my back and earned an amazing reward," she said with a wink as her eyes continued to scan the work on my desk. A wink of her eye was all she ever had to do to melt my heart. This wink was no exception.

I mumbled, "Stupid number twenty-seven, always too absorbed in my work."

"No worries. There will be a second chance for redemption, believe me, there will be. Say, this all looks like quite the project here. Are these Jim's notes that you told me about? My goodness! There are pages and pages of them." Rose now jumped off the corner of the desk, she leaned over the desk and I watched as her dark eyes studied the pages of Jim's notes that I had spread out on my desk.

"They are, and luckily, I have assembled them into some type of order and I think that so far, I am working rather well from them." Rose did not comment, instead, she curled her lip and slowly nodded her head while continuing to study the work.

"Do Jim's notes actually tell a complete story? Sorry, for the twenty questions, my love. I just find it fascinating to see you work off of another person's material. I have never seen this before on any of your other projects."

I enjoyed the fact that my wife was so interested in my work. She always showed me her full love and her respect, too. I rolled my chair out from the desk, smiled, and patted my lap as an invitation for Rose to sit on my lap. She smiled and eagerly sat down while putting her one arm around me. Rose then leaned in to listen and watch while I explained.

"Not actually any storyline that I can simply transfer to the pages. These notes are actually individual events, laced with tidbits of Jim's own thoughts and emotions. They seem to all record parts and pieces of his life to explain his background from his youth to just a few months ago. I am using my writer's privilege to assemble them chronologically and to add dialogue and, in some cases, characters. It has a great deal of my own assumptions and yes, it is very different."

Rose nodded, and I saw her eyes move from the papers on the desk to the words on the screen. I remained silent as she read a few words, then fiddled with the mouse and dropped a page and read some more. Then a few more. I usually did not share any of my work in progress, I did run draft copies of books by Rose for input, but usually not work that was in such infancy stages. This work, however, was very special and, as Rose correctly stated, very different for me. I think Rose deserved to share in this one. After all, James T. O'Malley is a huge part of her life too.

"This is wonderful, Paul. Very creative and different in how you shift from you, Paul, being the narrator and telling the story from a foot away, to a third person telling the story from a few hundred feet away. I must ask you, Paul, will you use Jim to tell parts of his own story? You know, first person, Jim. Verbatim or paraphrased from his notes?"

I now leaned back in the chair, Rose leaned on the desk, and my wife carefully studied my eyes. She could tell that I had not considered that before she mentioned it. Rose was amazing and although I understood her description of telling the stories from various distances, I had never heard those terms used before to describe writing styles. Not that I actually had a style. I sat forward, placed my hands on each side of my wife's lovely face, and deeply kissed her.

"My goodness, Rose, you are so amazing. Your mind is deep, and it is brilliant. I love you to the moon and beyond and now, I need to make some pencil notes."

In haste and excitement, I picked through the many papers piled on my desk, until I found the book outline that I had created earlier and I studied it while Rose watched me. My mind was a whirlwind of creativity as I ran the progression of the storyline through my head.

I then looked back up at my wife and said, "I cannot fit that in just yet, but I will at some point. In looking at Jim's notes, I think I know just the spots. Mostly, near the end of the book. Perhaps, here and there. Anyway, fantastic idea! I will mention you in the credits as a creative contributor. Thank you."

Rose laughed and kissed me again while mumbling as our lips remained attached, "You are welcome. Such a reaction to a simple suggestion. My goodness." She then leaned back, tugged at the neckline of her blouse to tease me a bit and added, "I thought that I always was a creative contributor in many ways."

"You are, dear Rose. You are, of course, I just cannot always write about and detail your, ah, creative ways."

"Good idea. You do not want to lose your family rating and give away too many details of our lives. Please make some pencil notes, my love. You are such a creative giant, and I must say that you are rather intense right at the moment. Suffice it to say that I guess that I should wait a little while more before starting to cook dinner. . .."

It was early February and the hardy residents of upstate New York held onto the icy winds and rode out another harsh winter. Winter was not for the faint of heart here in the upstate regions of New York. In the city of Mohawk City, the residents were used to it and they stomped their feet upon the frozen ground and worked through winter as if it was just another aspect of the landscape. Mountains, rivers, lakes, trees, and cold ice and snow. It was part of their heritage and part of their fortitude.

Another part of their heritage was in the old city's nickname, Sin City was what they called the old city, a leftover adage from the corruption and madness of a particular era in the 1950s. An era no one here was proud of, yet, was still part of history. An era, which made the lawmakers in the capital city of Albany, some ninety miles southeast of Sin City, shudder and quake. It took a long time for the government corruption to settle out of Mohawk City, but the organized crime lingered. It lingered here and there, and as the textile mills closed and the manufacturing dried up, so did the economy and so did the jobs. The old city became perfect prey for the evil side of life to twist and manipulate and to use for evil gain. As the good residents and loyal people of Mohawk City fought to regain their city and seek a release from the grips of evil, they recruited good soldiers of the law and courageous persons equipped to fight for all that is righteous, just, and honest.

On this cold morning, from deep in the shadows of a dark alleyway in the downtown area of Mohawk City, New York, a silent evil lurked within the concealment of the enveloping gloom of the intense cold. From the shadows, a young man watched the rear door of a local café. A coffee and sandwich shop where you picked up the daily newspaper, grabbed a piping hot cup of coffee, and exchanged some words and the daily gab with the owner and some locals.

Wily police officers plant the seeds of the plants of information along the way. The seeds might sprout plants with leaves ripe with the heartbeat of the streets.

There were a few of these types of establishments in downtown Mohawk City, but this particular café was a favorite early morning stop of a certain Mohawk City police sergeant named James Reilly O'Malley.

The good police sergeant was one of those aforementioned good soldiers.

Upon starting his day and beginning his daily shift, Sergeant O'Malley stopped here every morning to pick up coffee and a morning snack. He parked his police cruiser in the rear of the cafe. Sometimes, his partner came in with him, other times, his partner remained in the car and Sergeant O'Malley picked up coffee for both of them. When it was a cold day, the sergeant usually went to the coffee shop, while his partner stayed in the car. Cars cooled off quickly in upstate New York winters and heaters in police cruisers were rather feeble.

This was a Tuesday, and the good sergeant worked solo on Tuesday. It was his partner's day off.

The young man watching from his concealment within the dark alley pulled his collar up and around his neck. He gave the knit hat on his head a tug or two. The hat felt warm, and the hat helped him to believe that his concealment was secure. His eyes darted from the watch on his wrist, to the narrow alley that led to another alley, and then to a side road. His escape route was perfect. He could clearly see the rear door of the café, but there were no other windows in sight from any of the surrounding buildings. A perfect location for a deadly ambush and an easy escape. The young man intensely studied the location, and he ran everything from the angle of the shot, to which way to turn to escape, to how the shadows fell on the alley, around in his mind. He shivered, yet, despite the intense cold of the early morning, he felt some sweat on the back of his neck. Sweat sprouted from wretched thoughts of evil planning. His fingers rolled over the hard metal of the gun in his coat pocket. This was an easy shot. In his military days, he had pulled off much more difficult shots for far less of a payday. What payday? Oh yes, he thought with a chuckle, a meager pay of forty dollars a day, free meals and free medical care. Military pay was awful, but his job for today, paid beyond his wildest dreams. He was desperate for money now, for a ticket to ride, for a payday to lead him out of his misery, and this evil and vile mission would provide the payday that he needed. The young man was far beyond believing that honor and fighting for your country was something that he believed in. Now, sadly, he believed in cold, hard, cash. Nothing much more than that. However, he would not complete the mission on this particular day. No, not today. The evil still required some more reconnaissance to pull off the perfect kill. He made a note that on Tuesday; the sergeant rode solo.

Tuesday was the day.

A day of evil.

He had heard that Sergeant O'Malley was an old-time war hero. A fellow military man. The young man was Navy and O'Malley was Army, but he was a brother in arms. O'Malley was a soldier and deep inside; the young man felt some pangs of regret at that fact. At one time, the young man was amongst the Navy's elite forces. Now he was just a broken wreckage of a man with little to no sense of any remaining military honor. Cheap shots on fellow soldiers and teammates were despicable, but that is the way it goes.

Either an old soldier dies in battle or the old soldier simply fades away.

Dead is dead.

It is the way it is.

Sometimes, when you are twisted and desperate and feel as if life has dealt you a poor hand, you lose sight of what is righteous, just, and honest.

You lose respect for the world and for your own soul.

Yet, eventually, there are those who come along to teach those little life lessons and even the score for the good people of this world.

Her beauty was a magnificent presence that surrounded me. An Irish mist of such exquisiteness that the presence defied description by mere words while it enveloped me. Kate came to me and gently kissed me, and held me close to her naked body. Her hair hung down over her breasts and it tumbled over me in great waves. Kate's skin smelled indescribable, something as if it were a cross between roses wavering in the breeze and the freshness of the air within the dawn of an early spring day. Her green eyes flickered while she looked at me and smiled. I gently reached behind her, held her bare backside with both of my hands, and pulled her close to me. She pulled at my pants and tossed my pants aside. Her face was full of passion as she pulled off the remainder of my clothing and tossed them aside, too. Her green eyes were wide and intense and I am sure that I locked my eyes on her naked glory, too. She gasped in deep breaths while she gently held my body in her hands, and while my hands voraciously explored her nakedness. I could feel her breathing grow deeper and steadier while she gently worked her hands over all of my body.

I asked her, "Are you sure, Kate. Sure? We are so young. You must be sure."

Kate seemed surprised at my question and her answer was quick, empathic, and honest.

"What does our age have to do with this, James? Nothing. You are eighteen, I am nineteen, and we are adults and we are madly in love. I am sure, James. I've never been surer about anything in my life. I loved you from the first moment that I ever saw you and I will, never, ever, stop."

I smiled, we kissed, and our love filled this entire world. Just the two of us . . . I honestly thought that there were no other people in the entire world other than the two of us. It was as if explosions were going off all around us. Kate ran her hands through my hair, and when the final moments of sharing our love arrived, she gripped the strands of my hair so tightly that I thought she would pull all of my hair out of my scalp.

Then, we collapsed together in a tangled web of love and sweat and I rolled over and whispered, "I love you with all of my heart and my soul."

Her lovely breasts rose and gently shook as her chest heaved in great waves of an afterglow.

Kate said between deep breaths, "I am lost in waves of true and glorious love. Beyond my wildest dreams, you are, James. Beyond my dreams."

After a few minutes of holding each other and sharing some kisses, Kate rolled her eyes as she spun away from me and landed on her back on the bed. She stared first at the ceiling, and then gently moved to her side and stared at me.

"I am not confessing this. There is no way that God views true love as a sin. Don't, you agree, James?"

I nodded my head and said, "No way this is wrong, Kate. Love and lust are so different."

Kate answered, "I agree. What is wrong with us sharing our love? Nothing. Yet, I think that everything is wrong about confessing to a man who works as a priest. I am done with confession and I am done with the Catholic Church. Call me a heathen or rebellious or call me a sinner, but I am nineteen now and it is time to make my own decisions. Just as I did when I decided, it was time for us to prove our love. Forgive me, James, but we just made love and there are no secrets between our thoughts. We are now and forever, one-person. The priest, well, he judges us? Why? He cannot see our hearts, nor can he touch our souls. I know we are both Catholic and all that we know are the rules and the rituals, but, honestly, I am no longer comfortable with most of it."

I rolled over on my side and I gently toyed with Kate's hair and tucked the waves of glorious auburn behind her ears.

"I agree, Kate. I feel the same exact way. All I know is that I love you deeply and will do so, forever. You are correct, there is so much more to religion than dwelling upon our sins. For us, it is time to separate our religion from God. I have to think that God knows our hearts and judges us by them. God knows all about us. Who we are, and all that we can be. There are no secrets from God."

I can recall thinking about how deep a thinker Kate was and how right now I thought that, despite her fabulous naked glory on display in front of me, how her mind was the most beautiful thing about her. I leaned over and gently kissed my beloved Kate. I felt my passion rising again and Kate felt it too as she glanced down and laughed at the sight of my "return."

"Oh my, James Thomas O'Malley, oh my. Really? Okay, well, we can work with this. Now and forever."

That was all Kate said and all that she needed to say.

Our love took over from there.

In the end, despite the tumult that became my life and the turmoil that entered my mind and disrupted my soul, our love was all that ever really mattered.

Kate Eva O'Leary eventually saved my soul by stealing my heart.

I am James Thomas O'Malley, and I have to think that right now, I am the luckiest man in the world.

It was Tuesday in late February, and the same evil hid in a dark alleyway next to the café. The young man hid within the gloom of an icy morning. Doom hung low, along with gray clouds spitting and coughing snowflakes. Nervous sweat ran down his neck while his fingers slowly screwed a silencer on the barrel of a handgun. Gunmetal is cold in many ways and it holds an eerie silence before the explosions occur.

Sergeant James Reilly O'Malley had not broken his daily routine and the young man had watched long enough to know that routine inside and out. His elite military training emphasized stealth, and unfortunately, he was very good at it. In his warped and desperate mind, his execution plan was perfect, his escape carefully mapped out and seemingly foolproof. Unfortunately, there was a reason the evil hired him for this gig, because he never missed. Even after losing three of his fingers on his left hand in a military accident, he still never missed a shot. The military knew that too. In his heart and in his mind, he harbored great resentment over that fact, because he felt as if there was no legitimate reason for his discharge.

After all, he shot right-handed.

Now, he could not even work as an automobile repair mechanic anymore . . . bosses looked at his hand and shook their heads. A pinky and a ring finger did not cut it in a mechanic's world. No one would even give him a chance. Stupid-asses. If the government would have coughed up more money for the disability that they caused, maybe this would not have to happen, but they did not. And now, he was desperate.

Four city blocks away, on Sixteenth Avenue, Mrs. Emily Washburn walked her dog. This was unusual for Rollo, the black Scottie dog, to require an early morning jaunt, especially on such a cold morning, but Rollo had jumped up on the bed and begged to go outside. For some reason, today, Rollo's schedule changed. Mr. Washburn only moaned and rolled over, so Emily had the pleasure of a walk on this icy and snowy morning. Her old bones creaked almost as much as the ice on the wires did, but Rollo was worth it. He was faithful, a great watchdog and a good judge of character.

Mrs. Washburn always said, "If Rollo growls at you, then you have something to hide. He sees things that my husband and I cannot see."

When you are old and a little feeble, it is nice to have a Rollo around. A medium-sized dog, with a heritage from that pile of rocks known as the United Kingdom, which produces some very tough dogs and some fearless individuals. It is in the genes. A dog, which will fearlessly confront and tear apart much bigger things. A handy pal to have if, and when, it gets a bit difficult.

Her husband always warned her that, "Evil lurks in those old city streets. Always take Rollo with ya."

The young man knew the routine never changed and even though he knew the plan and had played it out a million times in his head, his heart still thumped in his chest. He leaned on the wall, pulled his wool hat down and unbuttoned a few buttons of his Navy pea coat. Buttons with anchors on them and buttons sewn in honor to represent the pride of their heritage. In this case, there was no pride and certainly, the heritage was lost forever. The killer braced his body on the snowy ground. Gun pointed ahead, arms tight and unwavering. Sergeant O'Malley was a well-trained street cop, he always took one-step out the back door of the café, his eyes carefully checked all around for anything out of place, then he took a sip or two of coffee and then he descended the few steps to the waiting police cruiser.

When he puts his head down to unlock the door, evil will strike.

The door to the café opened. The killer watched the policeman's eyes dart back and forth and then he turned his head and scanned the surroundings. In the dark alleyway, there were only shadows, and the evil remained undetected. Sergeant O'Malley took one sip of coffee and then walked down the steps. The killer's heart pounded as his fingers poised on the trigger and his eyes locked down the gun sights. They were only a mere ten feet or so apart in distance.

Sergeant O'Malley reached in his coat. He pulled the keys out and when he put his head down; the trigger squeezed and a great man left this world in a slump and a crash into the snowy ground. One head shot. One kill. One drop. Just as the military taught him to do.

First, the good sergeant's head twisted from the bullet's impact. His service cap went flying into the cold air, then the coffee container flew in the air and the now dead body hit the police cruiser and bounced off at an odd angle. When the body hit hard against the cold metal edge of the hood, the police badge on the breast of his jacket hit the car's hood and popped off and landed in the snow, a mere few feet away from the killer's feet. A great life snuffed out in a blink of an eye.

Tragedy is one of humankind's saddest plagues.

Despite the horror of just killing a defenseless man, the killer smiled.

'How ironic. A trophy. A deer head to mount over my mantle,' he thought. He picked the badge up, glanced at its spent glory and whispered, "Number Eleven. Sorry, number eleven, I hope Heaven is kind to you. I know that I will never know. After this, all I will ever know are the flames of Hell licking my ass."

He placed the badge in his pocket and ran down the alleyway. He ran for two city blocks, darting here and there, looking for witnesses, hiding when cars passed by him, he ran while cutting down alleyways between old apartment buildings and through parking lots and passages of abandoned buildings and empty factories that told no stories, except of the desperation and emptiness they represented. The killer stopped his desperate retreat in front of a rubbish dumpster behind an Italian restaurant on Sixteenth Avenue, and he removed his military boots and tossed them into the frozen mounds of trash. Then he picked up the other boots he staged a few hours ago and put them on his feet. Even though the snow and ice did not cover all the ground, he knew the alleyway had his boot prints. Now there was no trail to follow.

From behind the alley of the Italian restaurant, he ran to the main street's sidewalk and then he stopped short, when he almost ran smack into the chest of Mrs. Washburn.

Rollo stood defensively upon the sidewalk with his hair rising and Rollo looked at the young man and he growled.

Under the cover of thick eyeglasses, Mrs. Washburn's eyes blinked in the relentless cold, as the old woman looked first at Rollo and then at the young man who almost ran into her.

For a mere second, the killer fingered the gun in his pocket, and then thought, 'Bad idea. This old bag cannot even see. Her glasses are as thick as soda bottles.' He scooted to the side and pulled at his wool hat. Besides, he was convinced that she never saw his face.

"Wow! It's cold today. Sorry, Excuse me, ma'am. Late for work. Again."

He dashed off and Rollo continued to growl. The dog was very perceptive and a good judge of character. A very good judge.

Mrs. Washburn's bones creaked and ached, but her eye doctor was on top of his game. Her corrective lenses were very good and she could see quite well. The elderly woman never saw his face, or his hair color, but she did notice that he was missing three fingers on his left hand. He was missing his pointer finger; the middle finger was just a small nub, and the ring finger was gone. She spotted his missing fingers when he pulled his hat down and she noticed the Navy pea coat that he wore. Her husband was in the Navy and his pea coat hung under plastic. It smelled like mothballs and hid in a dark corner of their closet in the hallway of their home. Unlike the killer's pea coat, Mr. Washburn's pea coat still had honor attached to it.

"C'mon, along, now Rollo. Just a young man late for work. I know you did not like him and I am sure he is irresponsible. Late for work, again. Shameful that these young people nowadays, have no discipline."

In the distance, police sirens wailed and echoed across the old city streets.

Sin city had lived up to its reputation.

Heaven greeted badge number eleven. His tour of duty was over and the pain of this morning and gloom of the horror of it enveloped many lives. None more than a certain young man named James Thomas O'Malley.

At the bus station in Mohawk City, a young man purchased a one-way bus ticket to New York City. He only spoke the words of his intended destination and was very careful to keep his left hand inside of the pocket of his pea coat and his wool hat pulled down over his head as far as he could; only displaying minimal facial features. On the sidewall of the main lobby, a television interrupted the weather report for a bulletin about the cold-blooded killing of a local Mohawk City police sergeant. He paid for the ticket, nodded at the attendant in the sales booth, picked up his sea bag of his belongings and made his way to the waiting bus. Bus number 39. He looked at the destination posted on the bus and then at his ticket and thought, how he could walk to Hell's Kitchen from the bus station. He hoped that it was not quite as cold downstate as it was here. Somehow, right now, no place on the face of this Earth could be as cold as it was here.

There was no graveside service for Sergeant James Reilly O'Malley. The frozen ground would not allow anything other than dynamite to disturb it. It had been a helluva wicked winter in upstate New York this year, and the burial would need to wait. Instead, there was a church service at Saint Peter's Catholic Church and the burial would be a date in the spring.

When the ground thawed.

If it would ever thaw.

If this wretched winter would ever end.

All that James Thomas O'Malley could think of was that his father's body would be on ice until then. He could not shake that terrible thought. He tried, but it lingered. The flag-draped coffin sat at the front of the church, with a picture of his father in his police officer's uniform standing upon an easel sitting in front of the coffin, but James knew that very shortly his father's body would reside in a freezer at the morgue.

For now, the grave slated to receive his father's dead body would remain as empty as James Thomas O'Malley's soul was.

James did not hear the words of Father Callahan conducting the funeral mass. He did not hear anything. He knew that Kate sat on his right side, his mother sat on his left side, and Kate's mother and father were in the same pew with them, as were his cousins, aunts and uncles and his father's partner, Sergeant Lawson. The church packed to the rafters, jammed with people to the last pew, all the way to rows of persons who stood along the edges of the sanctuary. Coach Hess and the hockey club attended, all of them wearing number eleven hockey sweaters. Priests and nuns from the Catholic parishes of the old city joined hands with the Lutheran pastor from Saint Michael's Lutheran Church, and the rabbi from the temple down the street, and the pastor from the Baptist church around the corner. Clergy, all united hand-in-hand, heart-to-heart to honor a great man. There were police officers from all over New York, New York State Troopers, United States Army soldiers, firefighters, a representative from the Governor of the State of New York, policemen and policewomen from all over—from New York City, from Albany and Schenectady, from Vermont, Connecticut, and New Jersey.

Fredrick Spieth and his family attended.

An Irish bagpiper from the New York City Police Honor Guard Piper Band played a wretched death dirge on the pipes. There were some aspects of being Irish that James T. O'Malley could do without. A bagpiper was one of them. Right now, he would like to stick the bagpipes up the piper's ass.

Local media and national media crawled over the scene. The piper played between the tears and sobs, yet, for Jim it was a blur. A haze of despair enveloped him, but he did not feel anything. Well, no, that was incorrect because he felt one thing. No tears. Just anger. An anger rose in his soul and it was an anger that he never felt before in his young life. His fists clenched as he sat there, and he knew that this anger was going to be something very difficult to control. Maybe impossible.

A joint Honor Guard of police officers and United States Army soldiers presented Mrs. O'Malley and James with the American flag and it was over. All over, except for the endless handshakes, condolences, and greetings. It seemed as if it would never end, and all James could feel was anger. Even Kate's words fell upon numb ears and her gentle touch fell upon an empty soul contained within a body. Kate felt the anger overcoming her lover, and she knew the storm clouds that were brewing upon the horizon of their lives. The world was about to meet an unleashed James Thomas O'Malley, and that thought brought fear to her heart and a deep and powerful tremble to her soul. Yet even more bombs were about to drop in their lives.

The repast was an event that Jim could have done without, but it was all paid for by the Policemen Benevolent Union. As the son of the fallen officer, he knew that he could not leave his mother alone to deal with what Jim felt was just another extension of their grief. The last thing that Jim felt like doing was to eat. He would sneak a few shots of Irish whiskey, that was for sure. After all, as he was, most of the attendees were Irish.

Jim sat with Kate hooked on his arm and he sipped a glass of water, spiked with a hit or two of Irish whiskey, that Sergeant Lawson was kind enough to prepare for Jim. It felt good to become a little numb.

Jim and Kate sat mostly in silence when Jim's mother

came along; walking with a man wearing a black suit, black tie, and a white shirt. Jim looked up and studied the man; his features were dark and his hair jet-black and thick. His build was medium in stature and while he was not short, he was not too tall, either. Kate's grip tightened on Jim's arm as she, too, studied the man. Jim felt for a brief moment as if he was looking into a mirror in the future, because he thought how the black-suited man looked, well, as he did. Jim's eyes studied his immaculate appearance; the suit must have cost a small fortune. It was beyond expensive. Jim looked up but did not stand and his eyes went first to Kate's eyes and then to the face of the man and then finally to his mother.

He knew that Kate observed the same thing as Jim did.

He knew his lover.

Every inch of her.

Literally.

"Who the hell are you?" Jim growled. His defenses were up, and his protective instincts of his mother and his girlfriend were on guard.

"James, I would like you to meet an old friend from the city. This is, Mr. Bernard Flaherty."

The man reached out his hand and Jim took it and gently shook his hand while studying his face and eyes. James Thomas O'Malley, even at a young age, was brilliantly intelligent and keenly observant. It was not just his hockey skills that were always peaking, but his life skills too.

"I am so sorry for your loss. Your father was a great man."

"He was. Thank you. Nice to meet you too. This is my girlfriend, Miss Kate Eva O'Leary." Kate stood up and while she stood, she gently lifted her man to his feet by applying some gentle pressure upon his arm and then she smoothed her dress out and smiled. There is nothing like a good woman to guide a man along.

"Nice to meet you, Mr. Flaherty," Kate said with a smile.

"My pleasure to meet you, Miss O'Leary. I am so sorry. I wish that we could all meet under better circumstances. You are a lovely young woman, but then, again, James is quite the handsome young man too."

Jim noticed how he was about the same height as Mr. Flaherty was and he continued to study his face.

Caution filled his body and soul.

Jim spoke in a halting tone, "From the city, huh? As in, Hell's Kitchen . . . in the city. You knew my dad as well as my mom from there?"

For the briefest moment, Mr. Flaherty's eyes darted over to Mrs. O'Malley and then back to Jim.

Jim observed all of these interactions very carefully.

"Well, yes, James, we all grew up together. In the old neighborhood. It was a long time ago."

"I see, well, thank you for coming and for paying your respects."

"Yes, of course, it was the least that I could do for such a fine man."

It was easy to tell that this meeting had caused James T. O'Malley a large amount of discomfort as well as raised a number of questions in his mind.

Jim waved his hand in the direction of Mr. Flaherty and then asked, "What do you do for a living to afford such an expensive custom-fitted suit? From what I know of it, and heard of it, the old neighborhood was not famous for many high rollers and lots of cash stuffed into bank accounts. It looks as if you did rather well for yourself."

"I am a businessman. A very successful businessman."

There were a few moments of silence as Jim studied Mr. Flaherty and you could tell that he was testing the pulse of the situation. The young James T. O'Malley was wise beyond his years.

Jim finally spoke as he reached for Kate's hand, "I notice how you are remaining rather vague. A businessman, huh? Well, it appears as if you are very successful.

Congratulations. Life is hard and to be successful is quite an achievement. However, I guess, it depends upon how you measure success. Anyway, it is nice to meet you and thank you for your condolences. I need a refresh of my drink. Kate, please, will you come with me? Do any of you want something? Mom?"

Both women and Mr. Flaherty shook their heads, but Kate tucked her arm into Jim's, while Jim nodded and the two of them walked away.

Mr. Flaherty mumbled, "You are welcome," and watched as Kate and Jim walked away. When they were out of earshot, he leaned in and whispered to Mrs. O'Malley, "He has grown into quite the man. His young girlfriend is gorgeous. I am worried. Lillian, are you sure that this is the correct time to speak with James? I mean, on the heels of such wretched heartbreak. Naturally, he seems quite aloof and upset. His eyes would not stop studying my face."

"It is time, Barney. The three of us agreed long ago for you to meet him and to tell James the truth. Now that James is gone, it is more than time. The pain will not ease, no amount of time will ease the pain, but James Thomas is strong and powerful and he will overcome all of this. I know in my heart that he will forgive us and that he will overcome it."

"I hope so. I pray that he will be okay."

Officer Lawson paused before he dumped a short pour of Irish whiskey in Jim's glass, but he did so. His eyes told him of a pain that he could not even imagine. Instead, he made it a long pour. Officer Lawson was Sergeant James Reilly O'Malley's partner for over ten years.

"I loved your father. He was my military brother and my police brother. The whiskey only masks the pain. I do not even want to think about how you feel. Go easy, son. Kate, watch him for us. Grief runs deep for all of us."

"I will," Kate said with a nod.

Kate and Jim walked away in silence as Jim sipped the drink, and he continued to look back at where his mother was speaking with Mr. Flaherty. Kate knew Jim well enough not to say a word, but she felt it, too. She knew what he was thinking, because she was thinking the same thing. The two young lovers remained very connected. As if they were one-person.

They stopped walking when a short, stocky man stopped them and held his hand out. His suit was sloppy, his necktie was askew, and his hair stuck out in many directions and in unkempt waves, and his face had a five o'clock shadow. Maybe, due to the events of the last few days, his face had a seven o'clock shadow. Jim vaguely recalled meeting this man once before, and he knew that despite his rumpled appearance, he was a police officer of some rank that Jim could not recall.

"Detective Lyle Odell. Homicide detective. I am so sorry for your loss, James. Your father was the best of the best." They shook hands, and the detective nodded and weakly forced a smile at Kate.

"Miss O'Leary."

Kate nodded and weakly smiled in return. The day was taking its toll on Kate, too.

The detective's eyes were sharp, keen, and clear and even though Jim could smell booze on his breath, Jim could tell this man knew his job. His eyes looked at the glass and he smiled a little as he put his arm on Jim's shoulder.

"Go easy on that, James. I feel your pain. All of us are hurting, but I cannot even fathom what pain you are going through right now, son. Just remember that tomorrow, it might not feel so swift."

Jim nodded, and he understood.

Jim mumbled, "My father's blood and whiskey. Not exactly a winning combination." Jim was numb enough, and he was not going to be stupid.

"Understood. I gotcha. I want you to know, James, that I

will do everything in my power to catch this evil bastard who did this to your father. I will get him, them, or whoever. You have my promise that I will do my best."

Jim nodded, and he handed the glass of liquid courage over to Kate. He shook the detective's hand again with both of his hands and then the anger rose and overtook Jim's face and soul. His fists clenched in anger, and his body shook as he took a deep breath. Jim now knew that this emotion was impossible to control.

While the detective and Kate watched and observed his reaction, Jim finally spoke, "Thank you. I am sure that you will do your best. I will give you some time, but I have to warn you that if you do not find whom is responsible for his murder . . . that . . . I will. I know this has something to do with my father's past. A ghost returned to haunt him. Regardless, I am not afraid of anything or anyone. You might think that I am just some young man spouting nonsense and grief. An eighteen-year-old, grief-stricken, son of a fallen police officer, but now, I am a man. For many reasons, the last few months, and especially, the last few days, have made me into a man. I will wait and then if you fail, I will even the score. The cold-blooded assassination of my father has knocked me on my ass, but James Thomas O'Malley always gets back up and I always play to win. Always."

The detective nodded as Jim patted his arm.

"I know you are a man, James. You are your father's son."

"I am."

Jim took the drink back from Kate and they walked away. Jim swigged the last drop of the drink; he set the glass on a table, grabbed Kate by the hand and said, "Let's go, Kate. I cannot take any more of this bullshit."

"I love you, James Thomas O'Malley. Always and forever."

"I love you too, Kate."

Kate knew the thoughts that nagged at her beloved James. She felt it, too.

Together, they walked arm-in-arm into the cold evening air. Later on, they proved their love as Kate did her best to help to absorb Jim's pain.

Painfully and somewhat reluctantly, the night slowly gave way to the early morning light.

Harold Garner had picked up and dumped the trash dumpster at Franco's Italian Restaurant every Saturday morning for as long as he could recall. It was on his route and after twenty-five years on the job, Harold could drive these city streets blindfolded. Franco's restaurant was an institution in the seedy part of the city. The best pizza and the best calzones. The best marinara sauce. Perfect crust on Franco's pizza, in the perfect New York style and tradition.

Harold, as most rubbish men are, was also an opportunist, an entrepreneur of sorts. The term of being "a dumpster diver" had such demeaning labels attached to it. Harold preferred to think of his unique ability to spot items of value in his trash dumpsters as a reward for the job. A few extra bucks for beer money to hide from his wife always came in handy. Four o'clock at the local watering hole was something that Harold looked forward to in his world. When you pick up trash for a living, you need to keep an eye on the bright side of life because there was nothing too glamorous about his job.

It paid well, provided great medical and dental benefits and was an honest way to make a living and Harold always said, "Hell, someone has to do it."

The seasoned driver guided the blades of his truck under the dumpster and then he put the truck into the parking gear and jumped out of the vehicle to check the trash piles. The kitchen laborer for the restaurant was notorious for piling trash in all the wrong places. Spilling trash during the overhead tilt and dump made for extra work and it was a pain in the ass. Harold's keen eyes caught something and while rearranging the bags of trash, he picked up a pair of military issue boots. Boots in very good condition, too. Expensive. Harold had pounded some ground in the Army a long time ago, and he knew what a solid pair of military boots could cost these days. Harold turned them over, studied them, and noted the size, which was an eleven. Same size as his foot. He was in luck today! This was a worthwhile catch and Harold happily walked over to his truck, placed the boots in the cab of his truck, and then returned to adjust the load. All the time, he wondered why a person would ditch such an expensive pair of boots in such good condition.

"Some people must not have to work too hard for their dough these days. I ain't one of 'em," Harold mumbled.

Over on Sixteenth Avenue in the first-floor apartment of the Washburn family, Mr. Washburn settled into his easy chair and tuned in the early morning news report on the local news channel. As he sipped his coffee, he listened and shook his head at the terrible news of the cold-blooded murder of the Mohawk City police officer.

"Sadly, according to the lead investigator in the case, Detective Lyle Odell, there are no solid leads in the case," the newscaster solemnly broadcasted, "the only shred of evidence are some footprints from what appears to be deep soled boots in the snow. The prints led from a hidden alleyway alongside the café where the murder took place, out to the intersection of Fifteenth Avenue. There, the snow gave way to a hard pavement, and the prints were lost. Apparently, the killer shot Sergeant O'Malley from the hidden confines of the dark alley, and then turned and fled through the adjoining city streets. Police are urging anyone who might have seen any suspicious activity to call. . .."

Mr. Washburn intently sipped his coffee and then called

out to his wife, "Say, honey, where were you when that young fellow ran into you and Rollo on Tuesday morning? Didn't you say that Rollo growled at him?"

In his truck, while he shifted gears and headed for the next stop, Harold Garner listened to the local news on his radio. He fiddled with the volume control knob as the news reporter repeated the same information as what the television station just broadcasted. All the local stations had the same press release from the Mohawk City police department. Detective Odell was very good at his job, and he knew when to call in some assistance. Harold's eyes looked over to the boots on the seat next to him, and his mind whirled. Harold was very street savvy. He shifted gears to a lower speed, and then he stopped the truck at the red light looming in front of him. Instead of going straight, he made a right turn and turned his rubbish disposal truck in the direction of the local police precinct office.

Chapter Six

Truth and Despair

"I guess you lost track of the time or you forgot me, my love?" My lovely Rose stood in front of me, holding a pizza pie box. I looked up and blinked my eyes a number of times as I looked at the wall clock hanging on the south wall of my office. Geez, eleven-thirty at night. My goodness, that was a long stretch of writing. I bowed my head and then smiled to test the Rose waters, and my wife smiled back. Okay, a good preliminary sign.

"I am so sorry. I did lose track of the time, but I could never forget you. I was lost in the flow of words. This was a ton of writing that I needed to put behind me. The pizza smells good though. Right?" Rose shrugged and set the pizza box on the only spot on my desk that was somewhat clear of papers and other items.

"Not as good as my lasagna that I put off until tomorrow night. Luckily, Joey's Pizza Shop is open until one in the morning. Must be a ton of college students close by or . . . obsessive writers with their heads stuck in keyboards. Obsessive writers who forget their wives," Rose said while handing me a paper plate, opening the box and placing a slice of pizza on the plate.

'Ouch,' I thought while I thanked her, took it, and watched while she plopped a slice on a paper plate for her. While scrambling, I worked in some damage control.

"I am sorry, my love. I promise you, Rose, that I never forget you. It is just this urge to remove these words from my soul. I love you."

"I understand, Paul. I do. However, you have been at this for over twelve hours, Paul. No rest, just some bathroom breaks and no food. My goodness, you are a machine sometimes."

I nodded and shook my head. Rose was correct because it was too long of a day. However, the flow was so strong today.

"I did not hear the telephone ring, but I have been a bit lost here and once, again, I apologize for my waywardness. Any update from Kate about Jim's condition?"

Rose shook her head to indicate no.

"What have you been doing?" I asked.

Rose looked at me and smiled. I knew that I had left that one wide open, and my wife's sense of humor was going to take full advantage of it.

"Oh, nothing, aside from eating stale crackers and licking bowls for scraps of food to stave off hunger, all while watching reruns of game shows from the 1970s, alone on the sofa. Nothing."

Oh, oh.

"Interesting," was all that I said. Then I added, "But now, we have pizza! Pizza cures a multitude of various ills and woes."

Rose did not comment about my proclamation for the glorious benefits of pizza. She stood up, walked over to the wet-bar in my office, opened the doors, and flipped on the lights.

With her back still turned to me, she asked, "Do you want a beer? I am having red wine. Lots of red wine. Pizza, red wine and then, my Paul afterwards."

I smiled; Rose was fine with my obsession with this work and honestly, with my rudeness for leaving her hanging for so long. I was going to survive unscathed. For the most part.

"Beer, please and thank you for you, Rose."

I watched while she prepared the drinks, and her head nodded.

"I love you, Paul. You do know that I am teasing you. I did miss you terribly, but did not want to disturb you. Obviously, I sympathize and understand the current situation and I know that with the emotions running so high and hard that you need to get these words all out of your mind and soul. Be warned, I am not teasing about some Paul time after we eat, though. No teasing there. I am going to wrap you up in love."

Rose carried the drinks over to the desk and handed me the beer. We touched glasses in a toast and she took a sip of the red wine.

"You are beyond amazing, Rose. Thank you for understanding. And as far as after we eat, well, it's a date."

Rose sat in a guest chair in front of my desk; she picked up the slice of pizza and took a bite.

With one finger pointed toward my laptop, Rose swallowed and asked, "So, exactly how is it going there, Hemingway?"

I also took a bite of pizza and I must admit that it tasted wonderful. I was so hungry.

"Well, Rose, I think it is going rather well. I reached a critical juncture. I think that right now, it is at a point where it is a good place to stop."

Rose nodded and smiled as she took another bite of the pizza.

"Wise answer, Paul. Yes, please, you can pick it all up tomorrow. The rest of tonight is ours and ours alone."

This pizza sure tasted good, and the beer was wonderful too, and so was the promise of the rest of the evening. Yet, writing the words today made my soul ache, and the story of Jim's life worked along the edges. Being lost in the sharing of our mutual love with my precious wife would go a long way toward healing some of that ache. Tomorrow, I would pour some more emotions upon the pages. For now, I needed to recall why I was such a lucky and blessed man.

Turning points within our lives often appear cloaked in disguise. Often, they arrive in surprise and in wonderful moments of joy and happiness. Others cause great pain. These moments arrive within innocent meetings of people who turn into friends or business associates, or lovers. Other times, they arrive as golden opportunities dropped into our laps, which produce grand ideas wrapped in rolling waves of wealth and power. Sometimes, however, there is a great anguish involved with these turning points. Turning points that first drive stakes of pain into our minds and our souls. They arrive when we are at the lowest points in our emotions, scraping our bellies along the ground as we crawl to regain what remains of ourselves.

It is how we pick ourselves up after these incidents, which count the most. Not the fact that we fell down, not the fact that we felt pain . . . but how we pick ourselves back up and move forward is what counts.

The rebound from despair.

A few days after the funeral service and memorial for his father, James Thomas O'Malley walked into the dining room of his home. The lovely Kate Eva O'Leary tightly held Jim's hand. Her love surrounded and enveloped him. He was going to need Kate's love and a lot more.

Jim's mother had asked Kate and Jim to make sure that they both stopped by today after their work shifts ended and before Kate and Jim had evening plans. His mother indicated that it was quite important. Deep down, Jim knew that this request had something to do with Mr. Bernard Flaherty. Kate knew it too. Even if they did not discuss Mr. Flaherty's appearance and presence, Kate knew that her beloved James felt that another turning point had arrived within their young lives. As if his father passing was not enough of a turning point, this was another one. James T. O'Malley was an introspective young man and a private person within his own thoughts. Kate was used to her man being rather tight-lipped and deep in his thoughts, especially so until Jim was sure of the situation that he was dealing with. He shared more with Kate than he did with any other person, but she was not willing to bring the subject of Mr. Flaherty into the conversation, until James did so. The two young lovers remained deeply in love and tightly connected. Kate respected Jim's need for privacy and she knew when the time arrived that he would open up her heart to her and ask for her opinion, her love, and her support.

Now, as they walked into the dining room of the home, Jim whispered to Kate, "This is it, Kate. I told you the expensive luxury car was Flaherty's car and the other car was Father Callahan's car. I already know what they want to tell us. My heart is not lying to me, Kate, and I know that my instincts are correct. I know the way we now share our hearts, and I know that you know and feel what I feel. We have not spoken about it and I love you and respect you for your silence while I gather my thoughts and emotions."

Kate nodded in confirmation to the words and observations that Jim had told her before they entered the home and as they walked up the driveway. As far as what the subject of this discussion was all about, Jim was correct; Kate had a good idea about that, too. She held his hand even tighter as she felt her James tighten his entire body up and his tenseness increase.

Around the dining room table sat Mr. Flaherty, Jim's mother, and then Father Callahan. The old priest sat next to Jim's mother, and Mr. Flaherty sat opposite the two of them.

Mrs. O'Malley looked up at Kate and Jim as they walked into the room and she forced a tepid smile. The smile was forced and her eyes told of layers of pain poorly concealed within them. Mrs. Lillian O'Malley was a beautiful woman, with long red hair that gently tumbled over her shoulders in waves, with wispy curls at the end of her hair that teased the air and danced in the wind. Her green eyes glowed and her perfect bone structure framed a gentle mouth and soft facial features. Now in her mid-fifties, her figure remained generous, but remarkably fit, and it was easy for her to turn the heads of men, both young and old. No doubt she was gorgeous and glowing. As of late, her glow faded . . . it was now a victim of grief and of circumstances and now, of the burden of revealing hidden secrets of a past from long ago, but a past that no one ever forgot.

James T. O'Malley dearly loved his mother, but she had been stern and strict concerning Jim's religious upbringing and she had unwaveringly committed Jim to a life embedded deeply in the Catholic faith. A life laced with a strict Catholic education and stringent and unbending adherence to the many traditions, rites and rituals that went along with the practice of the faith. Lillian O'Malley wore her Catholic faith upon her sleeve, in her heart and on everything that she did in her daily life. As of late, as religious freedom and the chance to choose his own paths crept into Jim's life, he felt her religious beliefs to be rather stifling. Obsessive. There was little doubt that Jim had been closer to his father than he was to his mother, yet there remained that special bond that a mother and her son share. A bond that was about to be tested to the maximum level.

"Hello, Jim. Hello, Kate. Please, come and sit around the table. I have made some tea. We would like to speak with you about an important matter," Lillian O'Malley spoke softly and then pulled out the chair next to her as Father Callahan pulled out the chair next to where he was sitting.

"Yes, please, come and relax," the old priest offered, as they all tested each other's eyes for the levels of emotions.

James Thomas O'Malley stood stoically, still holding Kate's hand tightly and his eyes went first to his mother's eyes and he studied the pain there. Then he studied the eyes of Father Callahan, and he sensed prayers emitting from his soul to Heaven that all of this will work out well. Finally, the eyes and face of a confident Bernard Flaherty forced a ripple of repulsive and powerful anger to flow through, James T. O'Malley. Mr. Flaherty sat there, with the chair pulled out a bit from the table, his legs crossed, a fine blue suit hanging on his frame and a pair of expensive shoes on his feet. Shoes, polished to high heaven and a little farther beyond. The man displayed confidence as well as an air of smugness. The ominous feeling that Jim was looking into a mirror at his own image when he looked at Mr. Flaherty caused Jim to prepare a great release of his heartfelt thoughts. James T. O'Malley, even at the young age of eighteen, never held back his thoughts, pulled punches or was a man to dance around a subject. He dove headlong into the fray. He was not afraid of anything, or anyone, or any situation. Especially, while enveloping within the immense love of a supportive woman, such as his amazing Kate Eva O'Leary, was.

Together, they could love as hard as anyone ever could imagine, but they could also kick some major ass.

Various tensions hung in the air as if they were angry storm clouds brewing on a dark horizon before a July thunderstorm erupts. Intense, explosive, full of power that is ready to unleash havoc.

"An important matter. Is that all that this boils down to for you? An important matter. Well, yes, I would say that is a classic case of minimization of a life-changing event. Let's get this over with, Mom. I know that this man is my biological father. Tell me how this happened and please, explain in great details why everyone felt it was fair to wait until I was a man to tell me the truth. Moreover, why did you had to wait until my father, who by the way, is the only father that I will ever have, is on ice in the morgue, in order for everyone to tell the truth and arrange a meeting with Mr. Hot Shit here?"

Lillian O'Malley gasped. Father Callahan grabbed her hand in support and Bernard Flaherty frowned, then uncrossed his legs and leaned in with a purpose over the table.

As a gentle tear rolled down the lovely and graceful cheek of Miss Kate Eva O'Leary, James looked over at Kate and he knew that his lover had also known ahead of time that Mr. Flaherty was his biological father. Kate gripped the hand of her lover even tighter than ever. She loved James Thomas O'Malley with all of her heart and all of her soul and she knew the pain of this moment might never leave him or that it would affect him in a manner that caused dread upon her heart. Fear gripped her as she wondered what the truth would do to her beloved James. Truth and despair were usually an insurmountable combination to most people. Yet James Thomas O'Malley was not an ordinary young man. No, no, God blessed him with a spirit that few, if any, persons ever receive in this life. You see, it is the love within your heart and the power of your soul that counts the most in this life. Despite the truth and despair creeping into his life, James still held his immense love for Kate, for his father, mother, and God within his heart.

Even from the deep pits of despair, Jim knew that love would eventually prevail.

"How did you know that, Bernard is your biological father, James?" Mrs. O'Malley asked.

"Really? Looking at him is as if I am looking in a mirror. I always tried hard to convince myself that I looked like you, or maybe my grandparents, because there was such little physical resemblance between Dad and me. But now, it is so easy to put the parts and pieces together. This spitting image of me shows up at Dad's funeral, tells me he is from the old neighborhood . . . all the pieces . . . begin to fit together. Hell's Kitchen, we left shortly after I was born, hints and clues that Dad would occasionally drop that we all needed to talk someday, and for you and Dad to tell me something important when the time was correct. Now, you call a meeting, you ask Kate to come along and our family priest is here. Really, Mom? I am not stupid."

James put his free hand through the jet-black curls of his hair and he attempted to comb away some stress while he shook his head. Kate still firmly held his other hand, and she was not letting it go either. The air in the room was thick with tension and everyone could feel the pain and anger within young James Thomas O'Malley building.

That was not a good thing.

"Please, sit down, James. Sit down here, Kate. I realize this is painful and shocking, and the last week has been horrible, but we need to discuss the circumstances. Please," Father Callahan said while they once again tried to ease the tension and have Kate and James sit at the table. Jim's eyes glowed with anger and he felt his fists clench, but Kate gently touched his chest with her hand and she nodded her head to agree that they should sit.

"Come and sit, James. Father Callahan is correct. Let's sit," Kate softly told James, while she led him by his hand to the table and chairs. Father Callahan moved over to sit next to Mrs. O'Malley to allow them to sit together.

Jim nodded his head in acceptance of the suggestion, and while still holding hands, they sat next to each other. The old priest knew James since he was a small child and he had a keen sense that if any person could keep James under some type of control that it was Kate. The two of them were inseparable, and it was easy to tell how deeply in love they were. Still, the young O'Malley's patience ran thin and lean. Once they sat, his dark eyes focused hard on his mother.

"Okay, we are sitting. Tell us now. Tell us quickly. The

short version. No bullshit."

Mr. Flaherty had remained a quiet observer and when he heard the impatient words of Jim, he spoke, "You know, James, this is not easy for any of us and you should have more respect. . .."

Jim raised his hand; Kate blinked and held her breath while she held Jim's other hand tightly. Attempts to absorb his anger were futile. James had now transformed into a man full of pain and explosive anger.

"It is only due to respect that I have not yet, knocked your fancy ass all the way to Hell's Kitchen and sent you packing with my foot stuck in your ass and my fist buried inside of your mouth. My best advice is for you to sit there, shut your mouth and not say a word. Especially, do not tell me what to do in my own house. My father's house. My mother's house."

When he was finished speaking, James turned and pointed to his mother and waved his hand in the air. Mrs. O'Malley knew that her son was losing control and without hesitation, she took a deep breath and finally told the secret that harbored within them for so long.

"Bernard was one of your father's best boyhood friends. Poor Irish kids growing up lean and mean in the old neighborhood. We all attended parochial school and church together. We all were friends, forever. Inseparable. Your father wanted to be a police officer since he was in high school and Bernard . . . well, he was very active in our parish and he chose the . . . priesthood."

Mrs. O'Malley seemed as if speaking the last word would cause her to fall over, but somehow, she managed to allow it to leave her lips. Kate gasped and James could not help but smile, and he shook his head. Father Callahan reached over and held Lillian O'Malley's hand again, and Mr. Bernard Flaherty shifted uneasily in his chair at the memory.

"This just keeps getting better and better, Mom. I guess

my biological father here made one helluva priest and a fine representative of the Catholic clergy . . . impregnating a young woman in the neighborhood," James spoke with a sneer in his voice and then he turned and faced Bernard. "So, what did you do? Leave the Catholic Church and become a Lutheran?"

Bernard's eyes studied his son's eyes, and he leaned in intently. It was now readily apparent where the fearless gene came from that James held deep within his soul. James received the gene from birth, life, and his other father refined it into a tool.

Bernard's eyes told the fact that he was not a man to mess with as Bernard answered the question, "I was only a student in seminary. I never reached ordination. I left the religious world and ventured into a business education."

Mrs. O'Malley continued, "We were all so young, and the world was upside down. The Vietnam War raged on. Your father was overseas and I seldom heard from him. I was lonely. So terribly lonely. Your father and I married right before he shipped out to fight in the war. It was his wish. Just in case that he did not return. We were as Kate and you are, young and in love from our first sight of each other. Childhood sweethearts. So many of the poor men of the neighborhood were leaving in the draft. So many were dying and returning in caskets."

James interrupted his mother, pointed his finger at Mr. Flaherty and spoke, "So many left their homes and did not return. College kids . . . avoided the draft. Yet, you were just another poor Irish kid from the old neighborhood. Huh? Where did you obtain money for all this education?"

"My father, your grandfather, became successful in his business when I was in high school."

"What kind of business?"

Mr. Flaherty leaned back over the table; the expensive gold watch on his wrist caught the dining room light. Bernard stared into his son's eyes.

"Business."

James smiled, and his mind raced with thoughts. His father always told him that organized crime always referred to their operations as a business. His mind filled with thoughts, 'expensive suits, expensive shoes, fine cars and gold watches around his wrist. Poor Irish kid from the old neighborhood, my ass.' He filed the words of his biological father away for future use. All eyes turned back to Mrs. O'Malley for the remainder of the story.

"All the old friends of the neighborhood remained close. We often spent weekend nights together or gathered after mass and shared dinner and drinks. One night, Bernard and I drank too much wine, and we made a grievous error. A sin of which I have confessed so many times that I have lost track of the number and in repentance, I still fall upon my knees and I pray for forgiveness every night. Young, lonely, stupid, and full of lustful sin and too much drink. A poor excuse for unfaithfulness, but it is the truth." Mrs. O'Malley began to cry, and it seemed as if the full story would not leave her lips.

Everyone sat in silence.

The tears ran down Kate's cheeks, she dabbed at her eyes with her handkerchief, and James checked on his lover to make sure she was all right.

Father Callahan comforted her and after much struggle, Lillian O'Malley fought back the tears and managed to finish the story.

"Your father was such a wonderful, caring soul. Even though he did not always attend mass, his soul was full of faith. Heaven welcomed James Reilly O'Malley as a Guardian of Heaven. I am quite sure he joined Saint Michael's Army and fights for the glory of Heaven right now."

Another pause and another deep breath.

"Somehow, I had the courage to write my beloved husband, tell him the wretched story and the news. I cannot even imagine the pain that I caused him . . . there he was, over in Vietnam, fighting a war, risking his life, and receiving a letter such as that. I will never forgive myself for writing that letter, but there was no other way to tell him the news. In the letter, I told the truth. Because of our faith, I begged to keep the baby and pleaded with him for forgiveness and acceptance. He wrote back a glorious letter. I still have it, James. If you want to read it, please you can. He wanted the baby and wanted to be a father, but he told me that we would never have any other children. He only wanted this baby and never fully explained to me why that was. His wish, but regardless, he made that very clear."

Jim's mind paused and captured that thought. His father had taught him so many things. From hockey, to life, to being a man, but one thought stood out right now. Jim recalled a frozen pond, a tricky and unpredictable hockey puck and his father's words, "Never trust a hockey puck. In many ways, it is as a woman is . . . at times . . . difficult to determine their direction and hard to trust." In his heart, Jim smiled, because even with his father gone from this world, he knew that he still spoke to him.

"Your father agreed with me that we would never entertain any thoughts of adoption or disgusting abortions or such. He wrote in the letter that he would love the baby as if it was his own blood and I believe that despite the despair that I caused for him that he loved you and me with all of his heart and soul. When your father returned from the war, I was almost full term in carrying you. He spoke with Bernard and they made peace. Your father was a forgiving man."

James shook his head at the thought, and everyone at the table could hear Jim mumble, "That is an understatement. Some best friend. But my father was righteous, just, and honest and he practiced that in his life."

The sordid tale continued through sobs and a halting

voice, "We prayed and we cried. All three of us agreed that we would stay silent until you were old enough to understand. Now, I know that was foolish, and you matured so quickly that we should have approached you sooner, but it is done. We were close to telling you right before he died. We had just discussed it a few days earlier. When your father was murdered and Bernard contacted me to ask to attend the funeral and pay his respects, I felt as if it was time. Father Callahan agreed, and so did Bernard. And here we are. A horrible moment in time."

Mrs. O'Malley paused, and she wiped her eyes once again and continued with her words. The words were almost a whisper now and choked with raw emotions.

"Truth and despair. However, James, it is the truth and we all deeply love you. All of us. Loved, in Heaven and on Earth. I dedicated my life to our family, to the church and to repenting for my sin."

James nodded his head and, in his mind, the statement explained his mother's constant adherence to the Catholic faith and in his heart, he felt that his mother was successful and sincere in her mission. Now, if he could only find some way to quell the anger in his soul.

Mrs. O'Malley recovered some of the power in her voice and the story continued.

"Your father became a civilian police officer, and he dedicated his first few years on the police force working in an organized crime task force. He was a brilliant officer and so smart. His years during the war, as a military police officer, gave him a sixth sense for sniffing out street crime and after his involvement in some high-profile cases, and the memories associated with the old neighborhood, he decided to take a position on the Mohawk City Police Force. He and William Lawson knew each other from their military days, and Bill convinced your father to come here. It was the right thing to do. We left that life behind . . . until now. We had many good years. Much happiness and I shall grieve all of this forever."

Mrs. O'Malley looked over to her son and with pleading and teary eyes asked, "Will . . . you forgive me, James? Can you find some way to understand and to forgive?"

Kate remained silent, her grip remained tight upon the hand of James and her every breath donated strength to him.

Bernard cleared his throat and spoke in a low voice, "I am very sorry for all of this, James. Your father forgave me too. For obvious reasons, we were never close again, we seldom, if ever, actually spoke again . . . but I still felt as if I needed to be here and pay my respects. We had been very close as youngsters."

All eyes studied the dark piercing eyes of James Thomas O'Malley and Jim sat there, thinking. The intenseness on his face and the pain in his eyes told a story. Suddenly, without a word, he slowly rose and as he did so, he pulled at Kate and gently helped her to her feet. He leaned over and kissed her cheek, and James Thomas O'Malley inhaled her scent. A glorious, sweet scent of a mixture of some mysterious scent that Jim could only describe as a mixture of roses and of love.

"Kate and I will be leaving in the next few days. I will take that supervisor job that my current manager offered in the Albany store. Kate here . . . can also find a job there. My manager's best friend manages that market. We will find an apartment and I will find a hockey team. Albany is a great hockey city and I will find many teams that need a good center iceman. I will work hard. I will play hard and I will be the best damn hockey player ever to come out of Mohawk City. Certainly, out of New York State. Maybe, America. I will play every shift to win every game and if I lose, I will respect those who defeated me, but I will come back with a vengeance to win the next time. I never, ever give up. I play the game to win, I fight for respect, and I fight to be a winner. I always will until the end of all time."

Jim licked his lips and his eyes wandered across all the persons before him. His eyes were dark and full of power and emotion.

Jim said, "If the good detective stalls in finding the gruesome person responsible for my father's murder, then I will find who is responsible. I will win the game." His eyes grew even darker, his fists clenched, and then in a moment of relaxation, Jim almost smiled before he spoke again, "From out of this darkness, glorious and remarkable love will appear. Once I have settled in a career, be it in hockey or be it in the world, I will ask Kate Eva O'Leary to marry me. It will be my honor if this glorious woman agrees to be my wife."

Mrs. O'Malley sobbed as she heard his words and once more, Jim's mother looked at her son and asked, "What about forgiveness, James? I know how deeply this has hurt you and I cannot say sorry enough times to you and to Kate. I know how deeply you two are in love and always have been."

Jim studied his mother and then answered, "I dearly love you, Mom. I have bled before and I will bleed again. I am not afraid to bleed. Honestly, I have to search my soul for forgiveness and for respect for you." He turned to Bernard Flaherty and said, "I have no words or forgiveness for you. I feel nothing towards you. Nothing. The only father that I will ever know is lying frozen on a morgue slab. He stood for honor. You stand for nothing but bullshit and all that is wrong in this world. If it were true love that drew you to my mother and you both loved each other with all your hearts and souls, then I would forgive you and understand. True love knows little boundaries and I would not have been the product of conception in lust, but rather of love. That is not the case here. I am simply a product of your lust for a beautiful young woman. You are a scoundrel of betrayal. My father found the power to forgive you, but sadly, I cannot. If we ever meet again, it will be only for a specific reason or purpose. You should leave here and never return to our lives."

Bernard said nothing, but he first studied Lillian's face and then nodded as he pushed back the chair from the table and stood up.

Father Callahan wobbled to his feet, and he steadied his legs and walked over to Jim and Kate.

The old priest placed his hand on Jim's shoulder and said, "Bernard and your mother both repented and confessed their sins. Your mother confessed her sins in front of God, her husband, and now in front of you, James. Your father forgave everyone and God forgives her, too. Jesus preached forgiveness. We should all pray together and ask God to intervene. Can you not search your soul now and forgive? Can we pray?"

James wrapped his arm tightly around Kate and pulled her close to his body.

He looked at Father Callahan and said, "Not right now, no. I am sorry."

Father Callahan nodded and said, "You are very smart and powerful, but so stubborn and headstrong, James. I admire that, and you need to chart your own course and make peace in your soul. I will pray that God helps you find it. However, you should not live your lives in sin. You should marry Kate, now."

Jim almost laughed, and he shook his head and told the old priest, "God blesses true love. No way will you convince me to believe anything differently. Kate and James are true love. Always and forever. With all due respect, Father Callahan, your world of confession, rules, rituals, incense waving, prayers, and homilies of forgiveness, lies somewhere between bullshit and horseshit on my list right now. I have to think that it is all so complicated that even God cannot follow all of it. Man makes a mess out of everything. I love God and Jesus and all the Prophets and Saints in Heaven with all my heart and soul and I believe in the Bible and the words therein. I always will. God will judge my soul's worthiness, not a man wearing a white cloth around his neck."

Father Callahan did not comment. He only reminded James, "Once more, your father forgave and God forgives. Jesus taught forgiveness. It is a core message of The Gospel."

Jim paused and then spoke with clenched fists and pain on his face, "I know The Gospel and have read every word of each of them a thousand times over. Yet, I also know the words of Exodus Chapter twenty-one, verse twenty-four. Peter knew that verse and too, understood the message therein. Peter cut the ear off the Roman Soldier, to defend what Peter believed in and what he felt that he needed to defend. I will not hesitate to do the same. What you need to understand, Father Callahan, is that I am not my father or anyone else in this world or in Heaven. I am James Thomas O'Malley."

With those words, James and Kate turned and walked away.

While they walked away, Kate Eva O'Leary gently whispered, "I love you, James. Know that I love you, now, and forever."

James nodded and answered, "Me too, Kate. You are everything to me. All that I have now is God, ice hockey and my Kate."

In her heart, Kate hoped and prayed that her beloved lover's rising and growing anger would not destroy him or their love.

A few days later, after returning to clean out his belongings and pack his hockey gear, James Thomas O'Malley left, and he never returned to the family home.

Chapter Seven

Ice, Blood, and Love

"O'Malley, huh? Number eleven. A center iceman. We always need good, solid, puck handlers and center icemen. Hard to find these days and when you do, they are usually pussies who will not dig for pucks in the corners or come back to play defense and kick some ass in the slot. We do have a roster opening, due to an injury, but I was really looking for a defenseman. Anyway, Danny Hess is a good pal of mine and he is a damn good hockey coach too. Many years ago, we played together. He was one helluva center iceman and Danny says that you are one too."

James T. O'Malley stood on the sideline of a hockey rink in Albany, New York and after a study of his prospective coach's face, Jim spoke, "He is a good man and he is a good coach. I have seen him shoot in practice and handle the puck. He still can play center ice. Great shooter. Believe me when I say it . . . that he could still play."

While Coach Joseph Kelleher nodded and studied the paperwork that Jim had filled out and gave to him, Jim studied the coach, his posture and his face. Coach Kelleher looked as if he had played quite a few games in his day. There was a prominent scar above his right eye; his eyelash did not grow in that spot in order to cover the scar. There were folded lines in his skin under both of his eyes from some poorly sewn stitches of long ago and a large scar on the bottom lip of his mouth that extended from his lip to the right side of his chin.

'Goaltender,' Jim thought. 'He had to have played goalie. Those scars are from hockey puck blows to a mask. A mask that saves you from death but leaves hefty scars.'

While flipping through the papers, now mounted on a clipboard, and studying their content, the coach said, "Yup, Hess was great. I know about his shot. Many times, he nearly tore my mask off with a few shots in practice." The coach vaguely pointed in the direction of his face and explained, "One of these scars is cuz, of his shot. I was a goalie."

"I knew that."

The old coach looked at Jim with a rather surprised look on his face and before he could even question Jim about his statement, Jim said, "The scars." Jim pointed at his face and smiled, "they gave your position away. Mask saved your ass."

Coach Kelleher smiled and placed the clipboard with the papers on a nearby bench.

"You know your hockey. I can see, even though you are young, that you have a few scars too. The one under your right eye looks a little nasty. Coach Hess says you can fill a net with hockey pucks as drunken sailors fill beer mugs when they hit port. He says ya have a mean shot and skate a mean edge too. He also mentioned to me that you can kick some major ass. Are you a fighter or a hockey player, O'Malley? You are calm and straight, but ya got a mean-ass lick to your eyes. You are a little on the smallish side, but Coach Hess says ya pack a professional punch."

"I am a hockey player, Coach Kelleher, but I play to win. If that means I have to fight, then so be it. I will fight anyone, anywhere. In the parking lot or on the ice. If you bring it, I will end it. I play hard, I play mean, and I do not pull any punches or give anyone breaks. I play to win the game. All of the games, hockey and life. The game of hockey is hard and tough and that is how I play it."

The coach smiled and kicked at the rubber mat under his

right skate. It was easy to tell that he liked this young man's spunk. As painful as the next part of the conversation was going to be, Coach Kelleher knew that he had to bring it up.

Coach Kelleher reached out his hand and when he did so, it was with compassion as the words came out slowly, "Sorry . . . 'bout your father. It was all over the news here, and Coach Hess filled me in on some details. The local news here says the police are still tracking the bastard. I hope they nail 'em quick and nail 'em hard."

O'Malley reached out his hand and shook the coach's hand.

Without the slightest wavering of his voice, Jim said, "Thank you. There is a very good Mohawk City police detective on the case. A friend of my father and I know that he is working very hard on the case. I have to warn this world, just as I warned Detective Odell . . . the police need to find the person responsible for my father's murder because if they do not, then I will."

Coach Kelleher carefully studied the young man's face, and he had little doubt that James T. O'Malley was serious about his claim.

No doubt whatsoever.

"In the meantime, Coach Kelleher, please, how about a tryout for a position at center ice for this hockey club? I brought my equipment and I can proudly tell you that it will be worth giving me a try."

"You are very well spoken, O'Malley. Impressive for a hockey player. Let's give ya ass a whirl and see what the hype is all about with ya. Locker room is that way," Coach Kelleher said with a nod of his head and a thumb in the air of the direction of the locker room.

"I need to make a point, O'Malley. I feel terrible 'bout what happened to your father, but this tryout ain't in sympathy. Nothin' personal, but ya gotta make the hockey club. I was being honest when I said that I am short-handed but that I was lookin' for a defenseman and not a center iceman."

James T. O'Malley nodded his head, picked up his hockey stick and his equipment bag and said, "It is with the most honesty of statements that I say that the last thing that I require is sympathy, Coach Kelleher. And the last thing you need is to be a softie when you want to win hockey games. I will make this hockey club. I will be out on the ice in ten minutes. Tell your goalie to tighten his mask straps and adjust his cup. Tell all my future teammates to keep their heads up and on a swivel because James T. O'Malley is coming and I do not pull any punches or give anyone breaks. The game of hockey is hard and tough and that is how I play it."

With another smile and as he began to walk toward the locker room, Jim added, "Nothing personal."

Coach Kelleher could not suppress a laugh as the coach walked toward the open door to the ice rink.

Just before he hit the ice he yelled out to O'Malley, "Hey, O'Malley! Do play you mean kick-ass hockey because of how you feel about your father or because you love the sport and want to win every hockey game?"

Jim never broke his stride but yelled back, "Yes!"

A half an hour or so later, Coach Kelleher stood next to his fallen goalie as the goalie tried hard to recover from the force of a wrist shot that had plowed into his chest protector, directly in the soft spot where the leather meets the collarbone at the base of his neck. A wrist shot taken by a certain James T. O'Malley.

"Ya gonna be okay, there, Gordon?" The coach asked while he leaned in as the goalie tore his mask off, winced in pain, rubbed hard at the sore spot, then sat on his backside on the ice within the crease, and moved his arm around in circles. "We need you for tomorrow night's game. You know how hard Barclay Millhouse can shoot. Honestly, this shot here that nailed ya ass was the only one that ya stopped from O'Malley. The rest blew up the twine behind ya."

Gordon looked up and nodded, then pushed his stick and his goalie gloves aside as he held his hand out to ask for assistance in climbing back on his skates.

James T. O'Malley was the first player to offer assistance and as he pulled the goalie to his skates, Jim apologized, "I am sorry for the unfortunate wrist shot. Nothing personal."

"It is okay, just wanna say to Coach Kelleher here . . . make sure ya sign this guy before the day is up. Sumthin' tells me that jackass, Millhouse just met his match!"

A few minutes later, Coach Kelleher and his assistant coach watched O'Malley win a face-off at the side of the goalie, push the puck to his right-winger, barrel over the top of a defenseman twice his size and then execute a perfect give and go where O'Malley tucked the puck cleanly behind Gordon.

After watching Gordon sweep the puck angrily out of the back of the net, Coach Kelleher leaned over to his assistant and said, "This kid is one helluva hockey player. He single-handedly dismantled our entire team within one hour." The assistant coach nodded and looked to his boss for further instructions. With a wide smile, Coach Kelleher added, "Go and find Timmy and make sure those papers are ready to be signed. I can't wait to see O'Malley take on Millhouse tomorrow."

In the locker room after the practice, Coach Kelleher grinned widely and happily watched as James T. O'Malley scrawled his signature on the dotted line of a contract.

Coach Kelleher, between smiles, added, "Yes indeed, ya can read it there, O'Malley. All in cold, stark black and white. We pay ya ass fifteen lousy bucks per game and pay for emergency room visits. I see you have medical insurance with your full-time job, so follow-up medical care is on you. What ain't written there is that if ya score a hat trick, then I buy ya a case of beer outa my own wallet.

Score four and we share Irish whiskey together because your name is O'Malley, and my name is, Kelleher. Welcome to the Albany Wolverines, number eleven, James T. O'Malley. Welcome to the wild world of semi-professional ice hockey. Welcome to war on ice, too much drinkin' of beer and booze for athletes to do, dingy ice rinks, drunken and wild crowds that hate ya guts and low pay and lots of stitches. Sounds like a blast, huh?"

James T. O'Malley smiled and handed the signed paperwork back to Timmy, extended his hand to the coach, and the two men shook hands. "Even after that rather interesting description of what I am in for, I still want to say, thank you, Coach Kelleher, for the opportunity. I hope that I can drain that wallet of yours and enjoy a few beers on you."

"Me too. Can I sit here?" Coach Kelleher pointed to the bench next to where O'Malley sat dressing into his civilian clothes.

Jim nodded and pointed at the bench while he resumed dressing into his civilian clothes.

While sitting, Coach Kelleher explained, "Now, let me tell you 'bout this player. His name is Barclay Millhouse, and he is the meanest son-of-a-bitch on this side of Hell. A refugee from the Iron League and somehow, his sorry ass ends up here on the other side of Route 787 and over the river in Troy. I gotta warn ya, Jim, this guy is no joke."

Jim's dark eyes darkened even more than usual. He stared long and hard at the coach and his lips curled at the edges.

In a low growl, O'Malley said, "Neither am I."

Detective Lyle Odell was working late in his office in the dark and dingy building, which housed the Mohawk City Police Department. He always worked late. No reason to go home early. He would only watch television alone and suck down glasses of whiskey. At least, he knew that if he was working late and hung around his office . . . then he would not drink so much tonight. The heat struggled to keep up with the cold of the evening; this building had seen better days. Budget cuts and a struggling economy meant that heat and any other luxuries were optional around these parts. For what seemed to be the millionth time, he read the reports neatly bound within a plastic binder. Pages and pages of reports. Autopsy reports, bullet angle, proposed position of the shooter, footprints in the snow, size and type of the boots, type of bullet and the type of gun that fired the kill shot, the distance from where the shooter stood until it struck Sergeant O'Malley. The missing number eleven police badge from the jacket of Sergeant O'Malley remained a concern and a clue. It appeared as if the badge tore off the jacket when his body fell against the police cruiser, but it was nowhere around. The small tear in the jacket told the examiners that it was pinned there on his jacket, but now that question lingered.

Find the badge, maybe find the killer? The badge was a little strange, and it was puzzling. Did the killer take the badge as a trophy? Sick bastard.

Despite the missing police badge, Detective Odell now had a ton of information on this crime and now it was just a little of a waiting game. The New York State Police Crime Lab had been of immense assistance. When some evil menace guns down a fellow officer in cold blood, help from law enforcement agencies is abundant. The state team used a special dye technique and extracted molds from the footprints in the snow and that proved to be a huge piece of evidence. At least the bitter cold wave that simply will not break was good for preserving prints in the snow, prints made in a narrow, dark alley where the sun never shines.

In more ways than one.

Despite the amount of evidence gathered over the recent days, Odell released teaser press releases and information to the local media outlets, still working the vague detail angle to see what, or if anything else came out of the masses out there.

They even had the bullet after the doctors extracted it from what was left of Sergeant O'Malley's head and brain. Odell made a mental note never to allow O'Malley's son ever to read this autopsy report. Something told the detective that kid was Hellfire on ice skates, and Hellfire, and Brimstone off of ice skates. The young man would dismantle all of New York in order to find the killer. That young man was the real deal.

Now, thanks to an alert truck driver named, Harold Garner, the good detective had a good feeling that they had added a major piece of evidence with an expensive pair of military boots extracted from a rubbish dumpster a few blocks away from the murder scene. Boots that perfectly fit the molds made by the state boys. Boots that were now in Albany in the crime lab and the experts were analyzing them for evidence by the scientific team. These crime labs are very important in law enforcement these days; Detective Odell knew that he wanted an ironclad bank of evidence; because he was not sure whose side of the law these prosecutors, district attorneys, and judges were on these days. Odell stared at the telephone on his desk, wishing it to ring, but knowing better. The boots most likely just made it to the New York State Police Crime Lab in Albany, New York, earlier this afternoon. Too soon for any news on what the lab crew could find. He also nailed a bit o' luck' of the Irish, with a description of what he felt was the killer . . . thanks to the keen-eyed Mrs. Washburn and a dog named Rollo. Rollo the dog appeared to be a better judge of character than most people are. Not too much to go on, but the missing fingers on his left hand remained a very good start. Expert shot, military boots, a pea coat, missing fingers; something told the good detective that he was looking for a military man. The boots were too large for a woman. A military man who lost fingers in a military accident. If the crime lab crew found anything at all, then he was convinced that he could run background checks for recently discharged military persons, with missing fingers as injuries and make some solid headway. The good detective also asked for copies of the daily arrests, traffic tickets, parking violations, and complaint files for the daily flow of crime in Mohawk City.

The desk sergeant looked at the detective with a puzzled look at his request and Detective Odell explained, "Criminals in a hurry to flee from a major crime . . . often commit other crimes or violations in their haste to flee. They become nervous. They become careless within their own deviousness. They run red lights and stop signs and . . . I find them."

Detective Lyle Odell was rumpled, hard-drinking, but solidly functioning. He was dismantled in his appearance and, because of his appearance, his fellow law enforcement officers often doubted his abilities. Yet Odell was the classic case of not judging a book by its cover because the good detective was very good at his job.

Very, very good.

The lingering question remained as to why this cold-blooded murder of a respected and honest police officer occurred. The brutality of the crime was shocking. Sergeant O'Malley locked up his share of bad guys here in Mohawk City. He was a great cop, very honest and solid at his job, but nothing unusual stood out in his arrest history. Every officer on the Mohawk City police force locked up many bad guys. There was an abundance of them here. He owed no one any money. He paid his modest house off years ago; it was free and in the clear, no liens or weird-ass loans. He drove an old car. O'Malley kept to his family and his career. No women on the side and most of his notorious arrests were still in the clinker. His wife was a faithful, churchgoing woman and his son, a rough and tough kid, but a respected local ice hockey player with a great future in the sport, and a gorgeous, loyal girlfriend who also came from a solid family. Detective Lyle Odell picked up the file containing human resource files and the entire background on Sergeant James Reilly O'Malley. No doubt that the answer was in his past. This was revenge for something in his past. Sergeant Lawson was his old military buddy, and he told Lyle that O'Malley was instrumental in some high-profile arrests while serving in an organized crime task force in the big city downstate. The city. Hell's Kitchen. Irish organized crime and local gang warfare. After some kind of bullshit, either in his personal life or his career, or both, he joined the Mohawk Police Department and left his past behind.

Or so it seemed.

Odell knew that first thing in the morning, he needed to contact the old precinct that Sergeant O'Malley worked out of in Hell's Kitchen and tap some old-timer for information. Someone must still be working that knew of the inside scoop. He also needed to meet once again with Mrs. O'Malley, the old priest, Father Callahan, and go share a few beers with Lawson. Somewhere there are other clues. He tilted his head and focused his bloodshot eyes for a look at the clock. Nine-thirty on the ticker . . . plenty of time for one more glance at this file. There was no one else working this late in the office, just the front desk boys and the crew in the lock-up tank, so no one would complain if he lit up a smoke. Odell tapped out a cigarette from his pack, struck a match on the desk, and took a long drag. The smoke circled the room and hung like a blanket of fog for a few seconds before disappearing from the lack of humidity.

Young James T. O'Malley's words about his father's murder stuck hard and fast in his mind, "I know this has something to do with my father's past. A ghost returned to haunt him."

"Damn, I must'b missing something that has to be here, right in front of me," Detective Lyle Odell mumbled at nothing but the sounds of the blowing of steam off the radiator steam traps in the office and the ticks of the clock on the wall.

The Troy, New York River Rats hockey club, had a short trek across the Hudson River, a roll down a piece of Route 787 and a few right turns and they were in enemy territory. The Albany Wolverines played a portion of their home games in an arena and ice rink in downtown Albany. The downtown ice rink was a polished and professional arena, on the par with the big-league arenas. The Wolverines played the majority of their home games in a smaller and less flamboyant arena and rink in nearby Colonie, New York. The Wolverines shared the downtown rink with a few hockey clubs, including the local Eastern Hockey League affiliate team for the big league, Boston Bears, but when the River Rats came into town, the team management always managed to book the game in the big-league rink. This was an intense rivalry and even though it was a low level of semi-professional hockey, the level of play was of a good enough quality to quench the thirst of a hockey-crazy group of avid fans. It was a Saturday night; the tickets were inexpensive when compared to the big-league team; the beer was cheap too, and the nights were too cold for anything but settling into a seat and watching a good hockey game. The arena would sell out hours before the 6 P.M. puck drop with the overflow of tickets going to the enemy fans from the other side of the river.

In addition, Barclay Millhouse was coming to town. This game was good for a few on-the-ice brawls as well as a few in the stands too.

Barclay Millhouse stood six feet and five inches tall, and he weighed a few pounds over two-hundred and thirty pounds. On skates, and packed in his hockey equipment, he stood even taller and his sour demeanor, honed from years of bouncing around some of the toughest hockey leagues in North America, loomed above him and all around him as if it was a dark cloud of doom from a very dark place. He was a monstrous man. Millhouse played right defense, and given the chance, most offensive players chose to attack the River Rats on the left defense. Millhouse was originally from Ontario Province in Canada but long-ago relocated to the beauty of upstate New York. His reputation as an enforcer was legendary. Aside from his enforcing skills, Millhouse was actually a solid hockey player with a wicked slap shot from the point and some good stand-up defensive skills. Now, he was close to forty years of age; he had a cup of coffee in the big league many years ago with the hockey team in Minnesota, but never hung around very long in the big time. Rumor was that his hard-drinking habits and poor attitude always caught up with him and his wife tired of his life on the road and told him to come home to upstate New York. No one knew what he did for a full-time living . . . maybe nothing, and he let his wife be the primary breadwinner. No one was close enough to him to ask, and no one was stupid enough to push the subject. Now, he mired around in this semi-professional league in eastern New York, earning a few bucks, becoming a hero to the local fans for his roughhouse play and terrorizing goalies in this league with his slap shot.

In the Wolverine's locker room, James T. O'Malley dressed for his first professional game. He dressed slower than he usually did. Perhaps it was to relish the feeling and preserve the memory. Before pulling the number eleven hockey sweater up and over his head and over the top of his layers of equipment, he fingered the number and the name on the back of the jersey. If he was not feeling sorrow over the fact that his father, and for that matter, his mother too, was not here to see him play in this game, then he would be fooling himself. Thoughts raced through his mind, the pain lingered and then O'Malley moved on, pulled the jersey over his head, and worked the folds out from in and around his shoulder pads.

A beautiful young woman named Kate Eva O'Leary was in the stands and right now, that young woman was more important to O'Malley than anything else in the world was.

Hitting the ice with his new teammates was a thrill that O'Malley never experienced before in his young life. While gliding around the ice and looking up into the stands and then to the American and Canadian flags hanging from the rafters, it was difficult not to lose his focus. Yet, O'Malley had a mission, and he was not going to allow stars in his eyes to derail that mission. As they warmed up Gordon in the net, Jim just kept reminding himself that this was no different from playing on the frozen Summer's Pond or the rink back home in Mohawk City.

Jim's teammates were all friendly and gave him a warm welcome to the hockey club and although James T. O'Malley was a solitary young man, he did appreciate their genuine warmth and positive attitude toward his arrival. Even the starting center iceman for the Wolverines warmly welcomed Jim on the squad, even if, in the back of his mind, he knew this young man might take his position on the first line within a few games. All they wanted to do was to win hockey games and tonight the River Rats and their notorious leader were in their way.

"O'Malley, sit ya ass right here in the rotation on the bench, next to Davis and Johnston. I need to put my eyes on your line at all times. Be ready for a pat on the back for a line change. I want to see how they play, Millhouse. If he is out there, I want your line to match up with his shifts. Bring the puck to him, O'Malley, and I know that I don't have to say this . . . but . . . I will. Don't back off from him, keep the pressure on and wear his old ass down," Coach Kelleher barked orders to Jim and his line mates and as soon as the puck dropped, O'Malley felt his world change. Even though he knew the love of his life was in the stands and watching him, he even shut Kate out of his thoughts. His pregame wave to her from the ice and her blowing kisses to Jim remained a faint memory now. All James T. O'Malley cared about now winning this hockey game, bringing honor to his father, to his own soul, to his reason for being here. His dark eyes intently focused on the puck, and then he followed the movements of Barclay Millhouse. Jim felt that now familiar and slightly uncontrollable anger in his chest rise as Millhouse crushed a Wolverine right-winger into the boards when the player tried to move the puck along the boards after a routine dump in of the puck. The coach of the River Rats had pulled a strategic maneuver and started Millhouse on the first line rather than his usual second line shift. Since the Wolverines were the home team, Coach Kelleher could not switch lines and send O'Malley and his line out on the ice until after the puck drop.

Jim's new right-winger, Teddy Davis, leaned in and said, "Millhouse is a friggin' beast. Do you see what we meant when we told you that he crushes the boards? He does not pinch the wingers into the boards. He crushes them."

Jim did not reply with words. His eyes burned with fury, and Jim only nodded his head in acknowledgment.

The Wolverine right-winger struggled to his skates after the crushing hit and gallantly tried to make his way to the bench for a line change. Millhouse glided the recaptured puck up through the neutral zone. Coach Kelleher signaled for a change on the fly and he tapped O'Malley on the back and yelled, "Out two!"

The starting center iceman was first to make the bench

and O'Malley jumped the boards and hit the ice hard. His skates cut sharp and deep and the ice flew in small chunks behind his blades as O'Malley turned up speed and flew into the Wolverine defensive zone. His head was up, his stick was out, and his soul burned with an intensity that he never felt before. While he watched Millhouse shoot a ferocious slap shot from the right point that Gordon initially struggled with tracking, but at the last second, deftly turned aside with his goalie stick and pushed the puck into the boards, O'Malley was back checking furiously. It was a poor rebound to allow, but luckily, a Wolverine defenseman captured the puck off of Gordon's errant rebound and when O'Malley hit the high slot, the defenseman hit O'Malley with a sharp pass. Jim neatly caught the pass on his backhand, flipped the puck to his forehand, turned his skates hard and headed into attack mode. O'Malley's speed on the back checking, the outstanding stick save by Gordon and the quick capture of the rebound puck by the Wolverine defenseman, had caused the River Rats to stall a line change and now, the first line, including Millhouse were stuck out there for an extra-long shift. The River Rats were all sucking air now and Teddy Davis joined O'Malley on his right wing and a fresh-legged Royal Johnston on his left wing. As O'Malley's skates cut a deep edge in the ice, he pumped and wove through the neutral zone, and his line mates stacked up on the attacking blue line, James Reilly O'Malley's words to his son from so long ago, echoed in Jim's head, "Stand up, James, only bend at the waist a little. Stick out straight in front of you! Work the puck smoothly back and forth on the blade, eyes up!"

With his eyes up and locked on the defensive formation, Jim cut hard and fast across the blue line, neatly avoided the poke check of the River Rat's center iceman, and then Jim skated straight at the leg-weary Barclay Millhouse.

Coach Kelleher had barked out the plan and James T.

O'Malley was going to carry it out, "Bring the puck to him, O'Malley. Don't back off from him, keep the pressure on and wear his old ass down."

James T. O'Malley arrived and just before O'Malley collided with the huge defenseman, he neatly passed the puck over to Davis, who had set up in the low slot in front of the River Rat's goalie. The force of the collision was brutal as O'Malley hit the big defenseman and Millhouse did not give up much, if any ice, but O'Malley did! Jim hit the ice hard, his stick crashed on the ice, and the force of the hit pushed all the air out of O'Malley's lungs. It was if Jim had hit a brick wall at twenty miles per hour! Davis seemed surprised at the tactic of O'Malley to bait the huge defenseman into leaving his position on the side of the net, but he neatly captured the clever pass and held the puck on his forehand for a second or two. Without any wingers back checking for the River Rats, and only one defenseman and the goalie left to defend the net, Davis was free to fake a one timer and turn the fake shot into a nifty pass over to Johnston, who had an open net to bury the puck into for the first goal of the game. The red light came on and the home crowd team went crazy! In the stands, a beautiful young woman, who had hidden her eyes with her hands when Jim violently collided with Millhouse, now resisted the urge to jump to her feet and cheer the goal scored by the home team.

Instead, Kate O'Leary mumbled, "Oh, dear Lord. Is this what my life will always be? Always worrying about if James will get up or stay down?"

Yet, in her heart, she knew that her beloved James always got back up. Always. She was madly in love with a very special man and a genuine old-time hockey player with immense willpower and deep courage in his soul. With that love in her heart, Kate let her eyes scour the scene on the ice rink, she rose to her feet and cheered with the rest of the crowd. On the ice, James T. O'Malley slowly rose to his skates as his teammates celebrated the goal. On the Wolverine bench, Coach Kelleher fist-pumped the air, thumped the back of his assistant coach and admired the fact that not only did O'Malley possess tremendous hockey skills, the young man knew how to play the game with a hockey sense that you cannot teach; it is a hockey sense that you can only be born with.

Barclay Millhouse was incensed at the early goal and the fact that this new player named, O'Malley, had baited him out of position and had the nerve to take him on with a one-on-one play and set up a goal on his watch. His huge frame angrily hovered over the fallen O'Malley and as Jim rose to his skates to join his teammates, Millhouse cross checked Jim high and hard with his stick and nailed Jim across the chest, knocking Jim back down on his skates. The referee threw his arm up and blew his whistle to signal a cross checking penalty and the linesmen surrounded the two players.

The crowd screamed and Millhouse barked out, "Stay down, punk! If you get on your skates before I make the penalty box, I will beat your ass silly. You think that I just knocked you on your ass twice and it hurt, then you have no idea of what the hell I will do to your face!"

"No. James Thomas O'Malley always gets back up. I never stay down for too long," O'Malley said as he jumped to his skates.

"O'Malley, oh yeah. Ya, the son of that cop that got whacked up in that dumpy Mohawk City. Well, keep this bullshit up and you can join your old man. I will arrange the family reunion and meeting for you."

The anger was uncontrollable, and as soon as the words left the mouth of Barclay Millhouse, James T. O'Malley threw his gloves aside and squared up. Players and on-ice officials backed off, and the crowd went even crazier. Kate O'Leary covered her eyes again, and then she slowly opened her fingers to peek through the spaces.

Just the look of fury on the face of O'Malley was enough to cause fear in her heart. Poor Kate watched between the fingers of her hands that remained locked over her face.

Millhouse laughed at the reaction of the much smaller and younger O'Malley. Suddenly, his laughter came to an abrupt halt. His era of terror was over.

Within seconds, Jim landed seven or eight clean punches that had Barclay Millhouse spinning on his skates and holding onto the hockey sweater of James T. O'Malley for dear life. It was as if he unleashed the fury of Hell. Two blows hit his face so quickly, and so hard that Millhouse had no chance for defense, and he staggered on his skates from the force of the blows and reached over his face with his arms to protect and cover up. The next four blows blew through his arms with a force that he had never felt before, and it felt as if sledgehammers had hit him.

Millhouse fell to his knees, blood pouring out of multiple cuts on his lips and face, and he spit one of his few remaining teeth out onto the ice. For a brief second or two, O'Malley stood over the fallen Barclay Millhouse; he leered at him and gnashed his teeth in anger, poised as if he was a terrier waiting for the horn to sound in order to begin the fox hunt. O'Malley then pounced on his victim and began to pummel him through a rather feeble defense.

"Geez, for the love of Heaven, get him off of me!" Millhouse screamed.

On-ice officials rushed in, along with teammates from both sides and with great effort, they finally pulled the wild-eyed James T. O'Malley off the destroyed Barclay Millhouse. The home crowd went nuts, the fans from Troy remained silent in their seats and the Albany Wolverines had a new hero. A legend born out of despair, and a player who played every game to win and who fought for respect with every ounce of his soul. Kate cheered and clapped and, in her heart, she knew that James had a good reason for fighting and standing for what he needed to stand for.

She only hoped that his anger would not eventually destroy him.

In the Wolverine net, Gordon Wigmore used his goalie stick as a tool in order to push snow piles aside, and under his mask; he laughed and said, "Yup, I was right. Millhouse just met his match."

One of the linesmen escorted Jim to the penalty box, the other linesmen escorted the bloodied Barclay Millhouse to the side door to head for the locker room for repairs.

Even if he could return, he would not, as the referee announced the penalties, "Millhouse, number four, for the River Rats, two minutes for cross checking, two minutes for roughing, five minutes for fighting, and a game misconduct for unsportsmanlike behavior. For O'Malley, number eleven, of the Wolverines, five minutes for fighting."

Teammates dropped Jim's hockey gloves and his stick off at the penalty box and just before they slammed the door shut, the referee skated by, leaned in and extended his hand to O'Malley.

"Good job, kid. I heard what he said about your father, and he deserved that ass beating more than I can ever say. That is why I gave him the game misconduct. I am so sorry about your father, there are no words for how sorry I am, but just take heart that your father is damn proud of you fighting for honor and for respect."

O'Malley forced a smile and said, "Thank you, sir. Thank you. Sorry for the fight, but it was the right thing to do."

"Hell, yeah, it was."

High above the ice, in one of the press boxes, a man named, Gerald MacCallum scribbled some notes on a pad with a letterhead stamped in bold letters, "New York Colonials Hockey Club, Inc." Gerald then made a careful note with a red pen, "James T. O'Malley. Number eleven" and with a smile and a large stroke of the red pen, he drew a large circle around the name and number. He then made another note on the pad, wrote, "Get the line mates too." Gerald mumbled, "This O'Malley is one helluva feisty guy and an amazing, hockey player." He then sat back in the chair, grabbed his glass of Scotch, took a long sip, and watched the rest of the game.

A few hours after the game ended, Coach Kelleher proudly plunked the cash down on the counter of the local beer and package store around the corner from his home in Latham, New York.

"Keep the coins, Billy," Coach Kelleher said to the store clerk, not trying to suppress his enthusiasm one bit.

The clerk slipped the coins into the tip jars on the counter and said, "Thanks, Coach Kelleher. Hey, congrats on the new player. Heard he beat the shit outta that jerk, Millhouse, and that he scored a hat trick too. Sounds like the real deal. Gonna pick up tickets for the next game. Hopin' that I can get the night off. What's his name, sumthin' Irish? A guy came in before who was at the game and he said it was friggin' amazing."

Coach Kelleher smiled and said, "Yeah, he is Irish. Yeah, he tore the hell-outta the net and outta Millhouse too. All it took was 'bout seven or eight punches. All clean too. The big boob went down like a tree. Crying for mercy. Payback for being an ass for all of these years. His name is O'Malley. James T. O'Malley. Yeah, it was some game, and he is a great player. Don't miss the games. Gonna be a great year." As the coach picked up the case of beer, he waved and nodded to the store clerk and began mumbling as he walked to his car with the beer tucked under his arm, "Well, one game, one hat trick, and one win. This O'Malley kid is gonna make me crazy in the head and a helluva lot poorer too. And I have to admit that I am lovin' every minute of it too."

Later that same evening after the game, in the small, one-bedroom apartment of James Thomas O'Malley and

Kate Eva O'Leary, there was a quiet stillness in the bedroom. There was only a strong beating of two hearts and rhythmic breathing of the same as the two lovers held each other in the bed and basked in the afterglow of proving their love. Kate ran her fingers through that glorious jet-black hair and while she did so, Kate carefully studied Jim's face.

She quietly whispered, "I do love you with all my heart, James. Always and forever."

"I love you too, Kate. My promise is that once we settle in at the market and I am making a few extra dollars playing hockey, then I am going to enroll in the junior college here in Albany County. I am not sure what to study, but it will unfold for us. My thoughts are that our new manager, Mr. Morris, likes both of us. He told me that you are very smart and that I have a bright future."

Kate nodded and said, "I think he does. I enjoy working there. Everyone is very fair and friendly, too. Your plans are wonderful, James. They really are."

"And once, my career path is set and we have steady money coming in, my other promise has not changed and that is to marry you."

Kate leaned in and accepted Jim's gentle kiss and her body shook with the feeling and thoughts of sharing her life with Jim. She wanted nothing more than to be Mrs. James Thomas O'Malley. Yet there was a concern growing in her soul for her lover.

"I know that horrible man only got what he deserved tonight for making such a wretched comment, but please, tell me that you are not allowing your anger and your pain to turn you into something that you are not. Please tell me that, James."

Jim rolled over and gently kissed Kate's forehead, then he pushed her hair back and smiled while pulling her so close it was as if they melted into each other.

"I admit that it is difficult, but I am fighting it, Kate. The anger and the pain are piling on now. In my heart, I am trying hard to forgive my mother and, to some extent, my father too. I think they should have told me years ago, way before this. Perhaps, it is the timing that is eating me up or perhaps, it is the look in Flaherty's eyes. I think there are deeper issues here than just what we know. I feel it. The emotions are waves in my soul. They are doing their collective best to crush my soul. Your love keeps me going. Your love keeps me upright, and you are my life now. Yet, when I am on the ice, it is as if I am a different man and all that matters to me, is winning the game and defending my team's honor, and my honor. I play the game hard and I play the game to win. I love hockey because in many ways, it is a metaphor for all the struggles in life. It takes courage, strength, dedication, and willpower to push your mind and body to limits that, ordinarily, you would stop at and then take the easy way out. Nothing is easy in this life. Nothing. I change on the ice, and I admit that it is strange."

Kate nodded at Jim's explanation. The concern weighed heavily in her eyes.

"Do you still love playing the game, James? Or, is it an outlet for your pain?"

"I do love the game and yet, I admit it does help release some of my pain. If I make it to the big-league, then we will live well and I will fulfill a childhood dream. However, right now, it is more than just playing hockey. It seems as if I am on a mission always to win at all costs. It is as if winning buries the pain and restores my honor. My father's honor." Jim paused, and he was deep in thought. There was little doubt that the game of ice hockey had taken on a different meaning for him. Now, hockey was a vehicle to help to cover the pain in his heart at all that had happened in the last few weeks. Jim then spoke softly, while gently stroking Kate's hair out of her face and while studying Kate's eyes, "You need to promise me that if you see me changing into someone else and someone that I should not be that you will honestly tell me so. I will take a different course, honest, I will. For you, I will do anything."

Kate smiled, nodded, and then whispered, "I promise you, James. No matter how it might hurt you or me, I will tell you."

They made the lover's pact, kissed and once more went on to prove their love deep into the night.

I glanced at the clock on my office wall and sighed. Another day spent here on the laptop. I clicked the save button and then sent the back-up file over to a flash drive. Cannot take any chances with losing these files. Too deep into this project now. After watching everything on the screen blink and wink at me, I closed out the windows and files and watched my trusty writing companion become dark and silent for the nighttime. It is time for me to do the same. In fact, it is way past bedtime. I stood up, stretched, and yawned. I shut the lights off in my office and from the darkness inside of my office; I could look down the second-floor hallway and see the lights glowing from the downstairs level of our townhouse. I wondered if my lovely wife was still up. We had not seen each other or spoken to each other since after dinner. Wow, this project certainly was consuming my time, but Rose remained very understanding. Rose was amazing.

I am a very lucky man.

With a concerted effort to be light on my feet and gentle upon the stairs, I walked silently and carefully down the main staircase and noticed the fire expiring in the fireplace; the television was dark and only a single reading lamp was on next to the sofa. Rose had fallen asleep on the sofa right next to the reading lamp, her feet propped up on a footstool, and a book sat open, but upside down in her lap. I walked over, trying my best not to disturb her, and noticed that the book was my own composition, *The Time Bomb in The Cupboard and other Adventures of Harry and Paul.* I smiled at my wife and the thought that I could not help but wonder how many other people that I had put asleep with my books. With some quiet ease, I picked the book up, closed it, and placed it on the table next to the reading lamp. Rose was dressed in her sleeping clothes, and I gently slipped out of my pants and shirt, folded them, and neatly laid them on the floor of the living room. When Rose stirred, I picked her legs up, gently spun her, and laid her on the sofa. I then slipped in next to her, wrapped my arms around her, gently cupped her glorious breasts, and snuggled up into her. Rose smelled as if her skin was a combination of sweet pea blossoms waving their gentle mist of a scent in the fresh spring air on an April morning. Her olive skin was so soft and glorious to the touch and her scent, and the feel of her body next to me overpowered me.

I heard Rose deeply sigh then she snuggled into me. This was wonderful. My wife always smelled so wonderful.

"Goodnight, Hemingway," Rose mumbled.

"Goodnight, my love. Goodnight."

Chapter Eight

Dark Shades of Life

On the top floor of an old walk-up apartment located in and around West 41st Street in Hell's Kitchen, a business transaction was ending. A transaction enveloped within the dark shades of life.

"Well, here is the cash," a slightly built middle-aged man wearing dark sunglasses, a wool hat, gloves, and a heavy winter coat said with just the slightest hint of an Irish brogue to his voice as he dropped a hard-covered attaché case on the table.

Seated at the lone chair at the table was a younger man who looked up, waved and pointed at the older man's garb and said, "It is about time that I got my payday. It sure took 'em long enough. I am down to brass tacks and crumbs." He pointed at the heavy outerwear and his wool hat. He waved his hand to encompass all of the clothes and said, "Ya know that ya can take all that stuff off. I know it is colder than a well digger's ass out there, but I have heat in here."

At first, the older man did not say anything or react; he simply studied the younger man.

After a careful study of his face, the older man mumbled, "I ain't staying. I am done here. Well, almost done."

With a smile and a nod, the younger man reached for the case with his left hand, and the older man noticed the three missing fingers on his left hand.

He pointed at the hand and said, "Yeah, have to tell ya, the big man is not too happy with some of the reports he is picking up from his contacts upstate. Sumthin' 'bout an old woman who says she ran into a young man in quite a hurry while walking her dog on a city street a few blocks away from the murder scene. I hope for everyone's sake that the old crow did not spot your hand there. Kinda distinctive trademark there, pal."

"She didn't, at least, I think she didn't."

"Were you wearing gloves?"

"No, not at that point—I wasn't wearing 'em."

"Tsk, tsk, not too swift there, pal," the older man said with an element of sarcasm buried in his voice.

Sensing the older man's hint that he had made an error in the committing of his devious crime and the resulting hasty escape, the younger man leaned back in his chair and asked, "What the hell was I supposed to do? Whack the old girl? It was like a . . . two second meeting. She couldn't see shit. Tell the big man, he ain't got shit to worry 'bout. I am the one bearing this cross and takin' all the risk. Is the dough all here? I hope that I don't need to count it all." He flipped the case over, tapped the latches and the case shot open, revealing neat rows of bundled cash, all held together with rubber bands.

The older man tugged at his wool hat, pulling it down more over his forehead. It seemed as if he took offense to the younger man questioning the amount of money.

"It's all there. You know whom you made a deal with. He is many things, but a chiseler is not one of 'em. A deal is a deal. Now, give me the gun and the silencer that you used. A deal is a deal, and that was part of the deal. The big man does not trust you to dispose of it correctly."

The younger man nodded. He stood up from the chair and said, "Yup. That was the deal. I don't want it. Big guy paid for it, anyway. It is technically his. Be right back. I have it tucked away in the other room."

Within a minute or two, he returned and handed the gun and the silencer to the older man, who took them, slipped the silencer into his coat pocket, then carefully studied the gun for a few minutes, lifted the gun barrel to his nose and sniffed and then placed the gun into another pocket on his jacket.

With a nod and a hint of a deeper Irish accent, the older man said, "If I were you, I would hit the road and high tail my ass outta here, but that is up to you. We are done," the older man said and with a quick turn, he spun and made his way to the apartment's hallway door.

"Hey!" The younger man shouted, and the man stopped and turned just before he left the room. "Thanks, and here," the younger man said as he reached in his shirt pocket, pulled out a police badge, and tossed it in the air to the older man, who caught it and studied it.

A police badge from the Mohawk City, New York, Police Department. A number eleven badge, with a sergeant's rank stamped on it right under the name "O'Malley."

A badge cast in silver and stamped with honor.

"Give it to the big man. I was gonna keep it as a trophy, but I kinda think he just paid for it."

"Better lock this door when I leave," the older man said.

"The knob locks on its own. It is a pain in the ass. I forget and lock myself out. I will slip the deadbolt over too."

The older man nodded and did not say a word, but slipped the badge into the pocket on his overcoat, turned, walked to the door, opened it and with a gentle pull on the door to close it behind him . . . he was gone.

Alone with his evil reward, the younger man studied the piles of cash. He picked up a stack and thumbed through the bills. It sure was a lot of money. More money than he ever saw before, but no doubt, it was a deal with the devil. The cash even had a bizarre air about it.

It smelled evil because it came from the dark shades of life.

The younger man replaced the cash in the case, closed and locked it.

He sighed and mumbled, "Yeah, thinking he is right. Time to get the hell outta here."

There was a knock at the door and the younger man looked up, slightly puzzled at who could be at the door. The older man just left. He closed the case, picked it up, and tucked it behind a chair in the living room on the way to open the door. There was only one chair in the living room and a small television sitting on top of an upturned cardboard box.

He lived a sparse life.

He looked through the peephole and saw that it was the older man. He must have forgotten some piece of business.

While swinging the door wide open, the young man asked, "Did ya forget something?"

"Yes, this."

The gun in his face was the last thing the young man ever saw in this world. His blood and brains splattered on the wall were going to be difficult to clean up.

As the body crumbled in front of him, the older man quickly grabbed the body and kicked the door closed behind him. He dropped the body a few feet inside the door and let it rest on the floor. With a few quick spins, he unscrewed the silencer and tossed it in his coat pocket. He strategically dropped the gun on the floor next to the body. With a quick search of the apartment, the older man found the case with the money behind the chair, grabbed it, and made his way to the door. He paused and looked at the dead body, and smiled.

Then as he exited, the older man mumbled with an Irish brogue so thick that it hung like icicles on the apartment wall, "Sorry, pal, but ya screwed up. Those missing fingers would have come back to haunt you and us, too. Guess that you did not know whom you were dealing with after all, pal. Better, slide that deadbolt lock over on this door when I leave. You just never know who might come in. Can't trust anyone these days."

A few mornings later, it was still cold in Mohawk City. The cold was not as intense as it had been the last few weeks, but it still was cold. A light snow fell during the night, a snow that was not quite as crisp as its predecessors were. Hints of spring buried in the snow.

Hot coffee on a cold day. Coffee, cigarettes, and whiskey were Detective Lyle Odell's best friends these days. Detective Lyle Odell's extra effort and initiatives paid off nicely. While scanning daily complaints and the reports for the Mohawk City Police Department, he came across a landlord filing a complaint on a young man who skipped out on his last month's rent for a small apartment in the city. Detective Odell was sure that the renter's name was a false name and his identity was bogus too, and he was also sure that this rent skipper had a more serious crime looming over his head because the landlord's description of the young man included one distinctive feature. He was missing fingers on his left hand.

The lab reports on the boots, as expected, turned up carpet, skin, and sock fibers, no fingerprints, but the lab team warned and Odell knew from his long career that extracting fingerprints from boots was a difficult, if not, an impossible task.

The downstate contacts did turn up a significant fact, and that was that many years earlier, Sergeant James Reilly O'Malley was instrumental in cracking a case of a large illegal gambling number's racket in Hell's Kitchen. His diligent digging and expert testimony during the trials, and because of his roots being there, his extensive knowledge of most of the players in the Irish mob active in the area, put a major dent in the crime ring and put the crime boss away in prison for a very long time. The crime boss was a man named Landry O'Casey and a man who was a big-time operator in the dark shades of life in Hell's Kitchen. The contact that Detective Odell spoke with reported that the word on the street was that the Irish mob considered O'Malley's actions as a double-cross of sorts. Mostly, because of O'Malley's roots and the fact that he proved to be an honest cop who stuck to his mission, was immune to payoffs and despite his Irish roots and potential loyalties, O'Malley ignored it all, and did his sworn job. This was interesting, and it became even more convoluted, when Detective Odell dug deeper and found out that about three months ago, the parole board denied O'Casey parole. In a deeper twist, a twist that could lead to revenge, Landry O'Casey died in prison about a month after the parole denial.

The good detective knew of James Reilly O'Malley's reputation, and his courage was legendary. Before his police duty, Lawson told tales of his military career. O'Malley was a war hero, a man who did not turn and run unless it was for a very deep reason. There was more to O'Malley leaving downstate than locking up bad guys.

The detective could feel it.

A long sip of coffee almost burned Detective Odell's lips and throat as it went down, but he seemed oblivious while he remained in deep contemplation and nervously drummed his fingers on his desk. Sometimes, what a tangled web this life weaves. His next phone call was to obtain a search warrant for the rent skipper's apartment and to bring the crime lab team along with him for the investigation. Even beforehand, Detective Odell was sure he would match evidence there to the boots and the good detective was confident they could lift fingerprints from the scene that would match someone's prints on the list he requested from recent military discharge records.

After all, how many recently discharged veterans could be missing three fingers on their left hand? Combat vets come back in all kinds of destroyed shape. Missing feet, missing legs, missing other stuff—the whole disgusting package. Right now, thankfully, the country was mostly at peace. There were limited combat engagements right now. The Vietnam War was long ago in the rear-view mirror. However, he was looking for a veteran with missing fingers. One finger, yes, maybe two, but three? Detective Lyle Odell was a United States Coast Guard veteran, and he knew how it worked. The chances are very good that without some kind of glorified dispensation, a person could not enlist in any military service without the fingers, but a person, sure as hell, could leave without them.

Detective Lyle Odell was very good at his job.

Over the next few weeks or thereabouts, it was exciting, yet somewhat predictable to the good detective at how the rest of the pieces of the puzzle fell into place. Due to his outstanding detective work, some luck, some stupid mistakes by the killer and the skills of the crime lab team, Detective Lyle Odell had the name and identity of the killer of Sergeant James Reilly O'Malley staring at him from a piece of paper.

Peter Randall Buckley. The killer's name echoed despair into the good detective's heart while he studied the letters.

There was just one problem. His police contact downstate in the Hell's Kitchen precinct just called him and told the good detective that the police just found the body of Mr. Buckley in his walk-up apartment on West 41st Street. He had been dead for quite a few days. Odell was a few days too late, and this mess just became even more complicated.

The policeman described, "A messy scene, and the neighbors called because of the smell."

Odell could only imagine. Mob hits were never happy

scenes.

The investigators found a gun on the scene and its caliper matched the gun used to kill Sergeant O'Malley. Even before the final crime reports returned, Odell knew that it would be the same gun used to commit the murder. Right now, there was no need to make a trip downstate to Hell's Kitchen. Detective Odell picked up the file with the details of Buckley's military career and his life. For the umpteenth time, Odell read the notes.

Peter Randall Buckley was from Hell's Kitchen. He was an Irish street kid, His father died young, his mother just died two years or so ago. An Irish street kid, amongst many other Irish street kids. No significant criminal record to speak of, just some stupid stuff as a teenager. Drinking underage, open booze on a city street, petty shoplifting of beer and candy bars from the corner store. He barely made it through high school, but he made it and worked as a car mechanic in a local repair garage. He was good with tools and his boss testified that he was a whiz on repairs. At the age of twenty-one, Buckley enlisted in the United States Navy, served as a Machinist Mate, then tried out and joined an elite covert Navy team. The best of the best. He excelled as a marksman and, as a result, received the billet of sniper and communications officer for his battalion. A glorified mercenary. Some records remained sealed due to classification; apparently, he served in some type of secret deployment overseas and served honorably. A few ribbons, many medals, and a few rank promotions and eventually he was Petty Officer First Class Buckley. A weapon malfunction caused the loss of three fingers on his left hand. There were no other details, other than after intense therapy and recovery; the United States Navy honorably discharged Buckley on a medical basis. His monthly disability payout and early pension collection amounted to just under four-hundred dollars a month. With a sigh, Detective Odell closed the file and shook his head. Buckley was a bad guy, and now was a dead bad guy, but wow, that was all the dough he could collect? Lost fingers, served with honor for about eight years of his life, secret deployments and now, not really much of a chance to manipulate small parts and swing tools when your left hand had three fingers gone to the wind. Once the whiff of cash and lure of crime floated under his beak, Buckley never stood a prayer.

All the parts and pieces fit now. Buckley needed the dough. He had street connections; he was a crack military shot, and he agreed to kill Sergeant O'Malley in cold-blood for a handsome payoff. He was a professional soldier, perhaps, not a professional killer, and that explained pulling off a crack shot with a handgun, but also explained some simple mistakes that he made. Yeah, he received a payoff all right. Pushing up daisies is the payoff. Buckley made a deal with the Devil and the Devil collected. Nevertheless, the question remained . . . in this case, who was the Devil? His meeting with Mrs. O'Malley had been a dead end. The poor widow was still a wreck, and she had Father Callahan by her side to coach her words and her every move. The situation was interesting, and it had Odell's investigative radar up and on full alert. Detective Odell knew that Mrs. O'Malley remained a woman full of faith, but it seemed as if the old priest was very protective of her, or if not only of her . . . of something. His meeting while sharing beers with Sergeant Lawson resulted in no new leads, either. Sergeant O'Malley and Officer Lawson were good friends, but aside from old war stories and sharing some military yarns; he never revealed a word about what O'Malley worked on in his previous life as a police officer. Odell felt as if Lawson simply knew little or nothing else to tell him, other than what he already shared.

The next step in finding the hierarchy of this mess was going to be a tough nut to crack.

Detective Odell badly needed a cigarette. His soul

stirred uneasily as he gathered up all of his notes, slipped them into his case, and checked for his weapon in his shoulder holster before he put his jacket on. His soul stirred because he had pulled off some great detective work and found his man, but someone else got him first. The detective was no buttercup; he knew that finding that someone in the maze of Irish mob madness was going to be a difficult task. The Irish mobs stood their ground in Hell's Kitchen, the other mobs, Italian or otherwise, kept their distance from the Irish territory. The area was small, and it was Irish. Their roots were deep, and he imagined that is most likely why they viewed James Reilly O'Malley as a turncoat of sorts.

While standing outside and sucking on his cancer rod, Detective Odell thought about how he still had to make a trip downstate. This road trip was not going to take long, a short trek down the road to Albany. A short time earlier, he had a telephone conversation with Jim O'Malley's girlfriend, Kate, and they arranged to meet after Jim's hockey game in the city. The detective knew that the meeting was not going to be the easiest thing to do, but he had to do it. He did not want a murdered police officer's son to read about the details of his father's killer in some stupid slanted-view newspaper.

Especially this particular son.

"I had no idea that you were as good a hockey player as you are until I watched the game tonight, Jim," Detective Odell said as he lifted his coffee cup and took a long sip of the brew. Tonight, Odell appeared extra rumpled, with a deep shadow of stubble on his unshaven face, his hair sticking out in waves, and weary eyes. Detective Odell looked as if he had not slept in weeks. In fact, he had slept very little. "I mean, I heard of your skills, but to witness you in action is amazing. You wore the net out and half of the other team, too. Great game. Great player. You have an extremely bright future," Lyle Odell made the statement of his heartfelt testimony as to James T. O'Malley's skills as a hockey player. With a hint of a smile on his face, Lyle pointed with his finger at the coffee mug sitting in front of him and said, "Ha, the last thing that I need these days, is more coffee."

Lyle fiddled with the mug while his eyes checked the couple sitting across from him. Kate, James Thomas O'Malley, and the good detective sat in a booth at a restaurant, close by the hockey arena, and they nibbled on some food and sipped sodas, water, and coffee.

"Thank you, Detective Odell. The other team is a little weak, and I had a good game tonight," Jim said as he held Kate's hand tightly. It was easy to see the love in their eyes for each other.

"Bullshit. I am just an old gumshoe and hardly a hockey expert, but you sure look like the real deal out there. Please, Jim, call me . . . Lyle. No need for all the detective stuff. I loved your old man, and I swear that I have not slept more than four hours on any night in months now. Fuel my old ass with coffee, cigarettes, pizza, and good quality, Irish whiskey. No sense wrecking my liver with the cheap stuff. I told Kate and you that I would, nah," Odell shook his head to negate the words and said, "hell that is wrong, cuz, I *promised* Kate and you that I would find the killer. You are family to me." He paused and then said, "And I have kept my promise. I did not want both of you to read it in the Times Union tomorrow, so I wanted to meet with you, face-to-face."

Both of their eyes widened, and Jim let go of Kate's hand and leaned in closely.

Still wide-eyed, Jim asked, "Who? Name?"

"Peter Randall Buckley."

Jim shook his head and, in the light, Detective Odell

could see the scars on his face and on his lip, along with a fresh red mark forming under his left eye. Battle scars and this young man was just turning twenty-one years of age or so. The detective could see the rage burning in his eyes, and his teeth clench, and his lips flare. He could see the fear in Kate's eyes, too. Fear at her lover's reaction. Odell thought about how this young man could turn into one fierce son-of-a-bitch on a dime.

"We appreciate the meeting and your thoughtfulness, Lyle. We really do. Have to say that I never heard of him." Jim turned to Kate and asked, "My love . . . does that name ring any bells?" She fervently shook her head to indicate, "No." Jim turned back to Lyle and asked, "Who the hell is this monster?"

"You would not have heard of him, Jim. Someone hired Buckley to kill your father for money. He was not a professional hit man, but he was a professional sniper. Military trained and a crack shot. A United States Navy elite marksman. A military assassin. The best of the best. A mercenary. The only trouble is that," Lyle paused and studied the eyes of the two young people in front of him and he might have even said a quick prayer to bring peace to their souls before adding the truth, "ah . . . Buckley is dead. Shot dead in Hell's Kitchen on the day that I was heading downstate to find him and arrest his sorry ass. An ugly scene. His head is in pieces. Shot at close range with the same handgun that killed your father. Sorry for the gory details but I need to be straight up with you." Detective Odell lifted his eyes to Kate and said, "My apologies to you, Kate."

Kate nodded, but did not say a word.

"My gut feelings and detective instincts tell me that it is the Irish mob, and they rubbed him out before I could arrest him."

Kate reached for Jim's hand, and he instinctively took it in his grasp without even looking at her.

Just above a whisper, while maintaining complete composure, Jim said, "I don't know what to say, Lyle, except, thank you for all of your hard work and effort and I know that my father is proud of you. I am proud of you. I honor you."

"As I do too, thank you, Lyle," Kate said with a forced smile.

Detective Odell thought about how this young woman was a pure knockout. Her beauty was encompassing and fully captivating. He took another sip of coffee, and the cup was empty. He looked around for the server and signaled for her attention while waving his cup in the air for a refill. The server spotted his actions, smiled, and hustled over to the counter to pick up the pot of coffee and bring a refill. Jim and Kate had been picking at their food and drink and now they stopped all together.

After the server refilled the coffee, Odell mumbled a weak rumble of words of, "Thank you" and the good detective leaned into the mug and with a tilt, he swallowed more of the coffee. "Geez, I have to quit this caffeine stuff chased by the booze. I will be wide-eyed for a month." Detective Odell reached into the case that he had previously set on the seat next to him and pulled out a manila folder with a thick stack of papers in it.

He placed it gently on the table and said, "Look, Jim, you are the son of a slain police officer. A proud, honorable police officer, killed in the line of duty. Here is a copy of the file on your father's murder. Technically, I am not supposed to give this to anyone outside of law enforcement. However, technically, all of that is bullshit. As I have said, you are family in my eyes. I have to say that I removed the autopsy report and some graphic details from the folder."

Jim looked at the detective as he picked up the file from the table. O'Malley had a puzzled look on his face, as if he did not understand the motive.

"Why did you do that? I would shield my beloved, Kate from that but I could hack it."

Detective Odell shook his head and said, "I didn't do it to hide it from you, Jim, or to protect you. I did it to protect the rest of the world from your reaction."

Neither Jim nor Kate reacted since there was little doubt, they both understood.

The detective swallowed another sip of coffee and he continued to explain, "Anyhow, those are copies. I have all the originals. In my heart and in my mind, I know one hundred percent that I nailed my man, but it has to go up through the chain of my command. After a review of the case, the big boys will agree and the powers to be . . . will close the case. The top brass, the prosecutors, and the district attorney's office, will not allow me to pursue a mob-hit downstate. That fact will cause great pain in my heart and I have to think, in your heart and Kate's heart too. Great pain, because the three of us will know that someone will have gotten away with murder. You spoke very true words to me when you told me that this has something to do with your father's past. A ghost returned to haunt him."

Jim and Kate sat silently, both of them waiting for direction and further explanation.

The explanation arrived quickly as Odell carefully explained, "Buckley's murder is out of my hands. It is in the jurisdiction of your father's old police precinct, and we all know who controls most of those directions. His death will go unsolved. Maybe, even ruled a suicide for all we know. Yet, there are still a few old guards left down there, good cops, who knew your father and they will feed me information when they can. I need your help, Jim. You and Kate's help. Please, read these papers and if anything stands out in it, please, then give me a call. It might be poor odds, but I need to find out who pulled all the strings on this and for what reason. My soul needs it, your soul, and

Kate's too. The world needs it. I owe your father the closure."

Jim picked up the manila folder, and the intensity still burned in the young man's eyes. Detective Lyle Odell had to hold back a shudder at the power of the fury that he saw when he studied the eyes of James Thomas O'Malley.

Odell thought as he studied Jim's eyes. 'It was a good thing that Buckley was dead. Having his head blown off was quick and, most likely, painless. James Thomas O'Malley's method of revenge might not be so painless.'

"Have you ever heard of a man named, Landry O'Casey?" Detective Odell asked.

Without hesitation, Jim answered, "No. Never. Kate?"

Kate O'Leary shook her head to indicate, "No."

"I thought that would be the case. He was a mobster that died in prison a while back. A month or so before your father died. Your old man helped put him away. You will read about it in the files. I am not giving up on this, Jim and Kate. Not until I solve all the pieces of this evil madness. I am hoping to find a connection somewhere."

Jim nodded and said, "Kate and I thank you from the bottom of our hearts. Moreover, I understand the honor. No doubt, there are many people that my father and mother knew from the old neighborhood and they never mentioned them to me. We will read the files carefully. Ten times over and try to find something for us to go on in there."

Jim's eyes wandered as he grasped in the air for a thought.

"I have to ask because it is nagging at my heart, but did you find my father's police badge?"

Detective Odell shook his head and said, "Sorry, Jim. No, not yet. It was not in the listed contents discovered in the scoundrel's apartment belongings. It remains a mystery."

"Okay, thank you. I promise that we will read every

word of these reports and we will be sure not to miss anything. Once more, thank you for everything, Lyle. I owe you a great deal for your commitment to win this game. For your respect and for your honor. You are a great man."

Kate nodded and Lyle shook his head in disagreement at the statement. Jim and Kate studied the bags under his eyes that hung like dark shadows of gloom, his unkempt hair, his loosened and dislodged necktie, the deep five-o'clock shadow on his face that now approached seven o'clock and his bloodshot eyes.

With his mouth barely moving, Lyle said, "I am not a great man. Honestly, I am a borderline alcoholic, introverted, loner of a police detective that has seen way too much of the dark shades of this life in order for me to see the bright side ever again. Too much, but I do my best and when fine men such as your father are killed in cold-blood for no reason, I become much the same as Jim becomes when he sets his skates on the ice. A man with a mission. Jim scores goals and wins hockey games and I enforce the law and restore honor. I am many things, but one thing that I am, is an honest man. A man, who will never earn a million dollars. A man, too ugly ever to have a pretty woman on my arm. A man, too honest to step on people to get ahead, but someday, when they plant me in my grave, and I meet Saint Peter at the Gates to Heaven, my hope is that the good saint says, to me, 'Hey, old gumshoe . . . job well done, sir. Please, c'mon in.'"

With tears in her eyes, Kate motioned for Lyle's hands. The good detective reached up and grasped the lovely woman's hands, and then, with her eyes, she implored Jim to join them.

With all three of them grasping hands, Kate said, "Bullshit, you are a beautiful man. Above all, you are a great man. Saint Peter will welcome you with open arms and with all the glory and power of Heaven."

Kate gently tapped Jim's hand and followed her lover's

eyes while saying, "Now, James, I think that the good detective here needs to know something very important."

O'Malley nodded because he knew that Kate was correct. They could trust Detective Lyle Odell without any question or any hesitation.

Jim knew that his private past might hold a clue to the person or persons that all three of them sought, and without further hesitation, Jim candidly blurted out the truth, "I know that you have met with my mother in order to quiz her on the past, and reached no fair conclusions. Mom called Kate this past week and told her so. We only owe you fairness, for all of your effort here. First, you need to know that James Reilly O'Malley was my father, but he was not my biological father. You might have met a certain Mr. Bernard Flaherty at my father's funeral and the repast. He is my biological father, and he is from Hell's Kitchen. I am the product of an illicit affair that my mother had with Mr. Flaherty while my father was overseas, fighting in the Vietnam War. My father, because of his immense and unfathomable honor and love, forgave my mother and accepted me as his own son. I just discovered this information myself after my father died. My mother, Father Callahan, and Mr. Flaherty met with Kate and me and told us the truth."

During his many years in police work and interviewing witnesses and criminals, Detective Odell was very adept at concealing his reactions and it took all that he could muster in order to hide his reactions to this bombshell of a newsflash.

He kept a poker face on and when he went to speak, Jim held his hand up to indicate that, first, there was a bit more to reveal.

"Pardon me, Lyle. There is more for you to know and to digest. During your visit, my assumption is that you ran into Father Callahan and his overzealous guard over my mother?"

"I did. He guards her for more than religious reasons. Or so I presume," the good detective said.

"He does," Jim said with a nod, "Bernard Flaherty was a final candidate for Catholic priesthood when he impregnated my mother with a bastard son while enveloped within an affair with a married woman. If and when, I make it to the big-league, then finally, some way, somehow, the truth will come out. We all know that abhorrent secrets only die with dead people, and the good priest, although, well intentioned, guards his church with the same honor that we feel for our individual passions."

Detective Odell weakly indicated with his eyes that this information was of shock, as well as of significance, and the rumpled detective sat silently for a long time while he pondered the last revelations of this incredible case that Jim just revealed to him.

After some extended silence, in which all that you could hear were other restaurant patron's conversations and the background ringing of a cash register, Odell spoke, "I only briefly met Mr. Flaherty. Your mother introduced him to me as an old friend of the family. One look and I did not like nor trust him. Sorry. I am an old detective with many street bruises and bumps. I have cynical ways. . .."

Jim held his hand up and once again, interrupted the detective, "Pardon me again for the interruption. We are on the same page here, Lyle. I agree. He hides the truth behind false eyes."

"And you told me this about your past because you think that Flaherty is involved in what? Or you think this fact, combined with the cracking of Irish mob cases, caused your father to flee Hell's Kitchen for a better life in Mohawk City?"

James Thomas O'Malley looked first at Kate, whose face remained stoic, and then he looked at Detective Odell, just as the server arrived at the table and asked, "Will that be all? If so, here is the check."

Odell picked it up and looked at it, held his hand up to indicate that he would pay, and reached for his wallet.

He scooped forty dollars out of the wallet, handed it all back to the server and said, "Twenty-dollar tab and good service. Here, thank you. Please, keep the change."

"Wow, thanks!"

With business out of the way, the detective looked at Jim and with his eyes, searched for the answer.

"He is involved in, I do not know what, but he is involved. I feel it in my heart. And yes, my parents fled for those reasons," Jim said and then continued, "once more, I will give the downstate police some time to find the person or persons who are also responsible for my father's death. On the other hand, if before that, I hear they rule this monster's death, a suicide and close the case, well, then I will pay a visit to Hell's Kitchen to even the score. I guess after my visit, the Hell in Hell's Kitchen will be most appropriate."

Detective Odell smiled and as he fingered his wallet and then slipped it into his jacket pocket, the old detective said, "I cannot even imagine."

Chapter Nine

Mr. Gerald MacCallum

James Thomas O'Malley single-handedly tore the Eastern New York Hockey Association apart. Game-by-game, goal-by-goal and fight-by-fight. By the end of March, when the relatively short season of thirty or so games ended, O'Malley led the league in goals scored, assists, minutes played, and penalty minutes accrued. In addition, Coach Kelleher was a few hundred dollars poorer and the corner beer and package store was a few hundred dollars in the black. There was a playoff of sorts, or if a hockey fan could muster up enough courage and embellishment to call it a playoff, they might do so, but it was more as if it was a "gimme." The playoff was a rollover and play dead sort of series of games.

The remnants and parts and pieces of the team from Troy, New York, after Barclay Millhouse suddenly "retired" in mid-season, showed up for four games, and the River Rats hockey club of Troy, New York lost all four games, of which two, were shutouts, and the league championship trophy belonged to the Albany Wolverines. The first line of O'Malley, Davis, and Johnston was more than formidable. It was unstoppable. O'Malley led the league in scoring goals and in total points, but his line mates, with Johnston second in scoring and Davis third in scoring, also received many accolades. The league named O'Malley, the league MVP, the MVP of the championship playoffs, and he walked away with one-thousand dollars in bonus money for all the accolades. He also left a knockout record of sixteen wins and no defeats in on-the-ice fights. In fact, it seemed as if an opponent's hands never even touched him. O'Malley was a folk hero in a hockey-crazed city and the Capital Region of New York had a beloved hero. The local kid from up the road, whose father died a hero in the line of police duty, and he had a beautiful girlfriend, and was a stunningly handsome young man.

It was storybook material.

Storybook, except for the on-the-ice anger, which Jim O'Malley kept finding more and more difficult to control. All that Jim wanted to do was to win hockey games. Winning made his pain subside and made him feel like someone special. He knew that someday, his anger would cause issues in his life, with his love, and with his ultimate goals, but right for now, a hockey rink and a game became his solace from a world of pain.

It was now the off-season for hockey. It was now, late spring in and around 1977 or thereabouts, and Jim and Kate settled into daily life.

Unfortunately, their careful and intense studies of the files that Detective Odell gave to them to study brought nothing new to light, and that was the only element of their lives that created sadness. The newspapers, as predicted, wrote the story as if Buckley acted alone, out of some warped vendetta against policemen and fellow military war heroes. Typical media bullshit, supposition and twists, and turns of the actual truth with little to no facts to back it all up. Other than that dark cloud, Kate and Jim were doing quite well in picking up the pieces of their lives and moving onto the next phase. Jim ice-skated almost daily at a local rink. He hit the gym hard, ran over a mile every day and his physical conditioning increased daily.

Kate spoke to her mother and father at least once a week and to Jim's mother once a month or thereabouts. Jim still had not mustered the forgiveness in his heart to speak with his mother. He knew he eventually would, however, right now it was still too painful. Their jobs were going rather well. Jim took some of his bonus money and placed it in a bank account and used the rest to sign up for more courses at a junior college. Jim was brilliantly smart, and he generally breezed through the coursework and received excellent grades. Kate often asked Jim what his goal for school was and even Jim was not sure. His guidance counselor suggested a wide-open curriculum of courses and Jim agreed, but once he completed the required courses in math, English, history, and such, Jim took more elective courses in social sciences and he leaned heavily towards sociology. In her heart, Kate only wished that Jim would find his way and they could marry. That was all that she wanted and desired.

On an early Saturday morning, there in the late spring, Kate and Jim's lives were about to change rather drastically.

"Hello, yes, James is here. Who is calling, please?" Kate answered the telephone call.

The voice on the other end of the telephone line said, "Oh, good. I was hoping he was not at work. My name is Gerald MacCallum. I am a real estate investor, but I also am a huge hockey fan and I own a hockey club in Rockland County, New York. I am the owner of the New York Colonials Hockey Club."

Kate paused for a moment and then said, "I see. Hold please. I will find James." Mr. MacCallum thought it was very cute how his wife formally addressed her man with the use of his full name, James. In the short time that he had been researching James Thomas O'Malley, all he ever heard was his last name used as an address.

"O'Malley."

For some reason, MacCallum thought how his last name had a formidable sound to it and that it characteristically summed the man and his immense talents up. Gerald could hear some faint speaking in the background, but he could not make out any of the conversation. There was a shuffling of feet, the phone rattled and then a voice, "This is, O'Malley."

Gerald smiled, paused and recovered, "Hello, Mr. O'Malley. As I explained to your wife. . .."

O'Malley cut him off, "Kate Eva O'Leary is my lover and my girlfriend. We are not married. Yet. Soon, but not, yet. How can I help you, sir?"

MacCallum smiled at the young man's bluntness and his honesty. He immediately liked this young man. He was very special.

"I see. Well, as I explained to Kate, my name is Gerald MacCallum and I am a real estate developer and investor. My home base is in Rockland County, New York. Downstate near New City. I do a lot of business here in Albany and catch many hockey games. I am a huge hockey fan. You are quite a talent, Mr. O'Malley. Amazing."

"Thank you, sir, but you still have not told me how I can help you or why you have called. Or how you obtained my telephone number?"

Mr. MacCallum smiled at the impatience of young O'Malley. He was sure it was part of the reason that he was such a great player. His soul was restless. Even over the telephone, his assessment of James Thomas O'Malley seemed to be holding true. Well-spoken, honest, quite forthright and no nonsense. Polite off the ice, hellfire on skates on the ice.

"Yes, of course. I apologize. Coach Kelleher gave me your number. We go back quite some ways together in hockey circles. As I mentioned to Miss O'Leary, I am the owner of the New York Colonials hockey club. We compete in the Metropolitan Hockey League and are part of the New York Rover's farm system. I want to sign you to a contract. Can we meet? I am in Albany today and tomorrow and then I need to head home to attend to important business. My sincerest apologies for the short time frame but I would love to sew up some business here and one of them is to have your signature inked on a contract to take back home. I plan to make appointments with Teddy Davis and Royal Johnston too. I want to sign all three of you boys . . . but honestly, you are the prize, Mr. O'Malley. It is your contract that I want to hang on the wall of my office at the New York Colonial's home arena."

Upon hearing the words, Jim's mind whirled with a million thoughts. The number one thought was that this was not only the moment that he had dreamt of since he was a young boy playing and shooting on frozen ponds in upstate New York, but this could also mean that if the deal was solid, then he would ask Kate to marry him. As in, marry him next week. . ..

"Well, my goodness, Mr. MacCallum. Thank you. I . . . I . . . I . . . please, can we meet somewhere? My apologies, sir. I am stuttering quite a bit here."

MacCallum laughed on the other end of the line and said, "I understand. Out of the blue telephone call, right? Please, I have offices on North Pearl Street and we can meet there. The corner of Pearl and Main. The Tower. Nineteenth floor. The top floor. Penthouse offices. Since it is Saturday, there should be plenty of parking available. If not on the street, please park in the parking garage next door. Tell the attendant you are here to meet with me and I will plow the road and leave word with the lobby security officer to clear you through. It is ten now, let's say one o'clock and then, perhaps, if we work a deal, we can catch some lunch and celebrate. Please bring Miss O'Leary. I have a feeling that where O'Malley goes, then so does his faithful woman."

The tower was a polished building that stood guard, very proudly over the downtown area of the Capital of New York as if it was the shining spire of the empire. The Empire State.

Mohawk City did not have any shining spires. It seemed to have blankets of gloom right now for Kate and Jim, but no shining spires.

The tower possessed marble floors that flickered with your reflection back to you as you cruised over them, polished brass elevator doors and brass trim, lined with marble stones edges and lentils. Elegant chandeliers hung like elaborate icicles in the lobby, with cut crystal glass glowing as if they were diamonds hanging on chains. Spectacular was a word that summed up a tidy description of the building. This was definitely the high-rent district of the Capital of the State of New York.

Mr. MacCallum simply called it, "The Tower." The part that he left out was that it actually was, "The MacCallum Tower."

Kate dressed in her best dress, a flowery print that waltzed gloriously around her knees, clung nicely, but not too tightly to her glorious curves and her female figure, and had a conservative neckline to hide some of her cleavage. Her beauty was such that the young woman could wear anything and make it look elegant. She wore simple gold post earrings and a simple gold chain necklace around her neck. The pieces were not costume jewelry . . . they were actual gold pieces. Family heirlooms, handed down from Kate's grandmother to her. To Kate, they were worth millions and when you are the daughter of an Irish stonemason and your mother worked in a dirty, inner city laundromat as an attendant, they *were* absolutely worth a million dollars.

O'Malley wore his only suit. The same black suit that he wore to his father's funeral. All black, even his socks and underwear were black. He favored black. It matched everything, including his mood.

The lobby security officer was expecting them and after warm greetings and some exuberant hockey talk, the officer cleared them to ride the elevator to the exclusive penthouse offices of MacCallum Holdings, Incorporated. It turned out that he was an O'Malley fan, too. It seemed as if all of the persons living in the City of Albany, New York, were O'Malley fans these days. A tall, slender man greeted Kate and Jim as they stepped off the elevator and into the center of the office. There was no elevator lobby on this level.

The elevator landed inside of the offices.

"So nice to see you, and thank you for coming on such short notice. James, Miss O'Leary, it is my pleasure. I am Gerald MacCallum."

His handshake was firm, but not overwhelming, and his attitude was gracious. He gently shook Kate's hand and you could see his eyes study her beauty.

"My, such a lovely woman, pardon me, but you are simply stunning."

The praise embarrassed Kate, and she smiled weakly and squeaked out, "Thank you and it is nice to meet you too."

Jim smiled proudly. He immediately liked MacCallum and his mannerisms, and Jim put his defenses down. O'Malley at this point, from both the hockey world and the real world, felt as if he was a supreme judge of character. No doubt he was correct. Here was a super, high roller executive; yet, he was quite down to earth.

Jim replied in agreement, "I agree and thank you. Kate is stunning, Mr. MacCallum. Stunning is a good word to describe, my Kate, and it is our pleasure to meet you."

Mr. MacCallum smiled and then held out his arm and gently guided his visitors toward the heart of the offices. "Please, I apologize, but since it is Saturday, my assistant, Linda, is off and I am ill-prepared. As usual, I overbooked my week and left, calling you until the last minute. My error, but time seems to fly by these days. Typical clueless executive, lost without his faithful assistant. Please, this way. We can use the conference room right here. It has a pleasant view of the city. You can see the top of the arena and the Egg from here."

They walked to the conference room and to say that the office décor and finishes were elegant and fine would be a severe understatement. The carpet was plush enough to cause your feet to sink so deeply that you could not see your shoes; the polished oak doors were elegant and created by craftsmen of old, the fine silver door hinges and hardware. The impeccable glass was spotless and without any blemish. Fine art, paintings, and photographs of New York lined the walls. The Empire State Building, various scenes of the Hudson River and the bridges and spans crossing it, downtown Albany, Manhattan, of course, there was a picture of a hockey rink, along with stunning pictures of Saratoga Racetrack in the autumn of the year, with spectacular colors in the trees. On and on it went. It was certainly beyond high-class. They entered the elegant conference room and Mr. MacCallum pointed at the black leather plush chairs at one end of a polished stone conference room table that seemed to be the size of Australia.

"Please, let's sit here at this end of the table. We can stay close here. The table is rather imposing and I apologize for the atmosphere. I assure you that I am not imposing in nature. Would you like coffee, tea, or some ice water? I am going to have a glass of water and fetch the paperwork."

"Ice water would be nice. Thank you," Jim said, and Kate nodded in agreement.

"Sure thing. Please sit, relax, and enjoy the view. I will be right back."

Jim held a chair out for Kate to settle into, and then he sat next to Kate and held her hand. One wall was a huge picture window looking out toward the heart of the city. You could see the Plaza, the Center, the arena and the Egg. The river loomed in the distance.

Kate leaned in and whispered, "My goodness, James.

These offices are fantastic. It is amazing."

Jim whistled, nodded, and with an amusing lift of his eyebrows and a little smirk on his face, said, "It is unreal."

While they sat there admiring the surroundings and taking in all the experience, Mr. MacCallum returned. He set a pitcher of ice water on a large coaster in the center of the table near the end where they sat and placed three manila folders on the table near his vacant chair.

Mr. MacCallum said, "Good thing that I have two wet bars in these offices or I would be making a trip back to my office. I forgot the glasses."

With a push of a button, a wall panel slowly slid open with the slow drawl of an electric motor propelling it along. Behind the panel was a wet-bar, and with a few strides of his long frame, Mr. MacCallum plucked three glasses from the glass storage shelf within the bar.

"Here we go, now," He proudly announced while handing glasses to Kate and Jim. He then sat down in the vacant chair and while Jim poured glasses of water for each of them, Mr. MacCallum pulled some reading glasses out of his suit jacket pocket, perched them on his nose, opened one of the folders of papers, and began to study the papers. Mr. MacCallum was a proud man. He was the type of man that it was difficult to tell his exact age, but a solid guess would be in and around sixty years of age or thereabouts. He was exceedingly handsome, impeccably groomed, his face clean-shaven, with waves of gentle black hair speckled with lines and dots of salt and pepper effects. Not a single hair was out of place on his head. He wore a gray suit of the finest quality, a white shirt and a gray tie with some black stripes in a quiet pattern. He wore an expensive gold watch on his left wrist, but no rings, wedding or otherwise. Of note to Jim was the tie tack that Mr. MacCallum used to keep his necktie in order. O'Malley did his best not to stare at it, but Jim swore that it was a tie tack of a policeman's badge. The type of tack that his father had and Jim now had in his possession.

A replica of a police shield. . ..

"I will pull no punches here, James. I have watched you play many games here in Albany this season. In fact, I watched you play your first game with the Wolverines and right from your first shift, I knew what I wanted. I want you to play for my hockey club, and I am prepared to pay you handsomely to do so. I had my legal department draw up a contract. Here it is. I made copies for all of us. This is a straightforward contract, James. It is a standard form. No crazy language or gotchas." While sliding the papers to Kate and Jim, MacCallum looked over the top of his glasses and asked, "I do not suppose that you have an agent or a lawyer to review this contract and advise you?"

Jim shook his head and said, "We don't sue people, Mr. MacCallum. Money awarded in lawsuits seems to be the end-all, stop-all, for some people. You hurt or offend me and I sue you and obtain money and everything is okay now. Bullshit. I settle scores without money involved and I do not need any prissy pants, tight-ass, over-educated nitwit to advise me and take a scoop of my salary for bullshit advice about a word or two and debate whether a period is required, as opposed to an oxford comma. I am James Thomas O'Malley and I kick ass on the ice and play the game of ice hockey, hard, fast, and fair. You are willing to pay me to score goals, kick ass, and win games. I play to win. Winning ice hockey games puts ticket-paying asses in the seats and we all make money. What else is there for you to know? I doubt very much a man of your reputation and means, gathered all of this glorious empire by being a jerk and chiseling people over hockey contract wording. It is not in your soul and damn sure as hell is not in your resume."

Kate looked at Mr. MacCallum with a rather awkward look on her face, as she carefully studied his face as if to gauge the reaction to Jim's long speech, his no-nonsense words and painfully honest approach.

Kate breathed a sigh of relief when she saw that Mr. MacCallum smiled and continued to slide the papers over to Kate and to Jim.

"Well said, young man, and I completely and thoroughly understand. Thank you for your trust. Your reputation for toughness, fairness, and straight talking precedes you and does you great justice, James."

Jim picked up the bundle of papers, adjusted his eyes to the words, and said with a smile, "Thank you. I tell it as it is. Please, call me Jim or simply call me, O'Malley. Only my true love here and my mother call me James."

"Fair enough. Jim, it is or, O'Malley. I guess it depends upon the situation." They sat in office-predicated silence and read the contracts together. Kate pointed out a few things in a gentle whisper, and when Mr. MacCallum realized they were discussing their future, he stood up and said, "Please forgive my rudeness. If you would like some privacy . . . I will leave the room and allow you to discuss this in private."

Kate smiled and laughed. She waved her hand and said, "Please, no, Mr. MacCallum. Please, stay. I was simply whispering to James that this is a shitload of money to make for playing ice hockey. For two poor Irish kids from humble roots in Mohawk City, this number here on the last page of this contract just about knocked me out of my chair." She smiled, nervously fingered her gold earrings and added, with a hint of coyness in her glorious voice, "James is not the only honest one here. I might look as if I am a gentle woman but above all, I am Irish too. And you sir, may call me, Kate."

Mr. MacCallum laughed a hearty and uproarious laugh and his face broke into a wide smile. The businessman now was left somewhere on the floor of his plush offices, or in another room. This was now Gerald MacCallum, hockey fan and owner of the New York Colonials.

"You dear, Kate, are the perfect match for O'Malley here. You are glorious. So, do we have a deal?"

O'Malley looked over at Kate, who only smiled and told the answer with her eyes.

Jim smiled too and said, "We do. I have some questions and loose ends here. However, I want to play for your hockey club. Consider me a center iceman for the New York Colonials."

"The businessman in me says for me to summon, Linda out of her day off, take you both to lunch, and then when Linda arrives, she can witness the signing of the contract and notarize the agreement. However, the MacCallum in me says to respect the O'Malley in you and the O'Leary in you, dear Kate, and let's sign away. The last thing we need is, my goodness, how does it go? A prissy pants, tight-ass, over-educated nitwit to charge us a fortune and have a wild fit because we signed without the proper legal bullshit blessing. I must be honest, Jim. I do employ a number of prissy pants, tight-ass, over-educated nitwits. They will hyperventilate over this contract, question me next week, and guess what? They can kiss my ass."

"That works for us. Please hand me a pen, sir."

A half an hour later, the three of them sat at an exclusive table reserved for Mr. Gerald MacCallum at downtown Albany's finest restaurant.

"So, please, Jim, tell me about these loose ends?" Mr. MacCallum said while he fingered a glass of a top-shelf Scotch poured neat in a custom-cut crystal glass.

"Well, Kate and I need to find jobs downstate. The supermarket chain we work for, well, they only have a presence here in Albany County. No transfers available to any downstate stores because there are not any there. We will need to find other supermarkets and apply for positions. I am sure we will be successful in securing jobs, because we both have solid experience and good work records. I know that it is a nice salary to play for your hockey club and it is loaded with bonus potential, but we still need to work a bit. It is the off-season."

Jim took a sip of Irish whiskey and soda water, and Kate did the same. Same drink too. They both were Irish through and through to their souls. Mr. MacCallum did not speak, he sipped his Scotch and listened to Jim relate the loose ends. He could tell that there was a bit more for O'Malley to tell.

"I also need to find a junior college and transfer my credits and then we. . .."

With those words, MacCallum placed his drink down and interrupted Jim.

"Let's see. I do not wish to be rude, but I think that I can finish this. First, we need to find an apartment. Then we have to allow Kate to check out junior colleges too and have Kate select some courses and decide upon a career path, which might be or might not be a schoolteacher. We have to buy a new car, because you might not have mass transit to take anymore, and then there is a little matter of important business, which I am quite sure, will include an engagement ring."

Gerald MacCallum finished speaking. He smiled, took another sip of his Scotch, set the glass down and then, with the bread tongs, he selected a piece of bread from a bread dish in the center of the table.

While placing the bread on his plate, Gerald MacCallum explained, "Kate, Jim, I am a businessman and I am sure that you both understand that I do not make investments without checking into what I am investing my money in."

Kate smiled and so did Jim; however, it was Jim who spoke first, "Impressive, and yes, you would not have the empire that you have if you made investment errors. We understand. Thank you for sharing your ability to gather the required background information on us. Information that puts enough faith in you in order for you to offer us this opportunity."

Jim's already dark eyes darkened some more while his voice grew in intensity.

"I plan to work as hard as I can to be a success on the ice and make an impact for your hockey club, sir. I understand that this hockey career of mine is not quite yet, full time and while your salary is generous and wonderful, it is the off-season and I hope very shortly to have a wife and perhaps, much more to support."

MacCallum leaned in intently and explained, "There is zero doubt in my mind, Jim O'Malley, about your hard work on the ice and your commitment to our hockey club. Zero. We would not be here if I had a doubt. I do my own scouting, and act as general manager of the hockey club too. My hockey blood boils with satisfaction at scouting hockey talent. I never played much of the game, but I am an expert in the game. Does that make any sense to you?"

Jim nodded, and Kate abstained from commenting on inside hockey testimonies. It appeared as she left hockey analysis to the experts.

MacCallum continued, "Please know that I understand your situation and that is why I am offering you much more than what is spelled out in the contract that we just agreed to. Honestly, I am a hockey fanatic and I love the sport, but the Colonials are a sideline business for me. Please do not worry. I am fully committed to the team's success. I feel we will pack them in next year, make tons of money, and have fun, but obviously, hockey is not my primary business. It is almost a hobby of sorts. Primarily, I am in the real estate business, therefore, please, cross an apartment off your list. I have many quality rentals available and you will receive a nice discount on the monthly rent."

Kate piped up rather quickly at that news, "Oh, thank you, sir. That takes quite a bit of worry off my mind."

Mr. MacCallum nodded, stared at the nearly empty drink glasses on the table and waved to a server standing guard in a corner of the restaurant. Wherever Gerald MacCallum went, he commanded attention and the silent sentry of a server received the assignment of personal attention to MacCallum and his guests. With a mere gesture and a wave over the glasses, the server nodded and was off to obtain refills. Yet, MacCallum was commanding, but he remained sincere as he mouthed a genuine, "Thank you" to the server for his prompt efforts. Usually, men such as MacCallum only snapped their fingers or banged their fists upon tables in order to demand service.

"Kate, Jim, I also want to tell you that if you want, there are employment positions available with my other companies. Kate, if you would prefer some office work, or you desire to learn property management services, or bookkeeping, I am here to offer you employment in one of my many companies. We will work around your education schedule. Finding reliable and honest people to work for me, is one of my greatest struggles."

Kate's mouth dropped, but before she could even comment or thank Mr. MacCallum, the server dropped the drinks, MacCallum thanked the server again, and off he went once more, dropping life-changing opportunities in the lap of Kate and Jim.

"Jim, I have field work available for you. I own a number of construction companies and I would assign you to work with my field operations managers on some upcoming projects. It is perfect for you. Outside work, all day in the cold, somehow, I know from playing pond hockey in upstate New York you are impervious to cold weather and your keen observation skills will be well suited to be what we call an owner's representative for construction projects. Catch the corner cutting that often goes on with construction projects. My company does not cut corners, however many of the subcontractors these days do so. Something tells me with Jim O'Malley watching there will be very few arguments over cutting corners. We will teach you. Your background in supervision from the markets will help with the management aspects. You are smart. Very smart and honest. That is where we start. Even as a trainee, it pays triple-fold what a food market job will pay you. No matter what you decide to use your education on in the future, this experience will be invaluable. Are you interested?"

"Of course!" Kate jumped in on the conversation now. She looked at Jim, somewhat embarrassed at answering for them both. But Kate Eva O'Leary was no wallflower. With a quick wit mixed with words and a seductive smile that could peel wallpaper off a wall, Kate said, "Jim is too."

As rough and tough as O'Malley was, there was no argument from him, only a fold of his arms across his chest, a smile and a gentle nod of his head. It was obvious that despite her relatively quiet demeanor and thoughtful approach, Kate had a lot of pull.

The servers delivered some salads, everyone at the table began to enjoy them, and while they did so, a period of a few minutes of a quiet silence ensued. Jim O'Malley was deep in thought and not overly hungry. All of this hit at once, and there was more to digest than just some food. He carefully pondered his next words, because the Irish whiskey had taken some effect upon his inhibitions, and he was beginning to feel a little looser right now. Jim pushed his salad aside and his eyes locked upon the tie clasp that held Mr. MacCallum's tie in place. The replica police badge tie clasp. A little small talk continued over the table. The ever-vigilant server delivered, Jim, another Irish whiskey and O'Malley took a sip or too.

Never one to hold back any words, thoughts or emotions, Jim pointed at the tie clasp and gently but thoughtfully asked, "I think we have something in common . . . do we not? I mean, it is most appreciated beyond words what you are doing for Kate and for me, but I think you feel a bind of sorts. Nothing against my hockey abilities, but. . ..”

Gerald MacCallum smiled. His eyes signaled the server for another drink and he pushed his plate aside. Most of the salad was gone. Just a few rims of cucumbers and a dash of lettuce remained here and there. MacCallum did not earn a fortune and create an empire by misreading people. Mr. MacCallum knew that he had hit the jackpot with the signing of Jim O’Malley to his hockey club. The young man did not miss anything.

With a voice that began as forcefully as an early March wind, yet eased into the conversation similar to a late September breeze, he smiled and then explained, “A thought comes to mind,” MacCallum eased back on the throttle, “I have a good friend in this hockey business. He is a friend who in our hockey circles, is in a leadership role with the team that is our archrival and on the ice enemy. His name is Eddie Austeri, and he is the general manager of the Long Island Roosters hockey club out on the island. He is the best hockey man that I have ever met. I tried hard to convince him to come and work for me more times than I can ever count, but he has family ties to the owners of the club and will never leave them. We drink together and talk hockey in a marathon meeting of hockey and fun and old friends at least once a year, and his club will always compete with us for the league championship. I know that Eddie is in New Jersey right now and he is checking out some goaltending prospect that he has his sights on, and no doubt, he will sign and the goalie will be good. Maybe great. Eddie seldom, if ever, misses. A goalie in New Jersey? Really? Only Eddie could find him. C’mon, New Jersey ice hockey goalies, but anyway, you will meet Eddie Austeri someday and be thankful that you did and you will understand what I mean.”

The server dropped the drinks, gathered the plates and MacCallum continued his thoughts, “Anyway, to get to the point, Eddie taught me that great center icemen, see everything, behind, sideways, front and center. Most of all, he looks for centers with great visions and observation skills, and then he looks at the shot, the skating, the stickhandling, and the toughness. Without the great vision, they will be ordinary. You, Jim O'Malley, have great vision and observation skills. That is why you are a great player." He took a deep breath, held a pause and then said, "I was born in Canada, and my father served in the Royal Forces during World War Two. Infantry. Hellfire and brimstone. But he made it home. We are Canadian through and through to our souls. Hence, the love of hockey. Father and son. After the war, his military friend convinced him to relocate to the Rochester, New York area. My father became a police officer. His friend went into real estate and bought up various investment properties and after initial success and some accrued wealth, he branched out into various businesses. My father's friend bought a restaurant and bar and my father, in order to earn extra money, tended bar part-time on Saturday nights for his friend. One Saturday evening, a bunch of thugs held the bar up and my father announced that he was an off-duty police officer, grabbed his gun and shot it out with the thugs. One thug went down, one wounded, but my father took three bullets and he passed from his wounds. I wear this tie tack in his memory. Yes, we are kindred souls. Both of our fathers, killed in the depths of evils and within the grasp of honor."

Kate mumbled, "I am so sorry," and then she placed her arm around Jim. O'Malley slowly shook his head at the story.

"I am too, very sorry," Jim said with his voice weary with the sorrow, "of course, I understand the pain. Let me ask you, please, will it ever go away?"

"Never. It never goes away, Jim," MacCallum answered without hesitation. "I am sorry about your father. From all accounts that I have heard, he was a fine man and an outstanding police officer. Was it from your father where you grew your seeds of hockey from?"

"It was. He grew up next to the big arena in Manhattan, on the outskirts of Hell's Kitchen. Obviously, a huge New York Rovers fan. Ironically, some boyhood friends in the neighborhood were Irish-Canadians whose families settled in New York for work. He played roller and street hockey with them, and then later on after the war, Dad began ice-skating with his police buddies. He fell in love with the game and taught me every nuance about the game. My father actually possessed a great hockey mind, and I was a wide-open student. He would have been a wonderful hockey coach. As far as my hockey training and my life training . . . I owe him everything."

"I understand and please, understand that while I feel your pain and we share a common tragedy in our lives, I am offering you and your lovely, Kate these opportunities because of your abilities, smarts and the needs of my hockey club and my businesses. Not out of sympathy, perhaps, I see something in you both, but this is not a charity. . .."

Jim cut him off in his statement and waved his hands in the air while saying, "We understand and honestly, if we felt otherwise, we would be out of here by now."

Mr. MacCallum smiled, nodded his head and mumbled a few words, "Perfect. That was the answer that I wanted to hear."

The servers delivered the entrees and took away the salad bowls. While they ate, the conversations drifted to a mixture of comfortable small talk, about how wonderful the food, drink and service were, and then sprinkled with intermittent silence.

When they finished eating both entrees and a taste of sweet desserts, Mr. MacCallum ordered some after-dinner cordials to go around the table, with the comment that, "They are good to settle your stomach after large meals."

A few sips into the cordials, MacCallum leaned into his

chair, his face became slightly quizzical and MacCallum asked them, "Kate, Jim, please, if I may, let me ask you . . . are you religious? If you prefer not to answer, please tell me and I will drop the subject. However, this is not so much a personal question because of the relevance to our business. I must tell you that one of the construction projects that we have slated for is to build a very large church. I want to share the details of this project with you because, Jim, you will be heavily involved. It is my dream to build this church, and it is a personal project as much as a business project."

Kate answered first, and Gerald MacCallum made a note of how the two of them were so in tune with each other in their relationship. By the look on Jim's face, MacCallum knew that he wanted Kate to answer the question.

"Jim and I were raised, Irish and very Catholic. Strict rules and constant regulations. Everyone tells us what we are wrong about, and that we are seldom right. Honestly, since we grew together in our lives and our love, we both felt it was too judgmental of us, too overly concerned with rituals rather than our spiritual beliefs. We are wayward now. Even more so since Jim's father is gone and all that has happened since then. Yet, we believe in God and read The Bible, but we are no longer hanging on all of those man-made rules and regulations."

MacCallum smiled and tilted his cordial over and took a very gentle sip. His eyes studied Jim and then Kate and it seemed as if he knew that he had made an outstanding choice on all that he had offered these two young people.

MacCallum explained, "I am a wayward, Anglican–Episcopalian. We share many of the same thoughts about religion." He placed his glass down and fiddled with it, "This vision that I have. It is for a nondenominational church. A church where everyone is welcome and everyone feels comfortable. I am alone now. I lost my wife to cancer many years ago, and I have a sister and her family, with one nephew and a niece. They are involved in the business, but unfortunately, they do not share my religious vision. It is so strong and now, I have this vision to build this church and organization. Now, I feel as if by meeting you both that, God is leading me to where we all need to be. This has been a dream of mine for a very long time and it is now time to make it a reality. I am very excited."

He raised his glass and nodded for Kate and Jim to do the same. With a smile, they toasted.

"To a vision and to the future. I think this is an important day for all of us." When they finished tossing the drinks, MacCallum looked at Jim O'Malley and said, "Enough of the business and religious ends of things. Back to hockey. Now, it is the off-season, but let me tell you about a little hockey opportunity that is coming up for us. We sponsor, along with some other companies, a hockey tournament. I have a small organization . . . formed with some associates of mine . . . these are fellow hockey lovers and Christian fellows. We call our club . . . The Christian Skater's Hockey Association and we have an event coming up in a few weeks. We have signed up many teams and clubs. Jim, I want you to play some center ice for our club. It will be a great warm-up for the season. You can meet some coaches and teammates of the Colonials and I hope to have Davis and Johnston involved too. How does that sound? Let's start this all off with a bang."

In a few short weeks, the words of Mr. Gerald MacCallum would prove to be quite prophetic. In fact, "Starting off with a bang," would actually prove to be a huge understatement.

Chapter Ten

A Goalie Named Henson

Rose walked into my office and she seemed a bit startled by the sight. While no one would certainly classify me as the world's neatest person, I usually kept things in a reasonably neat and orderly fashion. At the moment, my office had fallen in a state of disorderly confusion.

I had set up an easel in the center of the office, and on the mounted board of the easel were many pieces of papers containing Jim O'Malley's handwritten notes. On the floor were more papers, and then on my desk, and on the counter of the wet-bar, were some more.

"Okay," Rose said with a long pause while she scanned my haphazard organizational attempts, "I see that you have some type of system going on here. Paul, I am not sure what it is, but perhaps, I am using the word system, in a rather overzealous manner."

Admittedly, the room was a bloody mess.

I stood with a stupid look on my face, my hands on my hips in front of the easel and pointed at the board while trying to provide an explanation for the system, "Well, these are what are left of Jim's notes. I have gone through the other pages and used them up. Those are spent notes that are in the folder on my desk. I have arranged the remaining pages chronologically. Right now, the ones on the easel are next in line for plugging into the storyline, and the ones on the desk are after that and the ones over there on the wet-bar, make no sense whatsoever. This is all becoming a bit confusing and I think that I might need just a bit of your help with the next parts, dear Rose. In addition, for some notes that make no sense, well, I might need to ad-lib some of those parts. I think these next parts are where I allow O'Malley's own voice to tell most of the story."

I looked up to gauge my wife's reaction and said, "You know, take your suggestion for telling his story with his own words."

Rose did not seem optimistic that my system had any semblance of order or functionality. She screwed her gorgeous face up as if it were a corkscrew uncorking cheap wine and shook her head while saying, "Okay, well, first, I think that I need a glass of wine. Maybe, two glasses."

As usual, my wife offered good advice and a workable solution to this dilemma.

In agreement with her brilliance and impeccably timed suggestion, I nodded my head and mumbled, "Scotch."

I was certainly glad to hear that Mr. MacCallum had worked out a deal with Teddy Davis and with Royal Johnston to play for the New York Colonials. We had developed quite a bit of chemistry together after one season in Albany, and I felt that we were a formidable line together. I had a feeling that luring Teddy over to the Colonials and moving downstate was going to be a simple task. Teddy was a single man, his good looks and single status made Teddy a bit of a lure for the eyes of the young women, and his job as a car mechanic allowed Teddy to find work rather easily no matter the location. Royal Johnston was a different story. He had married only a year or so earlier and his wife was expecting their first child. Royal was originally from Ontario Province in Canada and his family remained north of the border, so I always thought that a move farther south would only increase the separation more. I was not sure, but I thought his wife was from New York, and perhaps, the move worked out well for her and that made the decision easier. Royal worked full time in the off-season, and part-time here and there, during the hockey season as a salesman for janitorial and cleaning products, therefore, it seemed as if he would be able to move his sales territory and work would not be an issue. Regardless, we found our line intact and together once again, and that made the three of us feel as if we could set the Metropolitan Hockey League on fire. Our move went smoothly, although the manager of the market made some generous offers to try to keep us in Albany. He understood that the working world was only a small piece of the puzzle for Kate and me, and that the hockey world was the ultimate goal. No job could compete with hockey for the heart of James T. O'Malley. I was more determined to be a success in ice hockey now, more than any other time in my life.

Mr. MacCallum set us up with a beautiful apartment in a tidy complex just over the New York border in northern New Jersey. Kate and I had our choice of a number of properties on either side of the border, but Kate loved this particular apartment. The fact that the new church project was located in New Jersey, and the main offices of Mr. MacCallum's company were in Rockland County and only a few minutes away, made the choice rather easy. Teddy and Royal chose apartments in Rockland County and that worked out quite well for their individual needs.

Kate and I began our new jobs, we settled into our new place and our lives, and Teddy, Royal, and I took to the ice to skate and practice as much as our schedules allowed. Ice time was easy to find and schedule when Mr. MacCallum was your boss! I found out in a very short order, Mr. MacCallum not only owned the Colonials, but he owned the arena we played in and practiced in too. Mr.

MacCallum was a very special man and the more that I grew to know him, the more that I liked him and the more that I realized what a great stroke of fortune it was for us to meet at this time in our lives.

In my heart, I knew it was time to make the most important move and decision of the last few weeks within this whirlwind of events that recently enveloped our lives. I always vowed and promised that when I felt as if we settled in our lives and I had a clear direction that I would propose to Kate and I intended to keep that promise. With the extra money that I received from a payout of unused vacation time, along with some upfront bonus money from my contract signing with the Colonials, I shopped for an engagement ring in a local jewelry store close to the office. A store that Mr. MacCallum recommended to me. It was easy to see that our new boss knew everyone and had business ties throughout the area. When I mentioned to the store owner that Gerald MacCallum sent me and that I worked for him in his business, as well as, I was the new starting center iceman for the Colonials . . . I received a major discount on a gorgeous ring! A ring that I never would have been able to afford only a few short weeks earlier.

On the first Friday evening that we settled into our new place and I had procured the ring, I took Kate out to an exclusive and very expensive local restaurant that Mr. MacCallum had suggested to us. Of course, this was on the pretense of celebrating our new life and our change in fortunes. That was a smokescreen for my actual intentions. Looking back on the evening now, I think that Mr. MacCallum must have made a few phone calls and paved the way for a special evening for us. It all came together in a storybook sort of manner. We had a private dining nook, with lowlights, low music and the best of everything. We spent too much money on a fine meal, some extra glasses of Irish whiskey and soda waters, and some fine desserts.

Afterwards, in the quiet flicker of candlelight on our table, I knelt down on one knee, displayed the ring and asked the gorgeous, rare, and precious, Kate Eva O'Leary to marry me. With a few flickers of my heartbeat, she accepted. I slipped the ring upon her slender finger and the patrons, workers, and onlookers cheered and clapped. The manager bought everyone a round of drinks to join in our joy and when we returned home to our new apartment, the celebration became quite intense! We set a wedding date of Labor Day weekend of that year, a date that was just before the hockey season began and a date that would work for our families, friends, and everyone else that we planned to invite. And, with that glorious event, the countdown to our marriage began!

The tournament that Mr. MacCallum and some of his hockey associates had organized seemed as if it was the perfect event to hone our skills with during the off-season. Royal, Teddy, and I all joined up with the Christian Skater's Hockey Association and after a few practices and some routine organization, we had a solid little hockey club to enter the tournament with. The second line was moderately skilled and after that, there was a huge drop-off in talent level, but our first line defense was solid and the goaltender was adequate. The hockey club consisted of players from all over New York, New Jersey and some from Connecticut, with even a few Vermont players. All the players seemed to have some knowledge of, or attachment to, a large Christian organization of nondenominational churches within the Tri-state and beyond areas. The association also sponsored figure skating instruction and events, youth hockey, skating lessons, as well as other skating activities, with the hockey club being only one activity of the organization.

Our coach, a man named Jeremy Baldwin, who was actually a pastor at one of the churches within the organization, was an experienced hockey coach, having played some college hockey as well as some semi-pro hockey as a player and from all appearances; he was a solid hockey mind. His quick organization of the team impressed me. I was also impressed by the level of competition and the potential to win some prize money too. I could use a few extra dollars to pay off some recently accumulated bills related to our move and our engagement!

Of course, the main objective of the event was to hone our skills and Royal, Teddy, and I while having some fun by skating and playing with this organization, mostly desired to work together in our new setting and continue the success we had as a first line in Albany with our new team downstate.

Ironically, the tournament's opening rounds took place in an arena in New Jersey. A large rink called Ice Land, set on the outskirts of a large city, called Paterson. The tournament would move successive rounds and the final games, first, to my new home rink in Rockland County, New York, and then the final games with the championship game played in a rink in Westchester County, New York. I never asked, but it seemed as if Mr. MacCallum fronted quite a bit of the sponsorship for the tournament. The heavy promotion of the CSHA team as the flagship team for the tournament seemed to be part of a mission to attract attention to the nondenominational churches associated with the club. In my mind, even with this Christian tag attached to our team, I was not holding back or refining my style of play. Never. James T. O'Malley plays every game to win. I hoped that I did not dishonor the name of the club, but I am quite sure that Gerald MacCallum knew what I would bring to the game. It was not going to be a bouquet of flowers for the church altar and a book of hymns for a sing-a-long. Competition was competition, and hockey was hockey. This tournament had my blood stirred up and my body and mind chomping for action. It had been quite a long time since I hit the ice for an actual game and practice was wonderful, but I easily got tired of endless skating and shooting drills. It was time for some banging and some action. Little did I know that is exactly what I was about to face.

The first round of the tournament was easy, we quickly disposed of a team from neighboring Westchester County, a team that we beat up physically and mentally and when the score landed at six to zip at the beginning of the second period, Coach Baldwin pulled the first line and rested us. I think it was out of respect for the other team as well as some type of semblance of honor to the Christian stigma attached to our team's name. Our hockey club had the best of everything. It seemed as if everything associated with Mr. Gerald MacCallum had the best label attached to it. Our uniforms were striking, with a white background and a gleaming gold cross emblazoned on the front of the sweater, and underneath the cross, a superimposed and almost three-dimensional, "CSHA" proudly displayed our club's name. A large contingent of supporters traveled down from Albany to take in the tournament play. Our playing time in Albany accumulated a large group of rabid hockey fans and despite being sad about our leaving their team; they expressed their best wishes for my continued success as well as the success of my line mates. While we were grateful for the support and honored to be the focus of their attention, their behavior in the stands often was raucous and wild. Albany was a hockey city and, in all honesty, I am quite sure that my rough and tumble style of play caused the fanbase to be a bit on the wild side too.

It did not seem as if the CSHA had "Christian-like" fans rooting for them.

Fateful moments in your life often arrive as if they are silent sentries. They creep up on you, grab you by the soul, and infiltrate your mind. I never expected that a life-changing moment would arrive in my mind during this hockey tournament. Regardless, in my heart and in my mind and in looking back on the game, I have no shame in saying that the second game of the tournament changed my hockey life. Perhaps it changed my entire life. I cannot say, but a raw assumption would be that it did and heartfelt thoughts would say there were no questions and no doubts whatsoever that it did.

Part of a hockey game is setting the tone during the pregame warm-up skate. Even more so, for a game when you are facing an opponent that you never faced before. To me, watching the pregame skate was very important. That is where I spent my pregame time, assessing the skills of the opposition's shooters and most of all, for me, James T. O'Malley, where I determined the size, toughness and strengths of the defensemen and the skills and weaknesses of the opposing goaltender. It is during this critical period that you can assess the team and decide if your own pregame skate should emphasize the team's skills or toughness. Hockey is a war on ice and despite the haphazard nature of the game to the novice watchers of the game, hockey is a game of strategy. You must possess the puck in the opposition zone longer than your opponent does, throw everything that you can in the direction of the defensemen and the goaltender and when you do, you stand a better chance of winning the game. Part of my strategy is intimidation, and honestly, elements of brutality. If I intimidate an opponent by my actions and abilities, then I stand a better chance of capturing the puck from that player. I probe for the soft spots and weak players and then O'Malley preys upon their weakness. When I find the stronger players, then my strategy is to wear them down, to cause them to lose their cool, to force them into penalties and then strike hard when they commit them.

For the second round of the tournament, we drew a team from the New Jersey shoreline. A team, from

Monmouth County, New Jersey and a team with the name of the Red Jersey Devils. During the pregame warm-ups, we watched them carefully. My initial assessment, along with Royal and Teddy, was that this was just a quickly thrown together hockey club of chumps. Just a bunch of local hockey players entering the tournament for a bit of fun, exercise and adventure with little hope of capturing a trophy, or any prize money. The poor chumps wore poorly made hockey sweaters stenciled with some wild logo of a devil holding a hockey stick. The sad-sack group of players had their names and numbers scrawled on the back of their hockey sweaters with black marker pens. Needless to say, it looked quite amateurish and silly. I thought how this was somewhat ironic that the Christians were now facing off against the Jersey Red Devils, even when I knew the Devil reference is to the folklore creature that supposedly inhabits the Pine Barrens of New Jersey.

Devil inspired or not, this bunch was not very frightening and it looked as if they could not dent a cream puff sitting on a plate in the hot sun. Aside from one shifty, speedy, and very skilled skater, a player wearing the number "18" and the name CANTRELLI on his sweater, the rest of the team seemed to be below average skaters and the skill level was low and rather weak.

Rather weak, until I watched the goaltender hit the ice, along with a large and solidly built defenseman. The defenseman had a number "35" scratched on his jersey along with the name, REDMOND JR. on the back. The goalie wore "27" with HENSON on the back, which was for me a classic pairing of names for hockey players. Why? I was not quite sure, but my father's words of so long ago echoed into my mind. My father was always so close to my heart and soul and I heard his voice loud and clear between skates crunching and cutting new ice and the slap of sticks and pucks.

"The Iron league and downstate, huh? Kick ass leagues.

Might run into big city players and some New Jersey players. Hold on to your ass with them. Tough as Hell. Never underestimate those Jersey guys."

Something told me that Dad was correct, and it was finally time to grab my ass, adjust my jock strap, and hold on tightly.

The goaltender was huge. He had to be at least, six feet five or so, and even wearing a goalie's chest protector and shoulder pads, you could tell that his arm and chest muscles were powerful and solid. I had never seen such a large and imposing goalie. His skating was a thing of beauty, upright, confident and powerful. It was as if he was walking down a city street. He skated backward as easily as he skated forward. He wore a smile a mile wide, and his eyes were quick, small, and observant. His eyes told the power of his soul. For now, number twenty-seven wore his mask upright, tucked neatly on the top of his head. He had long blonde hair with hints of red in it, and he wore a full beard and facial hair. Honestly, the goalie looked more as if he was a hippie, and not as if he was an ice hockey goalie. But my father's words along with the gnawing in my soul about him told me otherwise. This was an athlete's body, and this was a champion's skill level.

I tried not to stare as I glided on my side of the ice and we made endless circles around the zones, but it was difficult not to take my eyes off of the two of them. Neither the goalie nor the defenseman noticed me while I skated around and I tried rather unsuccessfully to hold back a sneer while watching the two of them. The goalie glided effortlessly around the ice in his pregame skate, and the defenseman skated alongside the goalie. The defenseman was not as polished a skater as the goalie was, but his powerful strides and hunched style of skating told me that he generated strong and powerful strides with his massive leg muscles. Number thirty-five smiled and laughed during their discussion and his ruggedly handsome, yet unlike his pal's, clean-shaven face, combined with longish blonde hair that hung mop-like on his head to make the defenseman look as if he was a combination of a classic New Jersey tough-guy mixed with a Hollywood movie star. These two players were the best of friends. They were obviously very close and I made careful note of that fact. This meant they knew each other very well on the ice. Set plays, intuitive angles, all aspects of the game that experience can bring and give you an edge. A skilled defenseman working alongside an experienced goalie where the defenseman knows a goaltender's individual save motions, where he sticks the puck, how he clears the crease after rebounds, are usually a difficult combination to beat. Especially so when the two of them looked as if they were the sides of mountains.

When we broke into the pregame shoot, Royal, Teddy, and I caught glimpses of the Devils warming up their goalie. Even chumps such as the rest of the Jersey Red Devils were . . . knew the golden rule that you never tried to make your goalie look weak or bad in the net while the other team was conducting a scouting mission. It is a fine line, because you need to show off some firepower with shots and skills to impose the other team, but you do not purposely show up your starting goalie or unlock secrets of where to score on him. Therefore, the back-up goalie usually becomes the whipping post. However, with the Jersey Red Devils that was not a possibility. Number twenty-seven was the only goalie dressed. I made careful note of that fact. Knock out twenty-seven became mission number one in my mind.

As expected, number thirty-five and the speedy number eighteen were the only two players who could shoot and stickhandle the puck well. Number thirty-five's slap shots and wrist shots were heavy cannonballs launched in the direction of his goaltending pal. The goalie was the real deal, and I heard Royal whistle at a save as his huge frame stretched out to capture a blazing slapper that number thirty-five unleashed. The goalie gracefully and easily snatched it out of the air as if he was picking cherries off a low-hanging branch and then spun on his skates, set his blades, glided out and stood up to face the next shot. Despite his huge size, he was quicker than a cat, more confident in his moves than a good-looking gal on a barstool on a Saturday evening was, and his feet and stick work remained a fluid display of beauty. Above all, it was his glove hand where he excelled. His glove could capture a mosquito flying by the net.

I had never seen a goalie move like this goalie could move, and honestly, I never saw a better goalie, and when I heard Teddy mumble a low murmur of, "Damn," after we watched another one of his glorious saves, I added, "Yeah, we are in trouble, men. This twenty-seven is the real deal and number thirty-five is a bull on skates with legs like tree trunks. Time to buckle up and take it straight to them as hard and as rough as we can. Let's come out of the gate like Hellfire and Brimstone. After all, they are the Devils and we are the Christians. We need to suck it up and work an angle on this one. I have a plan. Let's move me to the right-wing and Royal to center. I think it might work if I can shoot to this goalie's short side and you both try to pick off rebounds or work deflections. Royal is better than I am when working close to the net in the low slot."

"Is that the plan, O'Malley?" Teddy asked me.

I nodded and tapped my stick on the ice to call for a puck, and after receiving a puck in a crisp and tight pass; I unleashed a wrist shot at our goalie.

After the shot beat our goalie's glove and rang the net's bell, I said, "Looking at that goalie and his defensive pal, I kinda think we do not have any other choice. Outside shots are not beating this number twenty-seven."

I approached our coach with my idea of switching to the right-wing position and he agreed. Royal was a skilled face-off man, and we all knew that this tournament was as good a time as any to experiment with our play and tinker with some new ideas.

When the puck dropped, I decided that I had to set the tone right away, and I nailed the Devil player next to me with a hard slash of lumber. Intimidation leads to submissiveness in most of these pussy hockey players. In my mind, I justified the slash because it fell under the game plan and I was simply setting the tone of intimidation, yet in my heart, I knew it was so much more. My anger rose in my soul and it never kept dormant and this game was like all the others before it. A way to hide, a way to overcome the pain of my life, a means to justify my existence.

Sad but true.

I looked up at the referee, who clearly saw the slash, but I was going to get away with it. No whistle and no arm in the air. The Devil player fell down hard upon the ice. Royal looked over and captured the puck, then broke toward the attacking zone. Royal knew that I was following the game plan and bringing some lumber hard and fast. I knew that the referee was a referee that I had seen in some of the upstate circles, and he must have put his whistle in his pocket for us.

I heard the big number thirty-five call for a penalty and then he yelled, "Okay, this is bullshit! Homer refs!" in a voice laced with disgust.

Number thirty-five was correct.

My possessed mind caused my mouth to shout out, "Tough luck, pal!" and with those words echoing above the ice, Royal tossed a perfect pass onto my blade, I handled the puck and crossed the neutral zone and then the blue line.

Within seconds of the opening drop of the puck to begin the game, we had a three on one breakaway on the Devil's goal. For us, it was the perfect opening scenario except for the fact that number twenty-seven stood in the net.

Only number thirty-five was back on defense and I worked the puck down into the high slot, with Teddy scooting over on the left wing and with Royal moving in on the high slot. My previous assessments and observations of the goalie and the defenseman being friends and having years of experience playing together were correct. The big defenseman slowly glided backwards on his skates, called out some code word and whistled a call of some sort. The goalie responded by gliding farther out of his crease and cutting down the angles and I kept my head up, worked the puck into the zone deeper, and watched them move into some set type of formation they must use for three-on-one-breakaways. No other Devil players were quick enough skaters to back check so we could easily set our own play. After a hard whistle, the big defenseman broke his backwards glide and instantly, he made two powerful moves and forced Teddy wide and then rolled over Teddy like a truck. Teddy slammed into the boards, lost his stick and his skate edge and hit the ice hard. Thirty-five was a beast. Technically, it was interference, but the official still kept his whistle silent for now and I guess the no call evened the score for my slash. Thirty-five was a smart player. He knew that the referee owed him one and he took the gamble and won.

Now, looking over the ice, I made a note of how our offensive world opened up with me playing right wing and I liked the strategy and the way my line mates responded. Perhaps, right wing was my new home.

Quickly deciding that their strategy was for the big defenseman to neutralize the third player and allow the goalie to take his chances with the shooter and a rebound, I faked a pass to Royal in the slot and ripped a hard slap shot that rocketed toward the top shelf of the glove side of the goalie. I was looking for a mishandled puck to cause a rebound that Royal could pounce on, but it turned out to be a mistake. Actually, it was a poor shot selection, because

I had just watched how good this goalie was on his glove side and made careful mental notes of it too. No doubt, it was a big mistake, and a wasted opportunity, as number twenty-seven quickly snatched it out of the air with ease and held it for a face-off. No rebounds and no effort on his part. This goalie was smooth as peanut butter and as comfortable on the ice as a penguin.

Time to storm the net and kick in more intimidation. Probe for the weak spots. Goat thirty-five into a penalty and force a power play. The goalie held the puck in his glove hand and I scooted in just as the linesman blew the whistle to stop play and I slashed repeatedly at his catching glove in a futile effort to dislodge the puck. The big goalie stood up tall and he towered over me. With one effortless extension of his arm, he pushed me backwards and please, believe me, his arm strength was remarkable. This was a powerful and finely tuned athlete. I could see his eyes burning under his mask. Teddy recovered from his steam rolling. He moved into the melee, and Royal did too. This was going to get ugly very quickly, but I had established the tone of the game and now we had no choice but to perpetuate the same tone.

The goalie screamed, "Okay, okay, play the whistle, Mr. Slashy! Easy now!"

The goalie spoke with a hard New Jersey accent. His eyes burned with fury and intensity and once more, my father's words of wisdom echoed in my head. We all pushed, shoved, and exchanged words and suddenly, number thirty-five arrived on the scene. I thought about how this hockey player could blow a hole in the Grand Canyon. He crashed into the pile like a freight train and I flew backwards and hit the ice harder than I ever fell before in my young life. Forget Fredrick Spieth, forget Barclay Millhouse, forget all the other bums that I had fought with and had hit me. They were cupcakes compared to this bruiser because this young man carried principle with his power. Great power combined with an outstanding principle is a difficult force to overcome. All the teeth in my head rattled and despite the pain, I quickly jumped to my skates and confronted this powerful monster wearing number thirty-five. He yelled at me and I yelled right back. In my heart, I already knew that he would not stand down and that intimidation was not going to be a valid plan. Number thirty-five would not run and hide from a rabid grizzly bear. We squared off, and I slashed at him with my stick while the on-ice officials tried hard to break it all up. I needed to get this big lug off the ice and even if I sat in the penalty box, perhaps, the second line and Royal and Teddy could put pressure on this goalie without his best defender and protector working the ice in front of the goal.

Perhaps, God, luck, or both would be with us and we could actually score on him too. . ..

At this point, the referee had enough of us, threw up his arm, and called out two-minute minor penalties to both of us. The crowd was going crazy and the noise inside the rink was deafening. The Albany contingent of fans screamed my name and they were becoming south of raucous and within a few seconds of the opening puck drop, this game turned into a melee.

War on ice.

While I sat in the penalty box and occasionally jawed at number thirty-five sitting a few feet away from me, I carefully studied number twenty-seven in the net. After a short shift for the second line, and after the big goalie easily turned away a few quality shots on goal from the second line, our coach skipped over the third line. Our coach sensed the need to press the net and to take advantage of every precious second that the big defenseman sat in the penalty box, and he sent Royal and Teddy out along with a second line player to take my spot on the right-wing side. For the remainder of the four-on-four situation, I watched in awe as the makeshift line buzzed the net and peppered the goalie with shots. Without Redmond Junior on the ice, the goalie was fresh meat and Royal and Teddy must have had ten chances apiece to score. Only the Devil player, named Cantrelli, seemed as if he could skate with us. The rest of the Devils were skating in mud. Cantrelli did what he could out there to assist the goalie and hold off the waves of the attacks, but even though he was a nifty skater, the poor guy was exhausted. The open ice, four-on-four play must have seemed as if it was a million years long to the goalie and Cantrelli. Even though this amazing number twenty-seven was the opposition, it was hard not to give this superb goalie his due and my intense admiration. Even the primarily pro-CSHA crowd and our rabid fan club quieted and watched in relative silence as they realized they were witnessing something very spectacular. It was amazing athleticism as his big body remained under perfect control as he guarded the net from every angle, sweeping the puck away as easily as a person waves a fly off their corn on the cob at a summer picnic. Split saves, stick saves, glove and leg pad kick saves. He crept out to cut angles, pointed out defenses and even cleared the zone by himself a number of times.

It was the most incredible display of goaltending that I had ever seen. In fact, it might have been the most incredible display of athleticism in any sport that I have ever seen. Forget just hockey or goaltending.

While I sat there watching the final seconds of the penalty tick off the clock, I still jawed with number thirty-five sitting next to me. He screamed encouragement at every save his friend made in the net and his pride rose upon his face quicker than a thermometer does on a July afternoon. I thought how these two must be very close, like brothers, and they must have been playing together forever. Maybe street hockey, roller hockey and now, on the ice. Teamwork and teammates. Truly, an unbeatable combination.

Redmond Junior enthusiastically thumped the boards of the penalty box with his hockey stick. And then, he glanced over at me. He must have read the admiration in my eyes because with a grin as wide as the Pacific Ocean, Redmond Junior said, "Never seen the likes of twenty-seven before, eh, tough guy? I ain't afraid of your tough guy bullshit and neither is twenty-seven. In our old neighborhood here in Jersey, you'd be just 'a nudder one of countless other smart asses that we'd roll over. Seen a million of ya. I will roll your ass and twenty-seven will shut the door. Good luck, jerk! You just met the greatest goalie ever to play this game. Mark my friggin' words! He will be in the big time someday. Big. Time."

I glared at him and said, "Sure he will make it to the big time, just like a million other wannabees!" I said with a sneer, while hiding the fact that I knew if any goalie from America had a chance to make the big league, this guy might head the list. There was just no way that I would allow him to know that I agreed with his statement.

The big defenseman smiled and shook his head and answered me with a shout, while he was waiting to race back out on the ice, "Big time! Watch and see and hold on to ya ass, O'Malley. Otherwise, ya might lose it out there!"

Deep down there might have been a ton of truth in his brave words. I took no exception to his defense. In fact, I admired him for them. No exception . . . except for the statement that he had encountered a million guys like me. In my opinion, there was only one, James T. O'Malley, and I set my heart and mind to prove it too.

While preparing to escape from my two minutes of confinement, I felt that uncontrollable anger rising up inside of me once again. The anger did not give me pride, nor did it give me shame. Instead, it was a mission. A mission to win. A mission to avenge all my pain by achieving victory in a game where I failed in life. To stand for the honor of my father and for the name scrawled upon the back of my hockey sweater. Other than my beloved Kate, all that I had left was hockey. It was where I fit in. If I was not in Kate's arms, I had to be here on the ice. Winning, scoring, hiding from my past, and out-skating, the pain. Even though I had great admiration for this incredible goalie and his courageous and powerful friend, they now stood in my way. They were now the enemy, and I had to take them out. Nothing personal, but the anger would not allow James T. O'Malley to play any other way. The anger overcame every other emotion.

Right, wrong, or indifferent.

The off-ice official watched the clock. He opened the door, and I shot out of my confinement as if I was off to the moon in a rocket ship. Number thirty-five was behind me, but he was not an overly fast skater. The puck had wobbled into the neutral zone and one of our defensemen had picked it up and pushed it over to Royal. Royal and Teddy quickly joined me in a rush and with my skates cutting hard and deep, and with the ice flying away from my blades in little chips, I yelled and tapped my blade on the ice while pleading for a pass. Number thirty-five raced to the front of the net and screamed some more code words to the goalie. The goalie pointed his stick and came out to cut off the angle. I could see the sweat dripping off the end of his mask like a river flowing from his face. Royal hit me with a neat pass just as I crossed the blue line, and I saw the big body of the defenseman move to face my attack.

I could just see the goalie's mask peeking out from beneath Redmond Junior's arm and when the goalie screamed, "Screen," I knew that it was the mistake that I had been waiting for. Sorry, twenty-seven, but all is fair in love, war, and slap shots to the head. I let loose a cannonball aimed directly at that mask. The puck hit dead on in his mask and I saw his head snap back and he collapsed in the crease. Royal, Teddy, and I moved in for the rebound, but remarkably, in another amazing display of ability and immense courage, while twenty-seven fell backwards, he managed to capture the rebound off his mask, and glove the puck, and hold it for a whistle. Despite my awe at his save, I stood over him as he gathered his head and perhaps his wits and teeth and I spewed some type of wretched nonsense at him, still trying my best to rile him out of his game. The big defenseman pushed me away, and I backed off as the linesman and number thirty-five checked on the goalie. The goaltender rolled around in his crease, stood up on his skates, flipped his mask off his face and it was then that I could see a cut on his forehead. A trickle of blood rolled down his face and his friend checked on his condition. With a glare in his eye, I saw number twenty-seven wipe the river of sweat from his long mop of hair and his beard. Blood trickled all over his face now, and I knew that fate had brought us together to fight for whatever it was that our souls sought. To fight not only on the ice but to fight for our places in this weary world. Whatever pain number twenty-seven harbored, it matched mine in some strange sort of manner. No one in their right mind would stand in front of a puck hurtled at their head, unless they sought some type of roundabout redemption.

I had met my match. This was a warrior. A man of intense courage and profound honor. His friend stood with him and together they were going to stand up to us with everything they had. In my heart, I knew that these two always stood together.

Forever.

The goalie's eyes never left mine. He flipped the puck to the linesman, and the linesman asked, "Are you good to go, goalie?"

With that deep glare and burn still locked in his eyes, number twenty-seven said, "I am fine. Let's go." He flipped his goalie mask back down over his face, but underneath it, his eyes still held the burn.

And go at it, we did.

I never exhausted my physical strength for so long and as hard as I did in that tournament game. In the third period, the speedy player named Cantrelli worked some type of nifty set up by the goalie and his friend and they scored a goal on us. After the goal, we threw it all at them and they withstood it all. It was an amazing hockey game, and we all left all of our souls out there on the ice. Every ounce of what we all had to give.

I learned a great lesson in that game. A lesson that I held deep inside of me and when the buzzer sounded and we lost in a one to zero shut out, I now knew that it takes more than emotions, brawn, and intimidation to be a winner. It takes smarts, it takes teamwork and most of all and above all . . . it takes a commitment to your teammates and to yourself. I made a vow to work as hard as I could to do better.

We lined up for the traditional ice hockey handshake and when I reached the goalie and his friend, I warmly thanked them for the game, for the honor of playing them, and wished them all the luck in the world. They both were very cordial to me.

Redmond Junior shook my hand and said, "I was wrong when I said that twenty-seven and I have seen a million players and guys like ya, O'Malley. Dead wrong. Ya one of a kind and one helluva player and a tough guy. It was madness out there, but ya a great player. I have tons of respect for you."

I thanked him, told the big guy that he was a great player too and that I very much appreciated his kind words. Henson, the amazing goalie, listened in and he agreed with his friend's words and conveyed the same thoughts to me. Henson, despite the sweat, welts and blood, was strikingly handsome, and very well spoken, and his eyes glowed much differently than they did during the game. They glowed with warmth and honor. Both players seemed surprised at how cordial that I was, considering the incredible battle that we just conducted. But for me, ice hockey is simply a microcosm of life. Never give up, never stop fighting and always pick yourself up off the ice when it knocks you flat on your ass. Today, it knocked me on my ass, but James T. O'Malley always gets back up. In my heart, I felt some honor and tons of respect for having lost to such great combatants and for learning so much, but I also knew that we would all meet again somewhere, somehow, in the future. It just had to be so. Fate would not allow any deviations. And when we meet, they better be ready for it.

Our team won the tournament championship, but I always felt as if the win was without merit or without honor. Our only loss was to the Red Jersey Devils, but they lost number twenty-seven and number thirty-five and that explained why they went on to lose their next games and as a result, they did not qualify for the final rounds of the tournament. The goalie and the big defenseman left the hockey club after our game, and in a way, I felt disappointment in them at having done so. While I understood their motives might have been just to play a game or two and earn some pocket money and their teammates were not up to par, I wished we could have met in a championship battle. Still, I understood. The goalie and the defenseman most likely had full-time jobs, responsibilities and their hockey futures to play out, and it was not worth risking a serious injury or getting beat up for a tournament game. Too much talent at risk there. Still, I longed for a rematch. At that juncture, there was no way for me to know that our paths would cross again and that fate would marry us together forever.

A few short months later, I heard through the hockey grapevine that the big defenseman did end up severely injured and he retired from serious play. I felt sorry for the loss to hockey of such a grand talent, but the goalie played on, and the name of Henson and his number twenty-seven, became a huge part of my hockey life and in fact, all of my life. Who would have known that, years later, the three of us would join up in life once again and together we fought life's battles as a team?

A team full of honor, respect, teamwork, and commitment. Just as we all shared on that ice together in that game of so long ago. Life's lessons arrive to your soul on gentle breezes or they arrive captured within roaring winds of turbulence, but they always arrive.

Here I am—the detailer and narrator of these events of so long ago, and the memories and emotions of that game still are fresh in my mind. Even so many years later, I still recall, climbing into my bed that night after that fateful hockey game, my body full of aches and soreness and just before sleep overcame my weary body and mind, I managed to whisper, "Yes, twenty-seven, we will meet again soon. I would not want it to be any other way and I know that you feel the same way too."

The long-awaited wedding of Kate Eva O'Leary and James Thomas O'Malley arrived quickly. As long as the summer tends to be, with dry, hot, and steamy days and sultry, sweaty nights, the wane of the season can also creep on you as if it is a wind announcing the arrival of a thunderstorm. Before you blink, turn and run for cover, you are drenched and the windy prelude was a warning that you missed or you neglected to heed. The wedding took place on the Saturday of Labor Day weekend. It was a dry day and a day when the daybreak arrived so much later than it did just a few weeks earlier in August, and the sunsets arrived so much earlier. A day, when the zinnias in the churchyard garden bloomed with less color and with blooms that had brown edges on them, and the marigolds tilted and fought to maintain their warning odors amongst their own fading glory. Yet, as summer waned and a flower's spent glory gave way to hints of the brilliance of autumn, in the church, love bloomed anew. The wedding ceremony took place in the nondenominational church that had now become their new home. A church, where Kate and James found their new Gospel and their comfort with religion. A place where rules, regulations, and strict orders did not exist, a church where they loved God and praised their love and their lives without restrictions and stringent orders. Pastor (And part-time hockey coach) Jeremy Baldwin married them in a simple ceremony. Detective Lyle Odell served as best man and Teddy Davis was an usher, along with Royal Johnston. Detective Odell looked as if he was a fish out of water, wearing a fancy tuxedo and perfectly combed and cut hair in lieu of his usual rumpled look. Kate had two bridesmaids. One was Mr. MacCallum's niece, who Kate had struck up a friendship with and the other was a cousin of hers from upstate. Her new best friend, a young woman that Kate worked with in her new office position, Alexandria McDermott, was the maid of honor.

In the audience, Sergeant William Lawson proudly sat in his police officer's dress uniform and wished with all of his heart that his friend and long-time partner could be here to witness this great day. In his heart, he knew that somehow, he was there. He could feel him there. Mrs. O'Malley sat and wept as the groom's mothers tended to do, and Father Callahan patted her hand, while comforting her as he always did. In his heart, the old priest harbored no resentment that this was not a Catholic wedding; he recently conceded that wherever Kate and James landed in their lives was a good place for them. A place away from their pain of the past, a place where their life could begin anew, and their love could fill the world. On the bride's side, Mr. O'Leary brooded over the loss of his little girl and a mother beamed at her daughter's beauty.

O'Malley would like to say he patched up the relationship with his mother on this glorious day and perhaps he did so. Deep inside, the pain would never go away, but a son and his mother have a bond that transcends time, and anguish, and their love is a gift from God and meant to overcome all strife.

A glorious reception followed at an exclusive club, with a talented band playing all types of music, dancing and merriment, fine drink and food, endless wine and of course, the best in Irish whiskey and Scotch. All bought and paid for with money thrown in the till by Mr. MacCallum, who beamed the entire day as if it was his own son who had married today. Perhaps that is what James Thomas O'Malley had become to Mr. Gerald MacCallum and in retrospect; there certainly was nothing wrong with that fact.

The day and celebration, as weddings always do, ended all too quickly, but the honeymoon began. Off the newlyweds went to a small cottage in a lake community in Vermont, on a resort property owned by Mr. MacCallum. It was a quiet and peaceful place for a honeymoon, with glorious New England beauty all around them and not too much to do.

It did not matter, and they did not care . . . they seldom left the cabin. Their love filled the world and their joy echoed in the night and continued to ride on the sunbeams of the daybreak.

And for a few glorious days, the pain of the past was far behind all of them and James Thomas O'Malley's normally restless soul rested in the love and arms of his enchanting wife.

For this world and for them . . . that was a good thing.

Chapter Eleven

Time to Even the Score

Rose was amazing in so many ways. Her beauty was beyond words, her deep intelligence matched her beauty, but most of all, my wife had the uncanny ability to see inside of my soul. Rose knew that these past few days of writing mayhem and intense creativity were more than just words on a page and a release for me. She knew that it was to share the details of the life of an extraordinary man. To tell a story that in my heart, I felt as if it required sharing, but also to honor a dear friend and a very special person in my life. In Harry's life, and in my wife's life too. A special person to this world.

She had assisted me with invaluable guidance while we sorted out the notes and the maze of papers that James Thomas O'Malley had composed. Papers, which contained a roadmap of his life and insight into his heart. The notes were all raw in composition, vague in spots, but with some deep probing and my wife's insight, you could capture his thoughts from the words and feel his pain. I needed to muster some skills as the writer and technically, as the interpreter, to pull those emotions from the papers and transpose them into some order of a storyline. It was not an easy task, and the work required quite a bit of fill-in and adlibbing, but I plowed onward in my task. For some reason, of which I just was not sure of, other than to honor Jim and to satisfy my own heart, I needed to finish the majority of this story while Jim remained here with us all.

Before he went to his final rest. Maybe, in some obscure way, and I am sure, imagined in my own heart and mind, it was to ensure that his rest and residence in Heaven was in eternal peace. However, now that I was deep into his story and saw the entire picture of his life, and what he poured out of his soul, I knew that I was incorrect in my original motivations.

Jim, long ago . . . as followers of The Bible tend to say, "Achieved a peace beyond all understanding."

Now, it was simply a mission of honor for our friend. Kate was still at the hospital while maintaining a bedside vigil next to her beloved, and Rose and I spoke with her many times. There remained no change in Jim's condition, and Kate assured us that Jim was in no pain. Rose supported me in so many ways during the past few days of my entanglement in a marathon of writing. With a new system behind us, a clear path and direction to the storyline within Jim's notes, and my wife's love locked in my heart; it was time to get back to work.

Detective Lyle Odell was the ultimate loner. Lyle never married, he occasionally had a few girlfriends here and there, but the romance never lasted very long in his life. Deep inside, he was a police detective, and deep inside he knew that he would make a poor companion to a woman. His obsession with his work would be unfair to a spouse, and the relationship would never last. Deep inside of his heart, he wondered what it might be like to have a woman companion. Someone to love him; help around the house, to share his life with and to reach for dreams as one. A good solid woman, she did not have to be a beauty queen. Lyle felt as if he certainly had nothing in the way of good looks to offer, but he just wanted an honest, solid woman. Maybe he would find a woman someday. Perhaps the Irish whiskey bottle would no longer be his only friend and companion.

His small house was more of an investment than it was a residence. The consensus was that he lived in his small office at the police headquarters in downtown Mohawk City, and that was most likely true. Lyle was never sure why he bought the house; the investment would be an inheritance to his one nephew when he left this world. Odell only had a younger sister for a relative and his family line was now dwindled down to just his sister and her family. He was not a good housekeeper, and he long ago conceded defeat on yard work and hired a landscaper to care for that situation. To say that the house was sparse in furnishings was an understatement. In fact, it was barren. A picture of police headquarters on the wall, a picture of his sister and her family on another wall. One table, two chairs, a bed in an upstairs bedroom, dusty boxes of storage in the spare bedroom, an antique television on a rolling cart in the living room. Lyle was quite tired of nearly poking his eye out on the rabbit ears sticking up from the television and he vowed that if they nailed him one more time, out the door, the television would land. Primarily, he used a radio for his news broadcasts and for listening to music and some semblance of entertainment. Television viewing was not high on his priority list.

He earned a decent salary as the Head of the Detective Bureau for Mohawk City, and his career had been long and storied. Detective Odell was a smart detective, and he had certainly solved many cases and locked away his share of criminals. His rumpled appearance and unshaven face and sad eyes often lulled criminals and fellow police officers into thinking that he was lackadaisical, and sleep walking through his work after all of these cases and years, but nothing could be farther from the truth. He was one smart cookie, knew, and performed his job very well. In a drawer, somewhere in his upstairs bedroom were boxes of ribbons and commendations that Lyle seldom ever wore or displayed or bragged about; he was not that type of man. He allowed his actions to display his valor, not the fruit salad, paper badges of honor or the decorations. Nothing missed his keen eyes, and there were no details of a case that escaped dissection within his sharp mind. Lyle spent very little of his salary. Instead, he simply socked the extra money away in a bank account. Someday, his nephew would thank him; he just would not be around to hear the words. He drank too much Irish whiskey, smoked too many cigarettes, slept too little and never relaxed unless you could count sitting on his front porch after work and smoking a cigarette and sipping whiskey as relaxing. Perhaps, to Lyle Odell, it was his escape. When you have seen a lifetime of the ugliness of human behavior and you seldom, if ever, escape the dark side of life, it taints even the strongest of persons. Lyle's idea of home cooking was opening a can of chili and sopping it up with white bread slices, and eating delivery pizza from the local pizza shop. Overall, he took little care of himself. However, what did matter was that even after a lifetime of police work, first in the Coast Guard and then in the civilian world, Detective Lyle Odell remained a driven man.

This was a typical day for Detective Odell except for a telephone call that he received late in the day from one of his contacts downstate in Hell's Kitchen. A long time had now passed since the cold-blooded murder of Sergeant James Reilly O'Malley and the unsolved case of the death of his killer, Peter Randall Buckley. Detective Odell never allowed the case to leave his mind for even a single day. Every day it haunted him, every day he opened up the case files and examined the words for something that he missed. Something to render a clue as to who hired Buckley. It was not there. The good detective visited Mrs. O'Malley often, and he sat with her and tried his best to extract some tidbit from her memory banks that might point him in the right direction. But she had already exhausted all her memories. Aside from the working aspect of his visits, Odell enjoyed his time with Mrs. O'Malley. Despite the pain in her eyes, she was a beautiful woman. Dark black hair mixed with blue highlights from the incredible sheen of her locks and just a touch of grey here and there. Perfect facial features and a gorgeous mouth with gentle lips. Her voice was smooth as silk and her demeanor gentle and touching. Odell had met Jim's biological father, and he was quite a handsome man, and between his two parents, it was easy to see where Jim obtained his own good looks. Mrs. O'Malley and Lyle often shared coffee and some general discussion when he stopped by to check on her under the disguise of checking in for her son and reporting to Jim how his mother was doing.

In his heart somewhere, he felt that perhaps she could be that woman in his life. It was a dream, a false hope. Odell felt as if he had little to offer. No doubt that a beautiful woman such as Mrs. O'Malley was had better things to do, and more handsome hearts to flutter than with this washed up, half-in-the-bag, old gumshoe.

Detective Odell also milked Father Callahan for information and he felt as if the old priest knew so much more about Jim's biological father than what he was willing to share, but the priest was old and feeble now and Odell was sure that whatever he knew would never be revealed . . . except in some type of awkward reunion in Heaven.

Odell maintained the pressure on his contacts and even rode downstate and met with the investigating detectives, delving into the strange case of Buckley's death. Lyle presented his details to the fellow gumshoes and while everyone agreed that the former Navy hero was the killer of Sergeant O'Malley, they would not budge off the idea that Buckley's death was a suicide. They claimed that Buckley was a distraught loner riddled with guilt of his failed military career, hampered by his disability, his lack of work, and then he became a deranged murderer by enacting revenge on a successful and honest man who was a military hero. The person that Buckley envisioned he should be, and when the realization of what he had done hit home, Buckley took his own life in sorrow and remorse. Odell did not buy their act one bit, the wise detective could smell a set up and pay off a million miles away and he kept the pressure up as much as he could, considering his chain of command closed the case and he had only opinions to offer when out of his jurisdiction. Mohawk City was a den of sin and corruption too, and he was no country bumpkin detective. Odell was as hardened as the best of them, and the downstate detectives knew this too. They walked and waltzed around him very carefully and tried to present all the correct answers and angles. Still, it bothered him terribly that fellow police brothers still felt some type of resentment towards Sergeant O'Malley and considered him some type of turncoat for his role in cracking the gambling ring and sending one of the Irish mob big wheels into prison for his role. Odell was sure that many police officers received extra money to protect the big boy and enjoyed playing the games, too. Even Lyle's own Irish heritage did not allow him much access into their secret and dark world.

About ten months after the death of Buckley and after the obvious stalling, manipulating, and behind-the-scenes shenanigans took place, the investigative reports arrived, and the coroner's reports and other evidence came into final examinations, and the dreaded verdict of suicide came down and the case stamped as such and closed. It was now a dusty file on the shelf and a number recorded in a file cabinet. Odell felt that it was all bullshit. The angle made no sense and the motive for killing Sergeant O'Malley was weak and held no water. The reports determined that from some vague family ties to Mohawk City through some long dead uncle of sorts, and with his life falling apart, he sought refuge in Mohawk City. Buckley hung around seedy bars, listened to street talk, and one night, O'Malley and Lawson rustled Buckley and a bunch of his pals around after he and some locals drank themselves into oblivion and caused a huge disturbance. Poisoned by his hardships, young Buckley learned of O'Malley's war record, and a jealous rage and a drunken fit, combined with street legends, that he was a turncoat cop on fellow Irishmen and caused Buckley to flip his lid. Buckley then stalked the good sergeant, and he killed O'Malley in some type of warped and drunken vendetta.

In a review of the archives of police records and in interviewing Lawson, there was an incident of the two partners responding to a barroom disturbance. In fact, there were quite a few of them. This was Mohawk City and there were bars on every corner and roughnecks drinking in all of them. The incident in question did not trigger any arrests. No names gathered, just a warning to calm your bullshit down and a wave in the air. Odell knew enough of the local bars, he knew most of the bartenders, and the usual locals and while some of the regulars recalled a vague incident with O'Malley and Lawson, no one ever heard of Buckley or recalled him hanging out and drinking with them. Surely, a supposed drunken young man, with his military record missing fingers on a hand, would have gathered some attention and recollection. A guy such as Buckley, being a former member of an elite United States Naval unit, was bound to boast of his merits and past after hitting the drinks. Nothing, zilch, nada. No one ever heard of the guy. Even the supposed dead uncle was bullshit. Just because there happens to be quite a few Buckley's living in Mohawk City. No kidding . . . it is just as Hell's Kitchen is, and is full of Irish families. There are at least twenty Buckley's in the telephone book and Detective Odell had tracked down most, if not all of them, and none of them had a nephew named Peter Randall Buckley who served in an elite branch of the United States Navy. All of Buckley's closest relatives were dead and woodpile relatives never really heard of him or knew of him.

He knew the downstate boys had obtained access to O'Malley's arrest records and police blotters through the proper channels, but this was a real reach. This was all conjured-up layers of unequivocal bullshit shadowed by payoffs and mob connections. No doubt.

Somehow, until this point, Odell had managed to prevent James Thomas O'Malley from losing his mind, riding into Hell's Kitchen with his hockey stick, and waging war on the suicide decision and those persons responsible for it. At first, the good detective was going to hide the verdict from Jim and stall a bit, but he was much too honest for that angle. Jim and Kate were doing well now, and his hockey career was taking off in leaps and bounds. Detective Odell was very fond of Jim and his lovely wife and ever since he recovered from the shock of being part of the marriage party and the ceremony, he realized that they were fond of him, too. The last thing that he wanted was for the volatile aspects of young O'Malley's hockey career to transcend over to his life off the ice and cause Jim to do something foolish. As wild as Jim was on the ice and as hard as he played the game, he was a perfect gentleman off the ice. Detective Odell wanted it to stay that way.

Lyle broke the news of the suicide ruling honestly and openly but also with the promise to pull some connections and have someone look at the case records once again down the road. That promise, as well as the fact that Jim was in the middle of his first season with the New York Colonials, caused Jim to pause and allow the good detective to do what he could to dig a bit deeper into the case. Detective Odell did just that, he met with his chain of command, and some legal eagles in the Mohawk City

District Attorney's office for advice. There, he offered his opinions of the case and presented the facts that he discovered on his own. No one disagreed that the ruling was a reach and had hints of corruption plastered all over it, but everyone held little hope that their efforts and inquiries could weed anything out of this mess. Yet, out of respect for the good detective's efforts on his own time of looking at the case, the fact that it involved a murdered police officer and the good detective's outstanding reputation, the chain of command did call in some cards and connections downstate. Their request caused another re-look at the case file, but it was just for pacifying them.

Another report came across his desk and it was the final ruling on the case after the reexamination. This latest and final report confirmed and agreed with the suicide ruling, and now Detective Lyle Odell had hit the proverbial stonewall. A dead end. But the cagey old detective had one more card to play. An angle and a hunch, and he knew that it was now time to unleash the force known as James Thomas O'Malley. He owed young O'Malley; he owed Sergeant O'Malley; he owed Mrs. O'Malley, and he owed his own heart. Now it was time to play that last card and hunch and see where it all takes them. Lyle knew that he could never rest until he had all the answers and that despite his efforts at maintaining a cover-up of his emotions, young O'Malley would never rest, too. Detective Odell knew where the answer was . . . it was just a matter of pulling that last card.

Life was grand for Kate and Jim O'Malley. Despite the fact that the two of them had been in love since they were teenagers, their love grew more immense every day. Hockey was good for Jim too, and his legendary status grew with each game, each goal, and each fight. He was the most feared player in the league and news of his feats seemed as if they reached every corner of the hockey world. The move to the right-wing position had been the correct move for Jim. He felt as if the ice opened up for his vision and his shot was deadly accurate when he shot from his natural side. Jim led the league in scoring, goals, points and, of course, penalty minutes. Led by the now famous, "O'Malley Line" of Royal Johnston, Teddy Davis, and O'Malley, the New York Colonials rather easily won the league championship and Jim won the Most Valuable Player Award. O'Malley was a local hero, and a feared enemy to all the other teams' fans in the league circles. The name James T. O'Malley invoked worship with his rabid fan club and horror for the rest of the league.

The word around the rinks was that big-league scouts were looking hard at Jim and after another year or so, he would move up. His part-time job with Mr. MacCallum was rewarding, and he learned a great deal. Jim loved being part of the construction crew for the church and to assist with Mr. MacCallum's vision coming to life. While the mega-church rose out of the ground, Jim felt a profound connection with the church and it grew stronger in his heart every day. When there were no games scheduled, or it was the off-season, Kate and Jim attended the nondenominational church every Sunday and they often read The Bible together at night and discussed the scriptures. A connection grew hard, it grew deep, and Jim found solace from his past in the Word of God.

Jim loved MacCallum and respected him too. The two of them had grown very close and for the first time since his own father passed, Jim felt as if he had a fatherly figure in his life. It was a great feeling and Kate and Jim realized how fortunate they were to have Mr. Gerald MacCallum in their lives. He was a very special man.

Kate also enjoyed her job, her church, and her life. She attended school part-time, as did Jim. The two of them were busy. Between hockey, school, and their jobs, there were very few days of leisure for the O'Malley couple. Once the hockey picture became clearer, and degrees hung on their walls and things settled out a bit, there was talk of a house, and some talk of a future full of happiness and hope. At this point in his life, Jim's bitterness at his own conception did not allow his heart to open up to the possibility of having children. Kate understood.

Yet, every day, Jim still felt the pain and the off-season was particularly hard for him. He did not have the ice and games, and the other team to use as a tool in order to vent his anger. He only had Kate and his Bible to assist with finding some sort of solace within his soul.

One night right after dinnertime, the telephone rang with all the power of Big Ben striking the hour. It was an ominous ring, a prelude to the events that were soon to arrive in the lives of the young couple. Yet, it was a ring that had to arrive.

Jim answered the phone on the fourth ring.

"Jim, Hey, Odell here. How . . . are things?"

"Hello, Lyle, yes, we are fine. You sound upset and a little bit on edge. Let me guess, the review verdict of the case remained the same. A bullshit, conjured up suicide."

Odell thought about how James T. O'Malley would have made an outstanding police officer. His instinct to read words and voices and moods is impeccable. Lyle had only said a few words, and he was spot on with his game.

"Yes, no change from the original ruling. I am sorry, Jim. I have worked so hard on this one and I feel as if I let Kate and you down. This one is so deeply mired in mob protection that I cannot dig through it all. It is a dead end."

"Nonsense, you let no one down. You have done a great job and we owe you a great deal of gratitude. You are a great man and I will never forget what you have done for us here. I know the pain you hold . . . I know it all too well. Now, it is my time and I plan. . .."

Detective Odell took in Jim's words carefully and held his tongue until the timing was right in the conversation. It was time to play the last card.

"Jim, easy now, please, hold on, son. Before you do something rash and uncontrolled. I have one last idea. I thank you for the kind words, but I am sure that your opinion of me is wrongfully elevated. Regardless, please, hear me out, son."

Jim paused on the line and took a deep breath to push the anger away from his voice, and in a voice just above a whisper, Jim said, "Okay, I am holding. What is your idea?"

"It is a hunch. It is where my instincts point me to no matter how many times, I open the file and review the case. It always comes back to one person. I need to find out who Landry O'Casey was."

Jim tried to hide his surprise at the idea and it showed in his voice, "Okay . . . but we know who he was. An Irish mobster that led a crime ring and my old man was a huge part of the team that broke the ring and sent the bum to prison. He died in prison without parole. Not sure that I am following you on this one, Lyle. However, I know your instincts are usually spot on . . . so please, go ahead and explain. I am all ears."

Lyle looked down at the folder in his hands, opened the cover, and stared at the picture of Mr. Landry O'Casey. The eyes, the mouth, the jet-black hair and the uncanny resemblance to James Thomas O'Malley and to Mr. Bernard Flaherty. It was just a hunch. It could all be just a coincidence. Merely a weird illusion conjured up by a spent and well-worn police detective, desperately trying to find a clue where there was nothing but emptiness. Yet, the old gumshoe knew he had to play this correctly. A loose and wild Jim O'Malley could cause an awful lot of trouble. Jim running amuck within the wild pangs of revenge could ruin his young life and his wife's dreams very quickly.

Easy now.

"Ah, detective. . .."

Jim's words shook Lyle into action, "Sorry, Jim. Yes, O'Casey was all that and more. However, try as hard as I can. There is no trail on this guy and it bothers the hell out of me. Nothing. No relatives, no family history, no children, no residential address. Every, single, thing, every record, wiped clean of this guy. Very unusual, even for a mob boss. Usually, they have heirs in place to carry on the empire of evil. These types of guys know that they eventually die or go to the clink. They set it all up ahead of time to perpetuate their legacy and the operations. This guy, nothing . . . just this huge cloud of mob relations and layers of various low-life thugs. This was a very bad guy, and he seemed as if he lived above the clouds and above the law. Until your father helped to bring him down. It was your father's testimony that finally nailed him. Did you know that?"

"I know. I read your files a million times too, but I am still not getting it."

"Jim, look," Detective Odell paused and thought about his next words, "Easy now. I am not sure. This is all just a hunch, but your biological father . . . well . . . he has only a smattering of a past too. Just this story of almost becoming a priest until you came along and all that chaos that surrounded it. I cannot find an exact family lineage on him either. However, I did find some information. Vague, but I found it with the help of your mother. Your mother told me that he always told everyone in the old neighborhood that his mother died during childbirth, he never knew who his father was, and that he grew up in Catholic orphanages and then a foster home sponsored by Catholic Charities. Eventually his background with the Catholic services and the church led him to the priesthood."

"Sad sob story, Lyle, but I really do not care about Bernard Flaherty. That is more than I knew about him.

Perhaps, Mom knew that I did not care one way or another, so she never shared the details. Honestly, I never let her."

"I know, and I understand, but let's just put away the emotions around your biological father and dig a little deeper and hold on tighter. Ya see—the trouble is that there is no record of a Bernard Flaherty in any Catholic orphanage in New York City, New Jersey, or Connecticut. Ever. Not just in the time frame required with a guess as to his age. I mean never."

"I see. Interesting. How about Father Callahan and his knowledge of the situation and his ties to the church? Can he help? How do you know that he was even in an orphanage? Flaherty comes across to me as being less than honest."

Detective Odell coughed and cleared his throat. Jim could tell that there was more to this story, and he waited as the nervousness of the truth crept in on his friend.

"Nah, I can tell ya that the old priest knows something, but his roots in religion are too deep. I can feel his struggle. It is painful for the old boy. He is more than tight-lipped. Locked up tighter than a drum. I think what he knows would hurt your mother, and you even more, so he never told anyone. Ever."

"Makes sense. He feels it is digging up bones. There has been enough pain and madness. Bad enough, the whole baby out-of-wedlock aspect, but when you add that Flaherty was a candidate for the blessed Catholic priesthood, going around all hot shit and stuff while impregnating the beautiful and lonely wife of another man, I guess it gets kind of rough for a priest to handle and keep the faith strong. Especially, when the husband is away fighting a war for us. Hell yeah, I would guess that constitutes a struggle. I get the sob story and the cover up. Lyle, I still do not understand the hunch."

"Jim, listen to me, son. Promise me not to overreact because this is just a name game and my gut leading me here. It could all be a simple coincidence. Promise me to hear me out to the next step."

Jim took a deep breath, and he now realized that his beloved Kate had crept into the room and she was sitting and listening to one side of the conversation. Her face color was awash . . . poor Kate was horrified and her eyes were sad and slightly lost. Kate knew that despite their happiness, this matter still would not go away. He looked at Kate, forced a smile, and then with pursed lips, Jim said, "I promise."

"Okay, good. There is no record of a Bernard Flaherty in any Catholic orphanages but . . . there is a record of a Bernard O'Casey."

Detective Lyle Odell was very good at his job. Today, he might have been too good.

A lesser man than James Thomas O'Malley might have howled in shock, or they might have dropped the telephone, but this was no ordinary man. Harry M. Redmond Junior nailed it when he retracted his statement that he had seen a million guys like O'Malley . . . because Harry was correct in his retraction. There was only one, James Thomas O'Malley.

Instead of shock and pain, Jim clenched his mighty fists, bit his lips, and chomped his molars together. The anger rose through his body and he felt his chest swell, yet he kept under control. A million words and thoughts rushed through Jim's mind.

Jim recalled his own words when he first met Bernard Flaherty, "What do you do for a living to afford such an expensive custom-fitted suit?"

"I am a businessman. A very successful businessman," was his answer and Jim's anger grew at the recollection of the words.

Then Jim recalled Lyle's words from his first meeting of Mr. Flaherty, "I only briefly met Mr. Flaherty. Your mother introduced him to me as an old friend of the family. One look and I did not like nor trust him. Sorry. I am an old detective with many street bruises and bumps. I have cynical ways. . .."

Jim never trusted Flaherty, and now he knew that his gut feelings were correct. Jim now made the evil connection.

"Under control," Jim mumbled, because he would not break his promise to a righteous man such as Lyle Odell was.

"How do we dig deeper? You said it was a dead end. How do we prove your hunch? Lyle, tell me the next step."

"I cannot do it alone. If Flaherty is really O'Casey's' son, and he ordered a revenge hit on your father, then the layers of mob-related bullshit will be impenetrable. I will end up dead trying to investigate any deeper. You will have no final resolution and Flaherty will skate away free. We need power, we need connections, and we need a person of influence, a man of wealth and of reputation. We need Mr. Gerald MacCallum's help."

Kate now stood behind her husband and her womanly instincts were to wrap her husband in her arms and hold on tightly. She knew this was painful for Jim and she wanted to support him and try hard to absorb some of his pain. Kate loved her man with all her heart and soul. To the moon, to the stars, and beyond.

"Why, Mr. MacCallum? He is Scottish and originally from Canada, not Irish, from Hell's Kitchen. Who is going to squeal to him?"

"Jim, money talks and bullshit walks. It is the way of the streets. MacCallum shares a bond with you. He knows your pain. He has the same pain inside of him forever. We are all part of the brotherhood of police officers. Inside the brotherhood, there are good people and there are bad people. MacCallum is one of the good guys. We fight and claw for the good people in the world. We do this rotten job for little money, for no power, and little prestige, but we do it for honor and respect and we do it because someone has to do this bullshit, and it is the right thing to do. Moreover, the good people stick together because in the end, we are all we have. Mr. MacCallum rose from the ashes of despair. Just as you have. Now, he has the money and the connections and he loves you as if you were his son. He will help."

A long pause ensued while James T. O'Malley thought long and hard about the poignant words of the good detective.

Jim broke the silence, "I get it, yes, you are correct. Mr. MacCallum is a great man and a man of honor. I will speak to him. Lyle, you are amazing. I cannot thank you enough. I can never repay you."

"Jim, if my hunch is correct, and this proves to be true, then please, do not confront Flaherty alone. I will go with you. We will enlist help. Maybe the feds from the organized crime bureaus. This is a dangerous man."

Jim laughed and almost in a whisper said, "He is not dangerous. He is actually my father and if it is for only one time in my life, I need to be his son. I will keep you posted. I owe you everything, Lyle. Everything. Please, know the honor that I feel for you in my heart, is beyond description. I can take it from here, but please, know that what I do from here on in, I will do with honor."

"You owe me nothing. It is my duty. As far as the honor goes, yes, I know and I understand, Jim."

"Thank you and good night, Lyle."

Both men hung up the telephones, and even though they both were miles apart, they stood and stared at the telephones for a long, long time.

"Jim, what is it? Is it, Flaherty? Is he involved in something to do with your father's death?" Kate asked, while trying to put the pieces together.

Jim nodded and held his wife and then he deeply kissed her and between kisses, he mumbled, "Maybe."

After kissing and hugging his wife, James Thomas O'Malley picked up the telephone and dialed the number for Mr. Gerald MacCallum. His boss answered on the second ring.

"Mr. MacCallum . . . O'Malley here. Sir, I am sorry to disturb you this evening, but I need your help with something very important."

It only took three days for Mr. MacCallum to speak with Jim and provide him with the information that he required. Jim was not shocked when Mr. MacCallum asked him to come by his office and before telling him the facts that he discovered, he poured Jim a tall glass of Irish whiskey and poured a Scotch for his own consumption. Jim already knew before the words left the lips of Mr. MacCallum that Landry O'Casey was his grandfather. Jim knew it already. Bernard's mother did not actually die in childbirth and the supposed foster family that was supposed to have taken Bernard in was really O'Casey and his long-time lover, Miss Marjorie Flaherty. At least, eventually, the bum finally married this woman. Therefore, his biological father for a time was a bastard son, just like Jim was. Interesting life. Even with no other heirs and with O'Casey being a crime boss, O'Casey hid the fact that Bernard was his biological son and decided to let him assume his mother's last name, join the priesthood and escape a life of crime. However, it became ugly and very complex, when Bernard could not keep his zipper zipped and seduced the beautiful wife of a mutual friend, and she became pregnant. Out of the priesthood, and into a life of crime, and a son followed in his father's footsteps. From a potential priest to a mobster. Nice gig. Yet, Bernard hid his actual occupation quite well. Even Jim's mother and Sergeant James Reilly O'Malley never made the connection and Bernard went through his life posing as the Chief Executive Officer of a sales and marketing firm that he began from scratch. He did do sales and marketing. It was just that Flaherty never told anyone what it was that he sold and marketed.

Jim thought, 'Interesting family line that I have. Amazing how loyalty melts on the streets when green stamps are involved.'

Jim was now sure that his father ordered the hit on Sergeant James Reilly O'Malley for revenge when his biological father and the man who was actually Jim's grandfather died in prison and without parole. He also suspected that Flaherty really did love his mother, and he always would. His motives were deep, evil, and powerful, and this was something that Jim needed to settle with his biological father.

Alone.

"Jim, please. Please, listen to me and to Detective Odell. Please, do not go to confront Flaherty without the detective with you or the police. This is something out of your league. This is not a fight on the ice, Jim. This is a dangerous man, and I cannot bear the thought that. . .."

Jim stood up and downed the rest of his drink. He reached out his hand, Mr. MacCallum extended his hand, and they gently shook hands.

"I cannot thank you enough, Mr. MacCallum, but you of all people, knows and understand that I need to settle this on my own. Most of all, I want my father's police badge. That is what I want. There is no evidence, except for the evidence in my heart, and Lyle's hunches and what you discovered. He will escape prosecution, but sir," Jim's eyes went down; he placed the empty glass on the desk. He then looked back up and said, "He will not escape me. Will you stay with Kate until I call you? Could you please call Detective Odell in the morning too? I do not want him to know until I am downstate in the city. He will try to come down and help. I am leaving tomorrow for Hell's Kitchen. I am sorry, but I will need the day off."

Mr. MacCallum nodded and sadly mumbled, "I do understand. I do not agree with your choice but I do understand. Of course. We will take care of Kate. Please call as soon as you can and God be with you, James. Godspeed."

"Thank you. I need to pay you back for the money this information cost. Please tell me how much it was."

"Nonsense! I will have no part of any such thing. James, you owe me nothing."

"Okay, well, we will work it out, sir. Do you have the address for Flaherty's office?"

Mr. MacCallum nodded and reached for a piece of paper from his desk and handed it to Jim. O'Malley glanced at it, extended his hand, and the two men shook hands. Afterwards, Jim nodded, turned, and walked away. Mr. MacCallum sunk in his chair and sat there solemnly for a long time. Then he poured another tall glass of Scotch and, as he sipped the drink, he prayed.

Mr. MacCallum prayed for a very long time.

Jim O'Malley double-checked the address and then looked up at the office building that housed what seemed to be a respectable group of corporations. Looks are so deceiving. Jim dressed in a black suit, black shirt, and a black tie. As if he was heading for a funeral. He entered the lobby, nodded to a security guard who barely looked up from his newspaper, and who seemed to read Jim's mind. The security guard pointed feebly at the directory mounted on the wall of the lobby rather than answering any questions. Jim nodded back, walked over to the directory, and checked for the details of where Flaherty's office was. Jim ran his finger along the names until he stopped at, 'Ninth floor, Suite 1200B. Flaherty, Sales and Marketing,

LLC.' Two strides and he was in the elevator and riding to the ninth floor. Remarkably, Jim was under complete control, but he knew that as soon as he confronted his father that all bets were off on his ability to control his anger. He just hoped that he could do one thing. He wanted his father's police badge. If he walked out of this building alive and with that badge in his pocket, then he would feel as if he could live the rest of his life knowing that he did what he could to avenge the death of James Reilly O'Malley. The elevator doors opened and Jim stared at a way-finding sign mounted on the wall opposite the elevators. Suite 1200B was to his left. Down the long hallway, Jim walked while a plush carpet with some type of blue and grey pattern danced under his feet. His eyes watched the suite numbers, and slowly, Jim reached the end of the road. Jim took a deep breath and then turned the knob to Suite 1200B.

The door was unlocked.

The main office was plush, with expensive wall coverings in a dull pattern of raised etchings, some leather chairs, a number of fancy wall paintings depicting some type of object art and a deep, plush, grey carpet underfoot. A table sat in the corner with a telephone on it. In front of Jim was a solid oak door with expensive brass hardware and the door was at the far end of a wall that had frosted sliding glass windows in it. Jim could see lights behind the glass, but no receptionist or person slid the glass open to greet Jim.

O'Malley was about to walk over and use the telephone when the door opened and a stocky middle-aged man stepped out into the office and looked at Jim.

"Can I help you?" The man asked in a voice tinged with a heavy Irish accent. Jim studied the man and noticed that he wore an expensive suit and the suit was custom tailored to be very loose fitting in the shoulder areas.

"I am here to see Mr. Bernard Flaherty."

Upon hearing his words, the man shook his head and pointed at the door.

"Get lost. Mr. Flaherty is not in. Hit the road, asshole. Go sell shit somewhere else."

Now, this was not the way that Jim wanted this to shape out, but here they were. Jim's anger was there. Full-blown. Uncontrollable. Jim's fists clenched, and the man noticed them clenching and his eyes locked on Jim's eyes.

"I am not a salesman. Technically, I am his son. My name is James Thomas O'Malley. Now, asshole, tell him I am here, get the hell out of my way or I promise you that I will kick your sorry ass all the way to Central Park."

The man reached into his coat, pulled out a handgun, and pointed it at Jim.

His voice was a low growl muttered in an Irish brogue, "Now, who's the asshole, punk?"

The door opened again, and another man appeared. This time, it was the man of the hour. Bernard Flaherty stood there, dressed in his fine suit, fine shoes, and with the same expensive watch still on his wrist. His face was smug and unconcerned at the sight of the presence of Jim in his office.

He first looked at his henchman, then to Jim, and with a motion of his arm, Bernard said, "Put the weapon away, Mike. This *is my* son. There will be no gunplay and no killing of my own blood son. If by chance, I underestimated the abilities of that drunkard, scattered-brained, Detective Odell and Jim here wants to see me without an appointment, for what I think my son wants to see me for, he will need to do just what he said. Kick your sorry ass all the way to Central Park. Otherwise, he can leave now. Son or not." Mr. Flaherty smiled a wicked and evil grin and then looked at Jim and raised his eyebrows and said, "Hello, son. Nice to see you."

"I am not your son. Consider me the product of wayward sperm."

Flaherty laughed and said with a smirk, "Okay, kind of

crude, but it works, I guess. My goodness, this hockey world has corrupted you. You usually are so well spoken. Anyway, unexpected visits are such a pain-in-the-ass. However, in your case, we sort of expected you. Odell never quit poking around and then some of my people on the streets say that some high roller, big shot, guy paid quite a bit of dough for some people to ask questions about my heritage, or actually, and specifically, our heritage. Unfortunately, people tell tall tales and cannot keep their mouths shut when dollars are around. Those cowards are gone now. I hope the dollars did them some good. Now, I will be in my office. I have business to attend to today with a police badge that I want to sell. I no longer have a need for it. Mike here is my best man and he will not so kindly show you out the door. If you are still alive, perhaps, you can visit at Christmas time."

Mike smiled, shouldered the weapon, took two steps towards Jim O'Malley and reached out to put his hands upon Jim's shoulders to "show" him the way out.

Bad move. A very bad move. It only took four swings.

It only took one right hook, a left cross, then another lethal right hand and then a direct punch to the face that blew right through Mike's best defense, for Mike's face to explode into blood and his nose to flatten on his face as if sledgehammers had hit him. Mike staggered backwards and bounced on the wall, spitting broken teeth out of his mouth, blood spewing everywhere, and he made a final effort to reach for his weapon, but it was too late. Mike's eyes rolled into his head, and he fell into a heap on the floor. O'Malley stood over him, his fists clenched and his chest pounding.

Jim then looked up at Bernard Flaherty and said, "Next thug in line. Please. Really, Dad? That was your best thug? Is that all you have? Best man, eh? You should've let him use his gun. Looks as if you need to put an ad in the paper for a new, best, thug, Dad. I guess you don't want Mikey here singing, so maybe, I just did you a roundabout favor by knocking this fat bastard out because chances are, he is the guy who wiped out Buckley. Oh, well, sorry, but his fat ass will be dragging for a few weeks and he might need a new nose and some teeth. In fact, looking at him . . . I think that he needs a new face. Might cost you some dough in hospital bills. Now, you are next. Warning, I play all the games to win."

Jim clenched his fists again and his face flushed with rage as he lowered his head and stared at his biological father out of the top of his eyes.

In a low growl, Jim said, "Hopefully, the hospital will give Mikey and you a double room and a discount."

Flaherty looked at the mess that used to be Mike, and the blood pouring out of his face and spilling onto the expensive carpet. And then he turned and ran to his office with Jim in full pursuit. Jim caught him, nailed him with a quick right cross, not enough to hurt him, just enough to snap his head back a little and then he tossed him into the wall, and watched as his father sunk to his knees and held his hands and arms over his head.

Jim stood over him yelling and screaming, "Oh come now, Dad, running for a gun! You just said that I was your son and there would be no gunplay. Not so much of a smart ass now, huh? Not so big and brave without Mike to protect you. Well, Mike is singing to the canaries in his head now, so I will cut you a break. Is the badge really here like a trophy for your wall or was that bullshit too?"

Jim's voice grew in intensity, and he was shouting now.

"If it is here, then give me the badge!"

"I have the badge," Flaherty said in a whisper while he wiped a trickle of blood running out of the corner of his mouth.

"All I want is the badge. You can live with the guilt. I can easily beat you to death here and honestly, I want to do so. I am an ass-kicker but unlike you are . . . I am not a killer. You are a sorry, disgusting, crumb of a man. And, you really were going to be a priest? A sad, sorry, sack of shit is what you are. A coward. Give me the badge and I will leave without making your face look as Mike's face does. I will walk out of here forever and never lay eyes on your sorry face ever again and be very happy to do so."

Flaherty looked up and his face was full of fear as he confessed in a whimper, "I loved your mother. I still love her and your father took her. He took my father . . . your grandfather, away from me. Your grandfather was a good man, and he died in that prison cell. I loved him. He was my father and not what the world made him out to be. Your adoptive father turned on us. He was a pal from the old neighborhood and he turned on all of us. He took my father from me. From us. And he had your mother's love. All I wanted was her love. I was beside myself with pain and with hurt."

Jim looked down and grabbed Flaherty by the lapels of his expensive suit, he looked him in the eye and then said, "You are breaking my friggin' heart with this sob story bullshit and feeble attempt at justification for murder and ruining people's lives. My grandfather was evil. You took my real father away from me and from this world! You ruin people's lives every day. You are scum. Listen to me carefully. Give. Me. The. Badge."

Flaherty nodded, slowly rose to his feet and slowly walked into the office with Jim watching his every move.

"Do you think that after you have the badge that you can go to Odell and try to tie me to the crimes? The badge does not prove a thing."

O'Malley shook his head and said, "No. I only want the badge. You can live with the guilt. You can live with the truth that you, a man who claimed to have at one time, known and loved God, and a man who did the things that you did when you left God in the rear-view mirror, now lives his life, while mired in guilt. You, a man, who wears the finest suits, and who drives fancy cars, has an overflowing bank account earned with evil, now lives with inconsolable guilt."

Jim pounded his finger into Flaherty's chest and Jim stated his verdict for punishment.

"Every hour, every minute, every second that ticks away in your sorry life, brings you closer to meeting the wrath of God and answering for your sorry life. All of your power, all of your wealth, all of your empire, will do you no good at all, when it comes time to face up to what you did. Now, I have the satisfaction of walking out of here and letting you think about that every single day. For you, I hope that your former life and knowledge of religion will unfold your ultimate fate before your eyes and that it is a slow torture for your soul. For me, my hope is that it will quell this anger inside of me. Anger that causes me to fight to prove on the ice and in my life that every second of my existence here in this world is worthy. Anger at what my past is and anger that I want to leave behind me so that I can live my life in some type of peace. Live my life, as my real father did, while I fight for respect, defend honor and while playing every game to win."

Jim once more grabbed Flaherty by his suit jacket lapels while his father's eyes widened.

Jim shook Flaherty by his lapels and said, "Yes, indeed that is a much better destiny for you. Knowing that you are watching the clock tick and living with the horror of your ultimate fate, well, honestly that is a whole lot better outcome than some jail term. A much better fate of a slow and deliberate torture. Yes, indeed, much better than you sitting in a cushy jail cell arranged with payoffs to corrupt judges. Sitting cozy and comfy for a few years for some roundabout, plea-bargained, cop-out term for some bullshit guilty plea of a lesser charge. Hell, knowing your fancy ass, they would serve you steak and cocktails in your cell."

Jim released Flaherty and tossed him aside. Flaherty

stumbled and then managed to catch his balance.

Jim growled, "Now, the badge before I change my mind about destroying your face."

O'Malley opened his hand while he stood there, glaring with the fury of Hell in his eyes.

Flaherty nodded; he opened a top drawer on his desk, fished around, and pulled out the badge. In silence, he handed it to Jim, and it was then that Jim saw the tears streaming down his face. Jim said not a single word; he looked one last time at his father, turned, and walked away. Down the short hallway he went, he stepped over the still unconscious and bloodied Mike. Jim turned to look at the office one last time, opened the main door and stepped out into the hallway and he closed the door behind him.

The single gunshot shook the walls, and then the silence signaled some type of obscure peace to all the madness. O'Malley paused for just the briefest of moments, he pulled the lapels of his suit jacket up and made sure that he squared it away, he tugged at his necktie to make sure the knot was tight and centered, and then he walked the rest of the way down the hallway to the elevator.

When he passed the same lobby security guard, he stopped for just a moment and the security guard looked up from his newspaper and waited for O'Malley to say something to him.

"I am very sorry about the mess on the ninth floor. I hope you can finish the article you are reading later today."

No sooner did Jim finish saying his words, when the telephone began to ring on the security desk and the guard's two-way radio crackled with a transmission. "Security two to security one. Hey, Reggie, we got something big happenin' on the ninth floor!"

James T. O'Malley then walked out the front door and disappeared into the maze of the city streets.

Chapter Twelve

A New Life

I always knew that I would once again meet the great goaltender named Paul John Henson and that the meeting would be an epic adventure with on the ice battles that paralleled some of the events of our lives off the ice. It was not until years later, when we both met and reunited as fellow clergymen, that Paul shared the pain in his life and I shared part of my story. However, for both of us, hockey proved to be our escape, and that was where we first met and where we earned respect for each other. Please let me make this statement and whoever writes this all down and records this forever, be it Paul on his own, or his son the sportswriter, or someone else, let it be known and said that there is no doubt, number twenty-seven, was the best hockey goalie ever to play the game. On any level. God's plan was different for Paul than he might have wanted it to be, but make no bones about it or debate it because he was the greatest. I would never admit it when we played, but I can say it now. Paul often told me that I was the greatest player that he ever faced, and coming from him, those were words that I held near and dear to my heart. In order to compete with an enemy on fair and level terms, you have to respect them. Henson and O'Malley were epic because of the respect that we had for each other. All that I wanted to do was to win, and number twenty-seven stood in my way! When a high-level scout for the Boston Bears approached me, about possibly luring me away from the

New York Colonials, and ultimately, away from the parent club of the New York Rovers and signing with their hockey organization, I refused to entertain his offer. The Bears held the contracts for Paul John Henson and there was no way this side of Heaven that I would play on the same team as number twenty-seven. I had to beat him! We were two warriors who would not give in or give up. It was in our souls; it was God's plan and in looking back; I am not sure that we defined victory in which team or player actually won the hockey games or the championship trophy. I think that we both were the ultimate winners. Winners, in life for the pleasure of having met as mortal enemies and combatants on the ice, to transpose that competition to a profound friendship after our playing days were finally over.

Harry M. Redmond Junior was the bonus to the meeting of number eleven and number twenty-seven. Harry was the ace in the deck. A glorious man who knew no limits to life, no limits to laughs, to knowing what it meant to be a friend, a father, a husband, and to being a man of God, a man of honesty and a man of immense courage and unlimited kindness. It was my distinct pleasure to know both of these extraordinary men and to call them my friends and companions. I often got down on my knees and thanked God for bringing them into my life, along with their remarkable families and for allowing me to be a part of their endless, amazing and wonderful adventures.

Yet, when I first stared into the eyes of number twenty-seven as he arrived in the Metropolitan Hockey League as a member of our heated rivals known as the Long Island Roosters hockey club, my attitude was anything but cordial. In the first game in which we met on this level, he stopped us cold. Royal, Teddy, and I had played together for years now, we won the championship the year before and we were not used to a stonewalling by a goalie. We always had our way. Not with Henson. Every trick we pulled, every set play, the big goalie had an answer for us. In addition, in that first game, he made the greatest single save on a shot that I have ever seen. It was on my shot and I swear that I see that save every day of my life in my mind's eye. It was a save of epic quality. It was an incredible maneuver. A move, made at the last second that he made, in order to bat away a flying puck, while he was sprawled out on the ice and helpless. Some would say it was pure luck, but I knew better. So did Royal and Teddy. They knew this goalie was superhuman and right then and there; I knew that the season would be a battle between our two teams.

That year, we won some games, and they won some games. I wore Henson out and he wore me out. My body ached after we played, and I know his body ached too. I bled from cuts and he bled too.

War on ice.

We both would never give up. I was his match, and he was mine. I loved to play against the man. He epitomized everything in the world about honor and playing hard and fair.

Whenever we scored a goal on twenty-seven, it was always some fluke goal, a weird bounce of the puck, a lucky hop or skip, or an error by a Rooster player. It seemed as if you never beat him cleanly. Sure enough, the season came down to a seventh game in the playoff for the championship and we lost by a goal. A shut out. One to zipper. Henson shut us out in the last game of the series to win the championship.

However, it was an epic season and a season that lives in my heart forever more. The players, and the fans, the press, and ownership loved it all. The New York Colonials versus the Long Island Roosters were the biggest and boldest games that the Metropolitan Hockey League ever saw. The arenas packed to the rafters with screaming fans from both sides, and there were as many fights in the stands as there were on the ice. Not only did the rafters pack with fans, but also there were many more fans standing and watching from every nook of the arena. Even more watching on television screens set up in the lobbies and fans listening on the radios in the parking lots while drinking beer and partying in the cold nights, in the snow, and in the ice. Henson had his fan club, and I had mine. Henson versus O'Malley. Fans still wear our respective hockey sweaters to this very day. That fact alone humbles and honors me. The rivalry filled the stands, and it filled our souls.

After that epic conclusion to that glorious season, in the traditional handshake lineup, I hugged Henson after the final game. I told him that I loved him and that he was a warrior. I told him that I respected every part of his being and he told me the same. We promised to meet again next season, but in my heart, I knew that it would never be the same. Henson's destiny was to move on in his great career and when he did so, the hockey games would never be the same. Sure enough, in that following off-season, Henson signed with a hockey club in a higher-level league and he was gone. Henson left the Long Island Roosters, and the Roosters were never the same glorious hockey club that they were.

A part of me left with him.

Now that all of my awful past and those wretched events were behind Kate and me, I had worked very hard to put my anger aside and to play hard and play fair, and I had made great strides at doing so. I still fought and battled my way through hockey games, but the wounds of my past had softened my approach and made me realize that you cannot conquer the entire world and appease the pain of your soul from a hockey rink.

Royal and his wife had a baby, and with no offers of a contract from the parent club, he retired four games into the new season. Teddy had chronic knee issues and his pain forced him to hang his skates up at the midpoint of the same season. I was alone and there were coaching changes, new goalies, and younger and younger players. It all became a blur, and hockey did not seem the same for me.

I had my chance to sign contracts with teams offering me fame and glory, and I always refused. I could have signed any of the offers and played at a higher level, maybe made it to the big league. Everyone told me so and offered me such. However, they wanted my fists as much as they wanted my hockey skills and I did not respect that fact, because above all, I was a hockey player. I only fought because I had to do so for a cause. For respect and to win the game.

Some games had the contract representatives of various teams and leagues lining up in rows to throw more money at me. My own parent organization of the New York Rovers had approached Mr. MacCallum many times about buying out my contract and moving me up through the organization, and each time that they did so, I met with Mr. MacCallum and asked this glorious man to keep me where I was . . . a right winger for the New York Colonials. Part of it was my intense loyalty to Mr. MacCallum and the fact that I could never leave him. I owed the man everything, and he was as if he was a second father to me. Another part of it was that something had changed deep inside of James Thomas O'Malley.

God spoke to my heart and told me of another mission.

The church construction was finally complete, and the facility dedicated and opened for worship. The facility was a beauty to behold. It was a dream fulfilled for Mr. MacCallum and I felt proud to be a part of such a grand facility. It had everything from chapels, to a huge sanctuary, to a television studio to broadcast services to the world and education wings and everything else you could imagine. The only thing missing was a hockey rink! Don't think that Mr. MacCallum and I did not think about adding one too!

Kate and I immersed our lives in the new church. This church was where we felt most comfortable and as if we belonged somewhere.

Pastor Jeremy Baldwin took the first appointment of the Senior Pastor of the Garden of Wonder Christian Church and the two of us became very close. He encouraged me in my Bible studies and he encouraged me to think about a possible career in the ministry. At first, it seemed outrageous, the fiery and feared, hockey goon and player, James Thomas O'Malley in the pulpit preaching the Word of God, but the more that Kate and I immersed our lives in the church, the more that God spoke to my heart. After I graduated with my degree in social work, I immediately went to work on a Master of Divinity degree and my beloved Kate stood by my side the entire way. She encouraged me; she loved me and without her; I was nothing. From that first moment so long ago, when we held hands and walked home from school together, Kate has been by my side and I have no doubt that she is my only soulmate and that we will be together forever.

The fateful moment came one night after a particularly rough and tumble game that we lost in a game for the ages. We had played the New Jersey Rockets, and they had a young bruiser named Cleveland Ackland playing defense for them, who turned out to be a mountain man and a load of pure muscle. Six feet, six inches tall, about two hundred and fifty pounds, with a head like a cement block and fists the size of Texas.

As Harry M. Redmond Junior said to me so long ago, "We have seen a million of 'em."

The newcomers always wanted a piece of O'Malley to hang over their fireplace mantle. They arrived in great waves of muscles, each time bigger, faster, stronger, and each time, I took them down. Down to the ice, they go because they lack heart and they fight only for the sake of fighting, or to enhance their egos, or for the sake of proving to the world or to themselves how wonderful they are or tough they are. They do not fight for the sake of a cause. When you fight without a cause . . . you lose. Every time. James T. O'Malley always fights for a cause. To win a hockey game, to stand for God, to stand for my respect and for my honor, my team's honor and for my father's honor.

On that fateful night, about midway through the second period, after jawing bullshit and barbs at each other since the opening face-off, Ackland and O'Malley tangled in an epic battle. I punched it out skate-to-skate with the young buck and finally knocked him out cold with a heavy right hook, but it was not without pain and injury. My left eye swelled closed, and I needed an ice pack to keep the swelling down and to see out of my eye, and I needed a few stitches in my chin. They stitched me in the locker room and I was back in the game after serving my penalty time. Ackland needed smelling salts, aspirins, a few stitches and an ice pack or two, but no doubt he was a beast. It took four of his teammates and one trainer to pick him off the ice on a stretcher and move him into the locker room.

The kid was a load.

He did not return to the game.

I scored a hat trick in the game and we won.

When I arrived home, bloodied and swollen, all it took was one look in the eyes of my beloved Kate, and I knew what was on her mind.

Later that night, when I lowered my beaten body into a hot water tub filled with soaking salts and the warmth worked into my aching muscles, the gentle knock at the door and the opening of the same, told me that this was the end of my professional hockey career. Kate walked slowly into the bathroom, and she weakly smiled at me. She curled up on the floor in front of the tub and looked at me as only she could look at me. Her beauty was deep and profound. Layers of captivating beauty that held me hostage within them. I felt as if there really was no lovelier woman in the entire world than my Kate was. I always felt that way. From the first moment that I put my eyes upon her.

I am the luckiest man in the world.

Kate always spoke her mind, and this time was no different. It was what I counted upon.

She brushed her hair out of her face, smiled and gently asked, "Do you hurt more or less than last week?"

I nodded my head, pointed at a large welt and bruises on my chest and said, "More."

"I thought so. James, it is time. You asked me so long ago, on a night where we made love at least five times, and a night where we held our love above all . . . do you recall what you asked me to do for you? You made me make you a promise."

"I do, Kate. I could never forget that night. Ever. For many reasons."

Kate wanted to force a smile, but she could not muster it right now. Instead, tears rimmed her eyes.

"James, you said to me, 'you need to promise me that if you see me changing into someone else and someone that I should not be that you will honestly tell me so. I will take a different course, honest, I will. For you, I will do anything.'"

Kate lowered her head and wiped away her tears.

Then, in a gentle whisper of her glorious voice, a voice that sounded as if it was a summer breeze whistling through the tree leaves right before sunset; Kate said to me, "I promised you. Now, I am honoring my promise because, James, I love you more than I could ever describe. Beyond words. Beyond time and space and beyond this world. You are changing into a man who is trying to deceive his own soul as to where he wants to be in his life. A man trying hard to ignore his true calling. That is not you, my love."

I nodded and tilted my head away from Kate and allowed my eyes to scan my naked body, soaking in the warmth of the water and the comfort of the salts. My legs looked like roadmaps of the interstate, with scars twisting and turning in every direction. My chest was full of welts and the bruises glowed with a shiny blue color in the water. There was no way that I wanted to look in a mirror because I did not want to see my face, by tomorrow; it will be just another badge of hockey honor.

Kate was correct.

It was time.

My heart was in some other place now. It was not on a hockey rink anymore. I needed to follow the call and follow my heart. Right now, I no longer wanted to be a hockey player. Instead, I wanted to be a pastor. I wanted to tell people how great God is and how he took the angry and fearless, James Thomas O'Malley, the ultimate tough guy, a hockey player who was the most feared player ever to play the game and calmed him, molded him, shaped him and made him into a voice for God. Made me into a man to stand for God and all that is righteous, just, and honest in the world. A man who is fair and powerful, but a man who never backs down from evil.

God did not make it easy for me. That is not what God promises. No, it was not easy for me to arrive where I was right now. I guess that in looking back on all of this, our adventures were beyond amazing. However, if everything in my life came easily and without some pain and suffering, then my testimonies for God would not be so powerful, so strong, and so heartfelt.

Nothing worthwhile is easy.

Kate reached over and waved for my hand and I pulled it slowly and painfully out of the water. There was a large bruise forming on my upper bicep. It was red now, but it would be black and blue by morning.

Cleveland Ackland was a beast.

I took her hand, Kate leaned in, and my wife kissed me deeply.

After we kissed, Kate said, "You are someone else now. The anger is gone from your soul and the love of God replaced it. In a far-off land somewhere beyond the stars, you will always be the great number eleven, but right now, you are someone else. The church is talking about calling a junior pastor to assist Pastor Baldwin. He is growing older now. He will retire soon. You need to apply. Your Master of Divinity degree is still a few credits away, but I think you have a good chance for the position. Please, do it, James. For me. For you. For God and for this world. It is time."

I smiled, nodded, and thought about how James Thomas O'Malley was the luckiest man in the world. With a deep breath to withstand the pain and then a laugh, I pulled my Kate off her feet and she landed in the water of the bathtub with me.

"James!" Kate shouted. "This is a new dress!"

Our joy, our laughs, and our love filled the entire world.

Do you know how hard it is to make love to your wife in a bathtub full of soaking salts while every muscle in your body ached as if a freight train hit you?

Take my word for it. It is difficult to do. Very difficult.

It was worth it.

Detective Lyle Odell was not sure as to why he was so nervous. He looked first at the lovely Lillian Patricia O'Malley and smiled, and then he looked at the telephone.

Lillian smiled back at Lyle and she waved her hand in his direction and said, "Go ahead, now, Lyle, please call him and tell him the great news. Ask him. Please. I am sure he will agree to do it."

Lyle nodded, and he noted how this woman could make

his heart melt. She was gorgeous beyond words, and honest, and of course, she was Irish. He felt as if for the first time in his life, he had a purpose in his life other than chasing clues in dusty rooms and tracking down criminals in seedy sections of Sin City. Criminals who all thought they were smarter than the old detective was.

Time after time, Detective Odell proved them wrong.

Detective Lyle Odell was very good at his job.

The old gumshoe smoothed his hair out, picked up the telephone receiver and dialed the number for Pastor James Thomas O'Malley. Pastor O'Malley answered on the first ring. His booming voice echoed through the phone receiver like a wind in a hurricane.

"Pastor O'Malley here!"

"Oh, hey, ah, ah, good morning, Jim. It is Detective Odell . . . err, I mean, Lyle here."

O'Malley laughed on the other end of the line and he wondered what had the usually composed and squared up Detective Odell all nervous and shaky. In the back of his mind, O'Malley had an inkling of an idea.

"Ha! You sound as if you sucked down too many cups of coffee today. Anyway, I recognized your voice, Lyle. How the hell are you? What is up? Everything okay there?"

"Oh yes, it is fine. In fact, wonderful. Say, I wanted to tell you that, ah, well, as you know, I have been seeing your mother for quite some time. Honestly, your mother and I have grown quite close, and well, last night, I asked your mother to marry me. To my utter surprise, she accepted."

There was some silence on the telephone and on the other end of the line—Pastor James Thomas O'Malley smiled widely at not only the nervousness of his old comrade-in-arms and his friend, but at the joy of the news.

"Ah, Jim, ya still there?" Lyle asked with a voice full of apprehension.

Pastor or not, O'Malley was not a man that you wanted

to be on the wrong side of. Downwind of a mean-ass right hook was not the place that you wanted to stand.

"Well, it is about time! Geez, for the smartest detective in the world, it sure took ya old ass long enough to find the clue that my mother loves you with all her heart! Atta boy, Lyle! I am sure that you have God's blessings and I send my blessings to Mom and you! I am thrilled!"

Lyle breathed a sigh of relief and Lillian, sensing the moment and the joy of her fiancé's heart, stood up from her chair, wandered over and wrapped her arms around Lyle's waist. She did love this man. He was full of respect, honor, courage, and honesty. He made her feel so safe and warm. He was a great man.

"Oh, well, maybe I am not as smart as what you think, Jim. Thank you, thank you with all of my heart. Say, one more thing, would you conduct the ceremony and marry us and would you . . . well . . . would you be my best man?"

"It will be one of my greatest joys and greatest honors to perform both duties."

Lyle breathed another sigh of relief and he spoke with a great deal more confidence, "Jim, thank you for this and for your blessings. I will honor and protect your mother with all of my power and my heart for all the rest of my days."

"I know that. You are a great man, Detective Odell. I know that my father smiles down from Heaven on this union too."

"That means a lot to me. I have given up the whiskey, just some beers here and there, and no more smokes. I even go to church with your mother and enjoy it, too. Gonna work two more years and then pack it in. No more chasing clues and evil. Retirement sounds good right now. You know, Jim, all we went through, all the pain, all the suffering, it is amazing how somehow, the horrible events brought us all here and now. Together."

O'Malley's voice grew even more powerful and the deep

resonance of it caused the receiver to rattle in the ears of Lyle Odell, "God is great, Lyle. Out of the ashes of despair, God rebuilds things. Slowly, quietly, and all we can do is pray and thank God for when it happens. God takes the worst situations and turns it in God's favor and all we can do is go along for the ride and pray to realize it. Pray that we open our eyes to all and open our hearts to the plan."

It was a simple ceremony, with Pastor O'Malley serving in the dual roles, and with Kate acting as a maid of honor for Mrs. Odell. Detective Odell's best friend from the police force, Sergeant George Grundy, and a handful of police officers attended, some church friends, a smattering of locals, but it was very low key. Detective Lyle Odell was proud and handsome. No more five-o'clock shadows, his hair now cut short, neat, and combed to perfection, he stood proudly in a smart police detective's dress uniform and on his chest, were pinned many medals, ribbons and decorations rescued from a dusty drawer and pinned on his chest with pride. Odell was the most decorated officer in all the Mohawk City Police Department, but until now, many people did not even know it.

After the wedding ceremony, at a small but glorious reception, Pastor James Thomas O'Malley pulled the good detective aside and Jim pulled the police badge out of his pocket. He held it out in his hand. A police badge from the Mohawk City, New York, Police Department. A number eleven badge, with a sergeant's rank stamped on it right under the name "O'Malley."

A badge cast in silver and stamped with honor.

"Please, Lyle, take it."

Lyle Odell shook his head and stammered, "Oh, no, Jim, I can't. It was your dad's badge. It is yours. I can't."

Pastor Jim grabbed the detective's hand and gently opened his fingers, and placed the badge in his hand.

"Yes, you can. Please. It is my honor and my father's honor and now, it is our shared honor."

The little house of the Odell's never was so clean. The stove had home-cooked meals; the pesky rabbit ears that nearly poked your eyeballs out were long gone now. The house even had curtains, pictures on the wall, and furniture. All the past, including the loneliness in the heart of the good detective known as Lyle Odell, went out the door with the old furniture, old pizza boxes, the whiskey bottles, the cigarettes, and those pesky rabbit ears.

This entire scene was surreal. The old arena of the New York Colonials packed fans into the rafters and into every nook and corner. Screaming, wild and crazy fans and most of them were wearing number eleven New York Colonials hockey sweaters. I stood on a red carpet rolled out onto the ice, with Kate on my arm, both of us wearing New York Colonials hockey sweaters with number eleven emblazoned on the back and on the shoulders and those broad, block letters above the number spelling out the name of, "O'MALLEY. We stood, smiled, and waved at them all. We waved and thanked each and every fan for their honor, for their respect and for their passion. After these many, many years, it amazed me that the fans even knew who James T. O'Malley was. Some of these fans must have been in diapers when I played.

How I wished that Mr. Gerald MacCallum was here today, but in my heart, I knew that he had the best view of this out of all of us.

A loud chant began, the famous chant the fans always roared with during the games, after I scored, or honestly, after a fight that I participated in. And it began loud and soft and then gradually built to a deafening volume.

"O-O-O-MALLEY, O-O-O-MALLEY, O-O-O-MALLEY, O-O-O-MALLEY!"

To feel their honor, honestly, it sent ripples of joy

throughout my soul. It sent ripples throughout me because it was when I realized that all of these wonderful people here this evening came to honor me. To them, I was not just a hockey goon, or a fearless brawler knocking out enemy hockey players, or a right-winger scoring game-winning goals, but to them, I was someone that made their lives happier and contributed in some way to their enjoyment. They saw me not just as their hockey hero, but they saw me as a man who played the game to win and who fought for respect. The feelings made me feel very special.

I looked over at Royal and Teddy, and their children, and their wives, and grandchildren, and they cheered, clapped, and joined in the chant too. They were such wonderful teammates and friends to Kate and to me.

When the chant finally died down and the crowd settled in, the public-address announcer continued with the ceremony.

His booming voice bellowed over the system, "Now, ladies and gentlemen, if I can direct your attention to the door near the side of the visiting player's bench. In order to help Jim and Kate raise his now retired jersey into the rafters of Colonial's Arena, we have invited a very special guest to this evening's ceremony. Please welcome back the greatest goaltender ever to play on this ice. Remarkably, this player is a member of the Metropolitan Hockey League, the American Hockey League and the Eastern Hockey League Halls of Fame. At one time, he was a fierce competitor. Now, he is Jim and Kate's close and endearing friend. Unfortunately, he wore a Long Island Rooster's jersey during his career and he is wearing it tonight too, but nonetheless, please, let's all give a warm, New York Colonials welcome back to the great number twenty-seven, Paul John Henson!"

The crowd went crazy again as in shock; I turned around to see Paul walking over the carpet to join Kate and me. The crowd was now on their feet, it was now standing ovation time, and it went on forever. An ovation in gratitude for the amazing memories and an ovation of respect. Paul, humble and respectful as ever, stood and waved to the crowd very briefly and quickly walked over to join us. He obviously did not want to be in the spotlight for very long.

I embraced Paul, as did Kate, and he bent down and gently kissed my wife's cheek. Paul is always the consummate gentleman. Paul walked over and greeted Royal and Teddy, and their wives, children, and grandchildren. The families were thrilled to meet the legend known simply as number twenty-seven. They were, of course, huge hockey fans and they heard the stories too. Geez, I think that Paul was even taller and bigger than ever. Still all the long hair, the beard, the whole shooting match. Moreover, he looked as if he could still stop the puck too!

"Thanks for coming, number twenty-seven," I said, as we warmly embraced once more. I could no longer hold back the tears and there were no better persons on this side of Heaven, finally to see them other than Kate and Paul.

"I would never have missed it, Jim. Geez, you always said that we would meet again on this ice and well, here our old asses are."

"Hell yeah, Pastor Paul. I would not have wanted it any other way. Would you?"

"No, Jim, no other way. Say, let's all of us pull this jersey up there where it belongs, eh? These fans are going to blow the roof off this joint. I have some cold beer on ice and we have some memories and love to share. Give me a hand, my shoulder has never been right since you nailed me with that slap shot in 1979."

"You are becoming quite soft, huh?"

"Yes indeed, really soft, Pastor Jim. Really, really, soft."

Together, with joy in our hearts and love in our souls, the three of us grabbed the rope and pulled the jersey up and yes, the crowd almost blew the roof off the old arena.

And yes, the beer was very cold too and the sharing of memories with the great number twenty-seven, well, of course, they were great memories of such wonderful times. I am sure that my beloved Kate had listened to these same old stories a million times before. All the same old huff n puff, about great saves, great shots, bad calls by the referees, because that was not an offside play, and that puck did cross the goal line after it hit the crossbar and bounced off your ass, horrible fights, all the same old, same old bullshit, but Kate sat and smiled the entire time. I might also say that she matched Paul and me beer for beer. After all, Kate is Irish. No doubt, that I am the luckiest man in the world because my wife is glorious and so are my friends. Yes, indeed, unforgettable times, shared with the best of friends.

All of this was truly priceless and other than the day when I first laid my eyes upon the stunning Kate Eva O'Leary O'Malley, this was the best day of my entire life.

Looking back on it all, I must say that this has been a remarkable life. Sure, some people might read this story and think that I had it a little rough, but God has been there for me, for us, during the entire time. I just had to open my eyes to the light. God never says anywhere in The Word that life will be easy and a happy stroll through rose gardens with gentle breezes on our face and glorious scents of roses in the air. Nowhere. That is why hockey was so important to me and why it was such a large part of my life. If you give up in a game, a simple game, where you simply battled for possession of a frozen rubber black disc . . . then you will give up in life too. If I have one thing to share with every reader of this story, it is that a person should never give up. Ever. No matter what the odds, the pain, or the suffering might be. Never give up. I fought as hard as I could on the ice, and in my church, working for God, and in my life. I never gave up. When God finally takes me home, it will not be because I gave up. It will be because God wanted me to change my address.

For two years as an Assistant Pastor and then thirty-three more glorious years as the Senior Pastor of the Garden of Wonder Christian Church, I had the good fortune to marry couples, to baptize amazing babies conceived in love and in the glory of God. I presided over funerals of young and old and mourned with their families at their loss and Heaven's gain. I preached countless sermons, celebrated countless holidays, praised God and shared in the lives of so many wonderful people that I feel as if I have not been just the recipient of countless blessings, but I feel as if I really am the luckiest man in the world.

To each and every person that was a part of my life, in hockey, in everyday life, and in my work for God, all I can say is, thank you from the bottom of my heart for all that we shared and all that you did for me.

My goodness, it is difficult to believe when I look back on all those countless hockey games and the brutal, on-the-ice-battles . . . I often feel as if before each game that I shook hands with the Hangman.

Perhaps I did so.

It was not for the money, that was for sure, but it was for the love of the game and for the love of life.

To the many guys that I tangled with on the ice. Well, sorry, but my name is James Thomas O'Malley and well, I never, ever give up. I play the game to win, I fight for respect, and I fight to be a winner. I always will until the end of all time.

Chapter Thirteen

The Final Game

I find it difficult to believe that an inanimate object such as a telephone can predict human events. Yet, I was about to write here that the telephone in our home rang with an ominous ring. Yet, now experiencing that fact, I will choose to write it, anyway. It was around eight in the evening, and ironically, I had just completed writing the final words to what was going to be the final chapter of this book, when the telephone rang. Knowing the great power of James Thomas O'Malley, then the timing of the call arriving just as I finished writing, had little to do with irony and more to do with the greatness of his soul.

No doubt that it was an ominous ring to the telephone. That is because . . . I knew why it was ringing and who was calling. It was about four days since we visited the great Pastor James Thomas O'Malley in the hospital and I knew that right now, Heaven was full of additional glory.

On the other hand, there might be a little hockey fight occurring in one of the corners of the clouds.

I ran down the main hall of our townhouse, quickly bound down the stairs, and met Rose in the kitchen. Rose already had tears streaming down her face, and I could hear her choking out the words with Kate.

I bowed my head, prayed, and thanked God for the glorious life of James Thomas O'Malley.

I then put my arm around Rose and pulled her in tightly as she finished her part of the conversation with Kate. Rose handed me the phone. My wife buried her head into my chest. She sobbed as I held her tightly, and I put the receiver to my ear. Despite knowing that this call was coming any minute of any day now, it did not make it any easier.

"I am so sorry, Kate. So very sorry, but Jim is in a place full of peace and glory now."

"I know that, Paul. Thank you for reminding me of the glory. I need to hear of the glory. I know that the pain is finally over, but I am going to miss him so-so-so-so much."

"I know, Kate. We all will. This entire, weary, world will. However, because of the life of James Thomas O'Malley, this world is a better place. Yes indeed, I believe that with all of my heart and all of my soul that this world is a much better place because of the great number eleven and all those little lessons that he taught to all of us. To this world."

My black suit and pastor's shirt and white collar sat on a hanger in my closet. Always crisp and dry-cleaned, and under plastic, it hung on a hanger as if it was a silent sentry waiting for a call to duty. Even though I was now retired for the best part of three or so years, my call of duty occasionally arrived. Sometimes, it was a joyous occasion, but sometimes, it was not.

This call was not.

I cannot even tell you how many funeral services and graveside ceremonies that I presided over and conducted, but I can tell you that it never was easy. Not even one was easy.

This funeral would be no exception.

The Garden of Wonder Christian Church packed parishioners and attendees to the rafters. Standing room only and then some. The sanctuary and facility always amazed me. It was over five-hundred square feet of glorious testimony to God and the glory of Heaven. In the adjacent gymnasium, the funeral service was broadcasted on the closed-circuit television system and in the hallways and nooks of this grand facility more persons than I could ever imagine or begin to count, stood silently to pay their respects to the life and legacy of the great, Pastor James Thomas O'Malley.

I stood in the pulpit and conducted the funeral service. To my side, and assisting me in the service, was Pastor Dylan Sheldon. Pastor Dylan stood next to me, just an inch or so shorter than I was, but at least fifty-pounds lighter. He was a glorious man, tall, proud, handsome and skilled. Above all, Pastor Dylan was a man of God. He was a light-skinned, African-American man of about thirty-five years of age, originally from a small town in South Carolina and now, he led this amazing church and an overflowing congregation as Pastor Jim's handpicked successor as the Senior Pastor of the Garden of Wonder Christian Church.

It is never easy to follow in the footsteps of a legend, but Pastor Dylan was the man!

I could tell, and Jim knew it from the day that he first met him. I recall receiving the telephone call from Jim on the day that he interviewed Pastor Dylan. Jim just about jumped through the phone with his assurance and enthusiasm at finding such a glorious man to assume his duties for his long overdue retirement. Now together, we stood in front of God and all of Heaven and did our best to honor Pastor James Thomas O'Malley.

A retired Lutheran bishop and one of Jim's best friends, along with a young man, just beginning his own pastoral journey. I think this was all part of the plan. In fact, I knew that it was.

We did the best that we could, but it is never easy to say the correct words, pick the perfect scripture readings, or sing the best hymns.

Especially amongst the tears and the shadows of the memories.

After completing the long funeral service, and greeting

and exchanging respects, with what seemed as if it was half of the population of the entire State of New York, we climbed in our vehicles and made the long, four hours or thereabouts journey up the New York State Thruway. We took a sad journey to a small cemetery on the outskirts of Mohawk City, New York. There, within the family plots for the O'Malley family, Pastor Dylan and I conducted a short graveside service and rather quickly, it was over.

Afterwards, we stood in a line in front of the grave, a grave now covered with a huge mound of flowers. All of us holding hands and in silence, we stood for a long time.

We all stood holding hands. Kate, then Rose and me, and Pastor Dylan. I watched as Kate slowly opened her purse and reached inside. Kate took out a hockey puck, and she kissed it and then gently tossed it in and amongst the flowers. I saw a few flowers jump and dance in the air. I smiled and reached inside my suit jacket, and Kate almost laughed as her face broke into a wide smile when she saw the hockey puck in my hand. I too tossed it into the pile, Rose squeezed my arm, and Pastor Dylan smiled.

"I guess we had the same idea, huh, Paul?"

"Of course, Kate. Jim was waiting patiently in Heaven with Harry by his side for the final touch. The flowers were nice and all but, hey, he was asking, okay, great, but where are the hockey pucks?"

Kate smiled and for the millionth time today, her eyes filled with tears. This was a remarkable woman. A woman of such strength and of such beauty that words can never describe the immense glory of Kate O'Malley. Her soul overflowed with love and her inner being glowed with honor for her husband. The wind blew hard. Kate pushed the wisps of her gorgeous hair from the front of her face, as I reached out for her and she buried her body into my arms.

I waved Rose and Pastor Dylan into the group hug, and together we wept, hugged, and honored Jim.

When Kate regained her ability to speak, and she managed to fight back the tears, Kate asked me, "Paul, do you know the only time in our fifty-two years together that I ever saw my beloved James cry?"

Without a second of hesitation, I answered, "Yes, I know. It was during the ceremony at Colonial's Arena when we all met at center ice and together, we raised his retired hockey jersey into the rafters. The great number eleven hockey jersey."

Kate looked at me; she tilted her head a bit and then wiped away her tears.

The wind blew hard once again and Kate pushed the wisps of hair from her face once more and said, "Why, yes. That is correct. That is amazing. How did you know that, Paul? He never even cried at his father's funeral, or his mother's funeral, or Lyle's funeral."

I smiled and looked over at the mound of flowers.

Now, it was my turn to fight the wind.

The wind blew my long hair in front of my face and I pushed the hair out of my face and said, "I know and I understand. He cried, because it was when Jim knew that the rest of the world recognized his commitment and that he never gave up. He cried, because he knew that it was when the world recognized that James Thomas O'Malley, the notorious number eleven, was more than just a fighter and a great hockey player and the local fan's favorite player. He cried, because he knew that he had made a difference in many people's lives and that his life was special and worthwhile. The world knew that James Thomas O'Malley was a great man, a man of God and that he always stood for respect and honor and always played the game to win. Even the last game that he played in was a win. Jim will always play the game to win. From now, until the end of all time."

The wind kicked up once again, and it blew hard and strong. A few flowers blew off the pile in front of us and they tumbled over each other, came to rest at our feet, and bathed handsomely in a band of waning sunlight that suddenly broke through the clouds.

They were red carnations, and they sat on the ground, winking at us in the sunlight and it seemed as if the red colors were more brilliant than any other red colors that we had ever seen before.

We stood in silence for a while longer, standing hand-in-hand, enjoying the brilliant display of color and sunlight that was no doubt, Heaven sent.

Then in silence, but still hand-in-hand, we all turned and walked away as the sun dipped lower in the sky and the glorious red color slowly faded from our sight.

The color faded, along with the waning of the day, but the brilliance remained in our hearts and minds forever.

THE END

Epilogue

It was just another farm pond located on a road on the rims and on the outskirts of Mohawk City in upstate New York. Named after an old farming family that originally settled the area, Summer's Pond was roughly an acre or two, and in the warmer weather, it was the local fishing hole, in the dead of winter it became a haven for ice skaters and it transformed into the local hockey rink. On this bitter, cold, winter's day, the pond did not live up to its namesake. Summer's Pond was nothing like summer today. Out on the frozen surface of the pond, the wind blew hard. It chased the little wisps of snow across the ice and they gathered in the corners of the pond, in and around the edges of the frozen dirt. The sun dipped low; the temperature dipped even lower, and the black ice grew thicker and deeper. Yet, the howling of the wind met its match with the sound of ice skates cutting the black ice hard, and the sharp blades created wisps of ice and lines that crisscrossed on the ice surface haphazardly in all directions. The echo of the wooden blades of hockey sticks striking the hard ice sounded in and around the wind and the distinct sound of a hockey puck hitting the same blades echoed across the pond in all directions.

Tonight, on Summer's Pond, there were only two figures left on the ice. The cold, the wind, and the dipping of the sun, chased all the other hockey players and figure skaters and other leisure skaters to their homes for warm fires, hot soup and warm houses to try to thaw their frozen toes and other body parts.

To these two hockey players, the cold meant very little. They remained impervious to the bitter wind and the dipping temperatures. After all, there were hockey lessons to learn and sometimes, those lessons come along the hard way.

Nothing worthwhile in life is ever easy.

A small boy of about eight years of age struggled to stay upright on his ice skates. His toes were numb from the intense cold, and his fingers and face reddened in response to the cruel wind. A few hours out on this pond could freeze the hardiest of humans, but this little boy persevered. Hockey was deep in his heart and the love of the game invaded his soul.

Winter only gave you a few precious days and hours of ice time, and you needed to take advantage of it!

The little boy used his hockey stick for leverage in order to keep his body upright, and under the watchful eye of his father, the small, budding hockey player accepted a crisp pass from the stick of his father. The father's ice skates were worn and old, and his hockey stick was a veteran of many games. The stick was nicked and beaten and it wore battle scars of hockey games of old, as if they were silent badges of courage and honor.

Just before it reached the blade of the small hockey player's stick, the puck skipped on a chunk of ice and it hopped, bounced, and jumped in the air. The spinning puck struck the young boy on his face, just under his right eye, and to the horror of the boy's father, he watched his son drop his stick and reach up to his face in pain. The father dropped his stick and skated over to his son as quickly as he could.

"Kenny! Kenny! Are you okay, son?"

The father shouted and asked as the young boy bravely fought back tears and checked his face with his gloved fingers for blood. To their relief, there was no blood. Just a little red welt formed where the puck had struck his numbed skin.

"I am okay, Dad. I am okay," the little boy bravely proclaimed as the tears welled in his eyes.

The father leaned in; double-checked his son's face and the lack of blood caused a wide smile to form on the proud father's face.

"Sure, you are, Kenny. You are a tough guy! You are just as tough as O'Malley was! Come on, it is getting dark and cold now. Time to go home. Your mother is going to have dinner ready and wonder why we are so late. We can practice tomorrow. Pick up your stick. Time to take our skates off, put our shoes on, go home, and warm up now."

Kenny was not going to argue. As much as he loved hockey, the little boy had enough hockey for one day.

Kenny nodded, picked up his stick and as his father put his arm around his little body and they skated over to where the father had dropped his stick, Kenny asked, "Who is, O'Malley, Dad?"

The father stopped skating, turned and looked at his son and smiled.

With the smile still locked on his face, he answered, "Why, who is, O'Malley? My goodness, and you are a hockey player from Mohawk City. And you do not know who, O'Malley is? James Thomas O'Malley just happens to have been the toughest and greatest hockey player ever to come out of Mohawk City, New York. In fact, he might be the greatest player ever to come out of New York! Maybe even America. He played right-wing. He was a superstar for the New York Colonials Hockey Club. He wore number eleven. He learned to play hockey right here on Summer's Pond. Just as you are!"

Kenny's eyes lit up as he watched his father bend down and pick up his hockey stick. While they continued to skate to the edge of the pond, he quizzed his father some more on the legend of O'Malley.

"Really? Right here, Dad?"

"Yup. Right here. He lived right down the road from here. In the big house on the corner of Walnut and Summer's Road. His father was a hero police officer with the Mohawk City Police Department, as well as, a war hero in the military."

"Wow," Kenny exclaimed in excitement.

They reached the end of the pond, they sat on a few rocks, and they unlaced their skates and changed into their shoes. Frozen fingers made this a difficult task, and the wind was unforgiving. As they changed, the legend of O'Malley grew even larger.

"Yes, indeed, O'Malley was the toughest and most feared hockey fighter that the game ever knew. The notorious number eleven, they called him. That was his number. Number eleven. He won the scoring title every year and could skate thirty miles per hour! His shot was so hard that it tore the net up. Pucks that he shot went right through the back of the net!"

"Wow! Right through the net! Do you think that someday, I will be able to shoot the puck as hard as O'Malley did?" Kenny asked, his eyes growing wider and wider with hockey excitement.

"Sure, you will! You have to practice hard, Kenny. Practice hard and you will. O'Malley never gave up. Ever. He played the game as hard as he could, every game. He fought men twice his size and beat them all. One time, he fought this mean man, a man who was five times bigger than he was and younger, too. Cleveland Ackland, the man's name, was, and O'Malley knocked him out cold! Ackland was six feet eight, and he weighed close to three-hundred pounds! Two punches and out cold . . . the big guy went. O'Malley took him out, and the Colonials won the game too! O'Malley won the game on a last-second shot!"

Kenny finished lacing up his shoes, grabbed his stick

and his skates, and looked at his father. His hockey fever rose even higher, his smile was a mile wide, and he begged for more information as his father put his arm around his son and together, they made their way to their car.

"Did you ever see O'Malley play, Dad?"

"I did. Once. It was one of the greatest days of my life. Unbelievable! I saw him play one game downstate, in the famous Colonial's Arena. O'Malley scored a hat trick, and he won all the fights too! Your grandfather took me to the game. When I was around your age. You can ask your grandfather 'bout O'Malley. He saw him play a lot."

Kenny stopped dead in his tracks and the little boy looked at his father and he frowned.

It was just a little frown as he realized that his new hero must have played hockey a long time ago.

"Is O'Malley still around, Dad? Is O'Malley alive?"

The father sensed his son's sadness, and he pulled him in tightly and answered Kenny honestly, "No, Kenny. I am sorry, but he died a few years ago. But, do you know something?"

The little boy wiped away some tears, and he shook his head to indicate that he required a little more information to prevent more tears.

The father grabbed his precious son by the shoulders and looked deeply in his eyes and with a bold and confident smile, said, "Old hockey stars never die. They live forever. In hockey rinks in Heaven and out on that ice right now. The spirit of James T. O'Malley lives forever, in the hearts of all hockey players. Young hockey players and old hockey players, all know of the legend of the great James Thomas O'Malley. Because, O'Malley, never gave up. No matter what the odds were, how big the mean player was, or what the score of the game was. O'Malley never gave up. Win or lose, he never gave up. Ever. We all can learn a great lesson from O'Malley. All of us. You should never give up, too. Never give up, no matter what you face. Try as hard as you can every day. Just like O'Malley did. Play every game of hockey and every game in life to win."

Kenny wiped away a tear and nodded his head.

"Dad, could I get an O'Malley hockey jersey for Christmas? I am going to practice shooting every day. Even in the summer. I will use my street hockey stick. I am going to stickhandle, and shoot, and be the best hockey player that I can ever be. I am going to be just like, O'Malley was. I am going to play the game hard and never give up!"

"Atta boy! I know that you will do it. O'Malley will be proud of you too! A number eleven jersey it is! Sure, Kenny. Absolutely, a number eleven, O'Malley jersey for Christmas. I might just get one too!"

Out on the frozen surface of the pond, the wind blew hard. It chased the little wisps of snow across the pond and they gathered in the corners of the pond, in and around the edges of the frozen dirt.

If you listened very carefully, between the howls of the wind, you could hear the sound of ice skates cutting the ice hard and deep. It is a very distinct noise and a sound that a hockey player and an ice-skater never forget.

Ever.

Along with the noise of the skate blades, you could hear the distinct sound of the blade of a wooden hockey stick knocking along the black ice and the noise of a frozen hockey puck hitting the wooden blade. It is a very distinct noise and a sound that a hockey player never forgets.

Gradually, as the sun finally set, the wind slowed, and the frozen howls faded away, the only noises left out on the frozen pond were the sounds of the skate blades, and the sounds made by the wooden hockey stick knocking on the ice surface while handling the frozen hockey puck. Those noises remained throughout the cold winter's night.

In fact, they forever remain a part of Summer's Pond.

Now, and until the end of all time.

** I nodded in agreement and answered, "He was, and is, indeed, the real deal. There will never be another player like him. Ever. I faced a million hockey players. I swear to you that, I faced a million of them. Jim made your body numb with pain and your soul honored to understand his endless commitment to his mission. James T. O'Malley, either as a pastor or a hockey player, is one of the special people on this side of Heaven. He taught me more about the sport, about honor, about God and life than I can ever relate. Him playing in the big league. It was not part of the plan. This was, as we have all experienced by having the amazing James T. O'Malley in our lives . . . part of the plan. It all interlocks. He had, as you can see, more important assignments."

** Quote from *Heaven's Gain*

Published by God Bless the Keg Publishing LLC
Henrico, Virginia, U.S.A.

ISBN: 978-0-9906979-5-4

ABOUT THE AUTHOR

If you ask Paul John Hausleben, he will tell you that he is not an author, he is just a storyteller. His mission is to continue to write and tell stories to warm your heart, make you laugh, and sometimes make you cry, just a little. Most of all, he deals in memories, and helps you to remember the good times of your own life, and the special people who touched you along the way. Paul was born and raised in Paterson, and then nearby Haledon, New Jersey, and began writing at an early age. He revisited a writing career later in his life, and he now is the author of a number of novels, compilations, short stories and audio and video works. Most of his work touches upon nostalgic remembrances of simpler times, and tells the stories of heartfelt, humorous, and special human relationships. Other than writing, among many careers both paid and unpaid, he is a former semi-professional hockey goaltender, a music fan and music reviewer, an avid sports fan, photographer and amateur radio operator. He now resides in Somewhere, U.S.A., but his heart always remains along Belmont Avenue in good old Paterson, and Haledon, New Jersey.

Other Work by Mr. Paul John Hausleben

The Time Bomb in The Cupboard and Other Adventures of Harry and Paul

The Night Always Comes, Another story from the Adventures of Harry and Paul

Reunion, A sequel to the Night Always Comes and Another story from the Adventures of Harry and Paul

The Miracle Tree, Another story from the Adventures of Harry and Paul

The Chronicles of Henson

Heaven's Gain
The Final Adventure of Harry and Paul

Geyer Street Gardens
Beneath the Mask of a Hockey Goaltender
Another story from the Adventures of Harry and Paul

Where the River Bends and Curls

Crows on a High Wire

And a few others too!

You may write to the author at ctte27@gmail.com

Published by God Bless the Keg Publishing LLC
Henrico, Virginia, U.S.A.

You may write to the publisher at
Godblessthekegpublishing@gmail.com

"Life's simple pleasures are so often the best ones!"

www.ingramcontent.com/pod-product-compliance
Lightning Source LLC
LaVergne TN
LVHW091115080826
845145LV00008B/1931

* 9 7 8 0 9 9 8 6 3 0 0 6 9 *